"Natural Products International."

"NPI, this is Chameleon control."

There was a click, a buzzing sound, then a man's voice. "Yes?"

"There was a break-in at the lab last night. McGinnis made a phone call to the police. He told them it was just some kids—routine vandalism."

"Has anyone seen the damage—besides McGinnis? What about the security guard?"

"I don't know. He left early. The technicians were given the day off before they got inside."

"Follow up on the security guard."

"Anything else?"

"I want to know if the P3 was involved in any way. Stay on top of it."

There was a click.

# THE CHAMELEON VARIANT

by

**Carol K. Mack**
and
**David Ehrenfeld**

FAWCETT POPULAR LIBRARY • NEW YORK

THE CHAMELEON VARIANT

This book contains the complete text of the original hardcover edition.

Published by Fawcett Popular Library, a unit of CBS Publications, the Consumer Publishing Division of CBS Inc., by arrangement with The Dial Press



ISBN: 0-445-04681-3

Printed in the United States of America

First Fawcett Popular Library printing: October 1981

10 9 8 7 6 5 4 3 2 1

To our parents,
Sylvia and Edwin Klein
and
Anne and Irving Ehrenfeld

# THE CHAMELEON VARIANT

# Friday, August third,

*at 6:03* A.M.*, was already uncomfortably warm. Paul McGinnis walked toward the massive chrome gate and gazed at the modern building complex beyond, set like children's blocks on a green felt lawn. Two details marred the otherwise flawless landscape: there were red paint smudges on the chrome, and to his left, the glass security booth was empty. He let himself in with a key, closed the gate behind him, and looked slowly around in all directions, alert as an animal. Surveying his property, he gazed widely beyond the trim acres, as far as the bordering woods. There was no sign of movement.*

*The words "McGinnis Pharmaceutical Laboratories" were carved in the polished granite facing of the main building. Blotches of red spray paint marked the tinted-glass entrance doors and ran in continuous looping designs over the granite. McGinnis pulled the handles to test the locks. The doors didn't give. He gazed through the glass to the reception area within. Nothing there has been disturbed.*

*The paint spelled out* PIGS *and* FUCK YOU *and finally somebody . . . that was illegible . . .* SUCKS *over the cropped front lawn. He bent down and touched the red stain on the perfect grass. It was already warm; no early morning moisture beaded it, and the paint flaked between his fingertips. He followed the paint stains with his eyes all the way to the foundation planting that hid the other buildings from his view. He stood and looked again for the watchman. A small muscle in his jaw tightened slightly, but otherwise his angular, handsome face was without expression. Then he walked quickly, with the loose agile stride of a tennis player, across the lawn, his navy blazer vents flapping up in back over his pale gray slacks. He approached the rear entrance of the P3, eyes on the trail of paint.*

*The outside metal door to the windowless unit was ajar. The lock had apparently been forced, and the entire side of the door had been twisted out of alignment, probably with a crowbar.*

*McGinnis glanced briefly at the alarm panel. The indicator light was off—last person out last night had forgotten to turn it on.*

*He pulled the ruined door toward him with a jerk and entered hurriedly. To the left of the entrance corridor was a small, white-tiled washroom with a large center floor drain. He walked in. No sign of disturbance. Nothing marked the immaculate walls, the hamper, or the neat stacks of paper-wrapped sterile garments. Quickly, he took off his street clothes, changing into white coveralls, cotton shoe coverings, and a surgical cap. Washing his hands, he turned the tap full to rinse off the orange Betadine. Then he walked to the interior door of the P3. A barely perceptible whoosh of air sucked in with him as he passed through the first airlock, entered the kitchen, and glanced around. Spray paint. This time both red and blue designs, and symbols on the counters and walls, no lettering. The paint trailed off where he stood, as if the vandals had left hurriedly.*

*He walked quickly into the animal rooms. The first, with the untreated control monkeys, was intact. He brushed by the hands extended for friendly contact through the bars and entered the second room. His gaze swept the treated monkeys as he passed by their cages. Some were chattering, others screaming, and a few were crouching silently; they all seemed oblivious of his presence. Then his shoe kicked something metallic. The key ring. It should have been hanging on the wall. He picked it up and looked again at the cages. One was unlocked and empty. It had contained a treated rhesus monkey that the technicians called Jackie. He examined the empty cage briefly, but suddenly his attention shifted to the small corridor that led to the main lab complex. Its door stood open, wedged with a lab stool . . .*

*"Dr. McGinnis? . . . Anyone there?" A husky shout came faintly from the direction of the kitchen.*

*McGinnis sprinted back toward the rear door calling, "Don't come in here."*

*At the airlock, McGinnis's steady gaze took in the wrinkled jacket, the blurred, faded blue eyes of the security guard. The stench of wine-soaked sweat rose harshly above the pale disinfectant odor that pervaded the corridor. "You know this is a restricted area, Jimmy. Only staff familiar with procedure may enter." He closed the inner door behind him.*

*Jimmy Walters looked down at the floor quickly, averting his eyes. "I'm sorry . . ." he mumbled. "Only, the heat was driving me crazy and that guardhouse was so close I couldn't breathe. When I went to check out the offices, I sat down to cool off a minute and . . ."*

*"No real damage," the icy voice interrupted. "Just some paint on the grass. And of course an attempt to open the outer door—but they didn't get any farther."*

*As they stepped outside, Jimmy Walters turned to look at the steel door with its mangled frame, its radiation warning symbol, and the rectangular plastic sign engraved with large letters:* BIOHAZARD AREA: AUTHORIZED PERSONNEL ONLY. *Then he squinted very briefly at the eyes of the man regarding him: they were gray, the color of smoke, unreadable. He swallowed uncomfortably. McGinnis was wearing a white outfit, dazzling as a snowfield in the sun, his face healthy and tan above it, and those eyes . . .*

*"I'm . . . I'm sorry. I was . . . just . . . gonna call the police."*

*McGinnis's eyes closed for a split second, as if he had a headache. "I have a call in to them, Jimmy. You can go home now."*

*There was something in the quiet, even voice as it gave the order that made Walters tremble with an unidentifiable fear as he backed off.*

*"I'll take care of everything," McGinnis was saying. "You report for work as usual tonight. But, Jimmy, don't let this happen again."*

*Walters didn't look back as he left the grounds.*

*McGinnis removed the stool that was wedged in the doorway and entered the main lab of the P3. He was aware of the steady hum overhead from the air-filtration system. Fluorescent light filtered onto the row of refrigerators, incubators, and freezers along one wall, and glinted off the glassware drying on black, polyethylene pegs on pegboards over the sinks. No spray paint. All the large apparatus was intact.*

*But the smaller equipment on the lab benches near him was a shambles. There was broken glass everywhere. Tubing was disconnected, an entire roll of chart paper was unwound, columns were smashed and wet ion-exchange resin dripped onto the floor. And then he saw the monkey. It was lying on a lab bench, horribly contorted, its mouth open as if to scream, its lips drawn back away from the teeth . . . dead. Its hand was in a glass water bath. In the water was a small laboratory hot plate, the red signal light still on. McGinnis's eyes followed the cord of the hot plate to the wall outlet: electrocution.*

*He walked over and unplugged the cord. He then crossed the room and unbolted the door to the second P3 laboratory. It was intact and clean. He relocked the door smoothly and stood with his back against it for a moment, contemplating the scene. The scintillation counters stood untouched in a glass-partitioned side lab, flashing their digital displays and clicking their print-outs as usual.*

*It was almost certain that the damage in the main room had been completely the work of the animal: it had defecated on a freezer; its foot was near two overturned glass cylinders. But the incubator had been left alone, the plates had not been moved. Petri dishes filled with a substance iridescent as raw abalone glistened under a reddish light, undisturbed. He walked over to check the bench-top fermenter, his face illuminated by the violet glow from the machine's interior. He glanced at the air and* $CO_2$ *gauges and bent briefly over the strip-chart to note the pH tracing.*

*His eyes traveled to the wall safe. It was closed. The corner refrigerator was locked. Nonetheless . . . he examined the padlock, then unlocked it and looked inside. The vials of white powder were exactly where they had been on the second shelf. He relocked the refrigerator and glanced at the wall clock: 6:41.*

*McGinnis went back into the kitchen and quickly wiped the spray paint off the counters and tile walls, using lab wipes soaked with hexane from a chemical cabinet. He put the empty cage into the large autoclave. Walking back to the lab, he picked up the dead monkey, carrying it firmly by one foot, his face devoid of expression. Taking it to the kitchen, he put it in a black plastic bag and placed the bag near the incinerator. He washed his hands again.*

*Taking a broom and dustpan from the maintenance closet, he began to clean the laboratory. He brushed the glass fragments from around the "glove boxes" on the lab bench along the east wall, threw out the disconnected tubing, and disposed of the broken beakers. Finally, he sponged and towel-dried the bench surfaces until, to the untrained eye, the laboratory appeared as it had the previous afternoon.*

*Closing the door behind him, he crossed to the incinerator and put in the garbage bag containing the monkey. Then he threw his coveralls, cap, shoe coverings, and paint-stained lab wipes in after it and flipped the switch to "on." He changed back into his street clothes, retraced his steps out into the sunlight, and entered the main building from the front. Sitting down in his own office, he phoned the police.*

*"This is Dr. McGinnis. I'd like to report some minor vandalism at the McGinnis Pharmaceutical Labs on Broadview Road. Nothing very serious; some kids apparently decided it was time to spray-paint our lawn. They tried to get in the back door, but something stopped them . . . scared them off." He swiveled in his chair, listening. ". . . no, I'm not interested in taking it any farther. I'm only calling because I didn't want you to get an exaggerated, secondhand report . . . Oh, certainly. Stop by later if you want to. Come to my office first, and I'll show you the graffiti outside and the damaged entrance door. . . . That's right. Just kids reacting to the heat wave. No harm done."*

# Friday, August third,

turned out to be a record-breaking day. The temperature reached one hundred and three on Main Street. Insects screamed in the grass, and nothing moved under the yellow sky. Sheffield was so still it seemed as if the population had evacuated the town. No one was to be seen on the sloping hills that widened at the shoreline and narrowed into forest at the city limits. No hum of lawn mowers or snap of hedge clippers interrupted the morning. Up in the Hill section, some gentle splashes could be heard from pools, but all in all, a great human silence pervaded the town.

Daniel Lieberman rolled up his shirt sleeves, washed his face in an examination-room sink, drank some lukewarm water from his cupped hands, and silently swore at his air conditioners. His armpits were swimming, and his concentration was as fogged as his glasses. He dried his hands, pulling the last of the brown paper towels out of the dispenser. If there had been time to get the machines fixed; if he had inherited his predecessor's nurse; if the new nurse hadn't gotten sick this week; if he had been able to find a better receptionist; if every child in Sheffield hadn't had a fever as hot as the sidewalk on Main Street. *Dayenu!* Enough! He glanced at the mirror above the sink for an instant, getting a fast impression of fatigue, a hint of reddish-blond stubble, uneven wire-framed glasses, the perspiration near his graying sideburns. A forty-year-old man staring back at him—a middle-aged stranger. Damn! If he could only get it together, then his new office with its red and blue stripes and white vinyl furniture wouldn't be sweating. Even his goldfish looked boiled. And his goddamn infected toe was throbbing again. He turned resignedly and handed his last loose, unmelted lime lollipop to Janie Garner. Another probable strep case; that made the entire elementary school set. A strep epidemic in August! What would January be like? He routinely streaked a red plate with the culture swab and put it aside, picking up his prescription pad.

This was an inch thicker last week, he said to himself.

"Louise," he said to Janie's mother, "I ordinarily wouldn't give an antibiotic till the culture was back, but seeing how strep throat is all around, go ahead and pick up the prescription now; start the medicine with two teaspoons before lunch and then go to four teaspoons a day for ten days." He was writing as he gave her instructions he had repeated so many times that week. "Give me a ring tomorrow, and we'll have the culture checked out by then." He signed his name, noting that it looked more like a worm than usual, then turned to Janie. "You'll feel a lot better by tomorrow evening, young lady, maybe even have a date with Maia over the weekend." He turned toward her mother. "You can send her back to day camp after twenty-four hours of normal temperature, but Louise, don't forget; even if she's feeling better, the medicine is for ten days."

Louise gave him a tight smile. "Thank you," she said, and put the paper neatly in her purse. She was a well-groomed woman; tall, with wide shoulders, dark blue eyes, no makeup. Her dark hair was streaked with silver, and she wore it pulled severely back in a chignon. "I'll take care of it right away," she said briskly.

Did he make her uncomfortable or was she always inside a steel shell, he wondered. "Try to keep Janie's temperature down with aspirin today, and call me if you have any problems."

"Dr. Lieberman, why'd you turn you air conditioner off?" Janie asked.

He ruffled her short brown hair. "Janie, it's the hottest day of the year, so it's out celebrating. Big fan party."

She rewarded him for his silliness with a nine-year-old gap-toothed smile, but with the same tolerant look in her eyes that his daughter, Maia, reserved for his puns. As he saw that precocious glint, he knew it had immediately attracted his city-bred daughter. His daughter! He felt a panicky stirring in his gut. He'd promised to pick her up at camp at midday and hadn't packed her lunch. How the hell was he going to get out of his office? He ushered the Garners out, wondering who was left in the waiting room.

He caught a glimpse of the fourteen-year-old bruised and puffy face of Wendy Dougherty half hidden behind a *True Romance*, which she'd smuggled into his collection of *High-*

*lights* and *Archie* comics. Her mother sat across the waiting room, thin-lipped and pale. He took a few steps toward Wendy. She was totally absorbed in the magazine, her lips parted, her eyes darting. He tried to get a good look at her face. An accident. But not an emergency. The bruises indicated that hours had passed; maybe half a day.

"Mrs. Dougherty? Wendy? Please come right in."

Wendy sullenly put her magazine in her khaki knapsack and slouched into his examination room, swinging her dark-rooted orange hair back off her round, slightly piggy face. No hello. Up close, Daniel could see a cut under her left eye, a scrape near her chin, and something that looked like cat scratches on her neck. Her mouth was distorted from swelling, but he didn't doubt that the deliberately hostile expression would be there, edema or no. Barbara Dougherty followed her daughter in, her shoulders curving in apology for this moody, clumsy adolescent who somehow belonged to her. She wrung her hands as she walked, unaware of her actions.

Folding her arms, she looked around the humid examination room, avoiding his eyes. "Dr. Lieberman, Wendy fell down a flight of stairs last night, but she seems quite herself this morning except for her bruises . . ."

Daniel Lieberman directed Wendy to a wooden stool near the sink. "When last night did this happen?" he asked.

"About nine or so," Mrs. Dougherty answered for her daughter.

"Whenever anything like this happens, call me right away. Don't be concerned about disturbing me at night," he said, gently moving Wendy's head from side to side. "Wendy, have you any pain at all when I do this?"

"No."

He checked her scalp for irregularities and cuts, probing gently. Then, sitting on a stool opposite her, he examined her eyes, peering through his ophthalmoscope. Her pupils were the same size and responded normally, and he found no trace of hemorrhage when he checked her retinas. "Tell me when you see this pencil," he said, covering her left eye and moving the pencil from side to center. "Look straight at my nose." He repeated the process with the right eye covered. Visual fields were normal.

"She pitched forward, just hit her face. It's lucky she didn't chip her teeth. Her braces just came off last month," the mother said, fingering her pearls.

Why the delay bringing her in? he wondered. Sitting on the

edge of the radiator cover, facing the girl, he spoke directly to her. "What happened, Wendy, did you trip on something in the dark?"

"Yeah, I think so."

"You didn't blank out or anything before you fell?"

"No."

"And after? Did you ever lose consciousness, even for a second?"

She shook her head.

"Have you any double vision?"

"No."

"I was there," Mrs. Dougherty interjected. "I picked her up immediately."

Nothing organic so far, Daniel thought, and other than in an emergency, teen-agers didn't come in with their mothers like this . . . the whole thing had a strange ring to it. "Wendy, let's take a look at you. Take off your shirt and socks and shoes, and climb up on that table," he said, and turned to the mother. "Has this ever happened before?"

"No, never," she said quickly.

Daniel listened to Wendy's heart, and she breathed cooperatively for him. He noted a small scratch on her midriff and another on her shoulder. They also appeared to be cat or dog scratches. He ran his finger lightly over a new scrape he found on her knee. "How'd you sleep last night, Wendy?"

She looked up at him dully. "Okay."

He ran a straight pin over the soles of her feet. Her Babinski reflexes were normal. He touched the pin gently to various parts of her arms, legs, and back. "Can you feel this?"

"Yes."

"Turn your head away and tell me when I touch you."

"Ouch."

He gazed at the few raw scratches on her shoulder. "What does it feel like?"

"A pin."

"And this?"

"Yes."

"Do you have a dog or cat at home?"

She stiffened. "No."

"You feel this?"

"Yes."

"Neighbor's cat scratch you?"

"No. I just fell down the steps . . . there was a garden rake and skates."

"I was up during the night to check on her," Mrs. Dougherty volunteered. "I woke her up each time, like Dr. Spock says."

The dark circles under the mother's eyes were filmed over with makeup. Daniel Lieberman looked at her carefully. Her brown hair was cut short in a neat cap and her nose turned up pertly, but her doll-like features seemed brittle, her mouth trembled slightly, and the colors of foundation and rouge appeared unevenly patched in the light streaming in through the window.

"Wendy, did you have nausea or vomiting?"

"No."

"Okay. Wendy, sit up. Now please answer these questions even if they sound silly. Where are you?"

"In your office."

"Doctor . . ."

"Lieberman."

"Okay, and why are you here?"

"Because I fell down the stairs last night."

"What day is it?"

"Friday."

"Good. Is Santa Claus real?"

Wendy looked thoroughly disgusted. "No."

"Okay. Get up and sit over there, please," he said, directing her to a stool near the medicine cart. "You have no headache?"

"No."

He watched her walk. She had an adolescent combination of baby fat and large breasts. Her nose turned up attractively like her mother's, but was out of keeping with small eyes and a heavy jaw. There was nothing abnormal. The girl had poor posture and, as Lieberman's mother would have said, was a klutz. But a normal one.

"I'm going to treat these cuts now, and I'd like you to take it easy today and tomorrow." He opened a glass jar of cotton balls, moistened them with alcohol, and cleaned the abrasions, swabbing the cuts with bacitracin ointment. "There's no reason for X-rays now. Wendy's neurological responses are normal, and she's walking fine. But if anything changes, I want you to let me know."

"I just thought you should see her . . . just a few steps really, going down to the garage. She tripped over some things at the top, Roy's skates, wasn't it skates, Wendy?"

"Roy's skates," Wendy replied in a monotone.

"When was your last tetanus shot, you recall?"

"Two months ago with Dr. Cameron," Barbara Dougherty said.

"Fine," Daniel said. He washed his hands. What had really happened? She was too young to drive, and anyway a car accident would have been reported . . . unless she had bumped into a parked car. That would be something to lie about; no license. But this looked like a fist fight—bluish tinge over the jaw bone, direct hits from a closed hand, not steps. But those scratches . . . an unrelated incident? Why the secrecy?

"Mrs. Dougherty, if anything like this happens again, call me right away." His voice was firmer than he intended, but he guessed that he was looking at a battered child. Wendy looked at him throughout with an implacable hostility. There was something in the set of her face that might drive many parents to a slap. But not Mrs. Dougherty. He remembered her bird-like fingers nervously moving the pearls around. Then who? The father? the boyfriend?

"I didn't want to disturb you so late at night, Doctor," she said meekly.

Daniel patted Wendy lightly on the back. "Call me anytime. That's what I'm here for." He ushered them out, making a mental note to check back in Wendy's file and see if she'd been treated for bruises by Dr. Cameron, or better still, give his predecessor a ring and see if he knew anything he hadn't put in writing. Mrs. Dougherty turned at the outside door, the lawn shining brilliantly as tin foil behind her; her flowered shirtdress was sticking to her body. She hesitated, then: "I do hope you will be able to join us tomorrow night . . ." she said nervously. "You did get the invitation, didn't you . . . the party?"

He'd forgotten the invitation in a forest of papers that had grown on his desk. He needed a secretary, a healthier nurse, a receptionist, a babysitter, a Daniel Lieberman organizer. Jesus, Lieberman, no wonder the woman is wringing her hands. She thinks you deliberately snubbed her.

"I'd love to, of course . . ." He blanked on her first name. "I meant to get to it, but this has been quite a week with the younger kids . . . I'd really love to. I'll tell you what—I'll see Wendy when I come over tomorrow night, okay? Unless something comes up before . . . then I want you to promise to call me immediately."

Mrs. Dougherty smiled timidly. "Thank you, Dr. Lieberman . . . see you at sevenish."

"Look forward to it. 'Bye, Wendy."

Mrs. Dougherty waited for Wendy to respond, but the girl just looked angrily toward the parking lot. Nervously, Mrs. Dougherty touched her hair, her pearls, then said unexpectedly, "Do you have an air conditioner man?"

"Funny you should mention that: I don't even have a classified directory, or if I do, it's somewhere under the comic books."

"I'll telephone my man and make sure he gets to you today. Um . . . will you be in all day?"

Panic. Pick up Maia. I have to pick up Maia! Quarter after twelve. No, he wouldn't be in and he couldn't leave the door open, because Dr. Cameron had told him the kids would get into his drugs.

"I'll be here from about two o'clock on."

"I'll try to get the repair man here at three or so, okay? And I'll see you Saturday!" she said, smiling, as she waved and mobilized Wendy to walk down the steps to the parking lot.

He waved. Bless you, Mrs. Dougherty. I appreciate that. But what really happened last night to your daughter? With relief he noted the waiting room was finally empty. Sweat was melting down over his eyelids under his glasses. There were cellophane candy wrappers on the red shag wall-to-wall carpeting. He pulled the white paper roll across the examination table, ripped off the old piece, and dumped it in his overflowing wastebasket. He washed his hands again, splashed his face, and reached for the empty towel dispenser. Dripping, he called his answering service, set the cardboard clock on his outside door for two, and hoped that nothing would happen in the next hour.

He stood by his old dusty Volkswagen for a few minutes with the door open and felt the heat from the interior rise up under his chin like flames. He had been in such a hurry that morning he had forgotten to park under the large oak tree just a few yards away. Twelve twenty-five. The car seat burned his shoulder blades, his thighs. He leaned over, opened the far window and headed toward the beach. As he gained speed, the car air conditioner began to respond. There was actually a cool breeze fanning his hair. It was great to get away from this dead humidity. He relaxed at the wheel. Driving through Sheffield with your windows down and your air conditioner on was a great thing to do. Better than lunch, which he had forgotten again. He passed under an arcade of trees planted before the Civil War. Cool. Good old Yankee oaks. Seedlings when his ancestors were maybe still on the outskirts of Odessa with not the vaguest thought of crossing the ocean. The white clapboard houses were set on half acres, and the sky was hazy and gentle. He took the long route past Main Street, admiring the compactness of the town. He could see the white steeple of the Congregational Church, which lay exactly opposite the Town Hall across the flower-bordered village green. He was sure he'd always be a tourist in Sheffield, delighting in every shingle of the ye-olde-shoppe fronts. There were no pedestrians out now, and Main Street looked like a set for a film about the American Revolution. At the intersection of Green and Newtown he turned onto the beach road.

The Sound was in view now; the breeze stronger, bringing with it the smell of salt and fish. Gull cries pierced the air. Boats and rooftops were shimmering, and the water glinted closer as he turned. Sunfish tipped gently in the marina. Suddenly the air was cooler by ten degrees. The quiet . . . the sand. Daniel parked by the beach, leaned back in his seat for a minute, and closed his eyes. Then the recollection of Wendy's battered face intruded on the moment. Teen-agers. He understood people till their mid-teens and then he had a big block till over thirty. He hoped he'd overcome it before Maia was fourteen. He thought of Maia's clear laugh, her big child's eyes. Maia's face would never turn sullen and closed like Wendy's, would it? Would he always understand her? His ex-wife said his block included all adults. Was she right? He had thought *her* smile wouldn't ever change either. And then it had disappeared, along with the rest of her.

He walked out onto the sand near the area used by the day-camp children. Beyond, the beach curved out, strewn with umbrellas and tourists. For the first time that day he breathed deeply, felt his muscles untense and his lungs expand. He found Maia with a group of other children, standing ankle-deep in the low-tide water, her strong, small-boned body wriggling with excitement. Her head was bent so that her light brown hair fell forward over her bangs. A slim young woman in the center was poking at the wet sand with a thin branch and talking animatedly to the kids, her long blond hair waving in the beach breeze as she turned to include each of them. And they, moving like little birds, poked their toes in the sand, tugged her blouse, fell over each other, all of them moving, never still, like the waves, the breeze, the gulls.

Daniel moved in closer, slowly and soundlessly, not wanting to disturb them. The young woman in the center was wearing rolled up jeans, a blue work shirt, and in her hands she held a squashed brown fedora, which she placed on her hair and pulled down. Tiny waves lapped at her ankles. She stretched out her arms and held the children for a moment of stillness, fascination. What was it? Something about mud snails. All the heads bent to watch something he couldn't see. Pieces of conversation floated over the water to him.

"They clean up . . . that's right, Tommy, they're the garbage men . . . see, they eat all the tiny dead animals . . . bacteria . . ."

"Yuck!"

Giggles.

"Yummy, yummy."

"Watch me, Billy. I'm going to pretend I'm a seagull and smash this mussel here for my dinner . . . it falls here on this stone. Ah, now I can get to the insides! Oh, but I lost it. I dropped the mussel near the mud snails! Oh, now watch. What will they do? Watch carefully . . . who can tell me?"

She bent over, limber as a dancer, her blue work shirt floating up in the breeze, her old fedora at a level with their heads, and they all huddled silently over the mud snails.

Suddenly Maia's voice. "They're wiggling."

"They're moving over to the smushy whatchamacallit you smashed up." Billy McGinnis's gruff voice.

"Right. And you know what they're going to do? They're going to eat it all up. That's their lunch."

Precise, accented English from one of the Santé twins: "They are pushing each other!"

"Mmmm, soup for lunch."

"Piggy, piggy, look at them wiggle over!" said one of the Lawson children sitting in the water.

Giggles echoed over to Daniel. Maia's voice again. "Could I take some home?"

"Sure, let me get you a jar."

The woman stepped out of the circle and immediately the spell was broken. Maia looked up and saw her father smiling at her. "Daddy!" she said and started to run toward him, stopped and then with grown-up politeness said, "I'll just be a minute . . . Laura's getting me snails."

He nodded. "Take your time."

The children dispersed, digging here and there, scooping up wet sand and snails, throwing mussels and stones out into the water. Some of them waved, their voices bounced to him like rubber balls. "Hi, Doctor Lieberman!" New in town, but he'd seen almost all of them, even if he didn't have their names straight. He waved.

Laura walked toward him hand in hand with Maia, very involved in feeding instructions for the snails.

"Sorry to interrupt . . ." he began as they approached.

Laura looked up with a direct gaze, the corners of her green eyes curved down; they were eyes that laughed easily. Her eyelashes were thick and honey colored, but her eyebrows, pale and light as feather tips, disappeared under her too-long, fringed bangs. Her wide, full-lipped mouth curved in a welcoming smile. "I'm glad to meet you, Dr. Lieberman. I'm Laura Benedict."

"I'm Maia's father," he said with a sudden wave of extraordinary clumsiness; his right heel gave way and sand spilled into his loafer. "Maia's told me so much about you, I'm sorry I haven't had a chance to say hello before this."

He felt the sand nearing the gauze bandage that covered his infected big toe.

"You must have had some week, moving in, and right away an epidemic!" she said. She swept the back of her sandy hand across her forehead and pulled off her terrible-looking hat. Her long hair was the color of wheat. "I'm really glad Maia's back with us, even if it's only for half a day."

"I hope I didn't interrupt your activities . . ."

"Not at all, we're breaking for lunch now anyway," she said, looking back at the campers and watching them attentively.

As she turned away from Daniel, her hair fell away from her long graceful neck and he felt the familiar loneliness descend for a moment. That was rare for the middle of the day. It usually started at suppertime; at sundown. He took Maia's hand. "Looks like your entire group was in my office last week. That must have been quite a way to begin a camp session."

She gave Maia a small hug. "I couldn't believe it. I'm much too old for strep, but I caught it too, so now we're all into peanut butter and jelly and penicillin for lunch. Sounds terrific, huh?"

"We have to put holes in the top soon as we get home, Laura says," Maia interrupted, thrusting the jar at him. "They can eat dead flies or anything we have around the house."

Daniel laughed. "We should be able to feed them well in that case!" He shifted his position and more sand filled the sides of his right loafer and trickled down under his instep. In a minute the sand would be inside his bandage, coating the wound like sugar. But he didn't want to leave the beach, the breeze, or Laura—even though she made him feel wrinkled and used and older then he'd felt in a while. She was lithe and cool and maybe twenty-six. He cleared his throat. "Are you planning on teaching . . . or what made you take up with this contagious group anyway?"

She blushed slightly, seemed suddenly embarrassed. "I thought I'd just try this summer . . . my dissertation work is in limbo and I . . . well I thought they needed a nature-study group."

"You're from Sheffield?"

"Yes . . . local girl comes home! My parents own the bookstore on Main Street."

"Benedict! Right, I passed it. . . . I really want to get there soon."

"I used to work there part-time. At least whenever I got a chance during graduate school. But this summer, well, I decided to try this."

"I think it's terrific. They look like they're loving it." Each of his words seemed more inane than the last. He felt Maia's tug on his hand.

"This beach is the most interesting ecosystem for miles—all this morning we looked at intertidal organisms."

"Like these?" he asked, pointing to the snails in Maia's jar.

"Yes, aren't they neat? Monday we'll do some bird watching, Tuesday we'll look at the salt marsh, Wednesday we'll look at the woods in back of the marsh . . ."

"I see why Maia is so excited," he said, grinning delightedly at her enthusiasm.

She flushed slightly and her green eyes darkened with a hint of anger. "They're never taught any real ecology in school, and I think it's important for them to know early on how their environment works, so they can take care of it." She stopped herself. "God, I sound like a textbook . . ." She let her breath out sharply, as if with impatience at her inability to express a strong feeling. "See, these children are my last hope for the town!"

Daniel's eyes widened as he heard the passion in her voice. He was suprised. Sheffield was so clean and free of litter. He had the only dandelions for acres. He'd even gotten a polite note in his mailbox about them. And since he'd been there,

*The Sheffield News* had had at least three editorials on pollution.

"You should see my hometown!" he said.

"At least in New York City you can see what's going on. Here the issue is all fogged over, you can't tell the good guys from the bad guys, you know? So who do you shoot?"

Okay, all graduate students were fanatics. Had to be. Went with the all-out pursuit of a single subject. He didn't really want to continue the discussion, but instead just stand there the rest of the day hypnotized by the breeze blowing her long hair . . . "I was under the impression that the people here were very concerned about the environment," he said. Lieberman, you have to get back to work, he told himself. Your cardboard clock is running out. "But then you're an ecologist . . ."

"Will be. Maybe I should show you around town."

"Don't expect me to be impressed. I'm from the land of genuine soot and grime, where the decibel level never falls below eighty."

"I know," she said, smiling at Maia. "And your daughter says you're a sucker for little white houses and fairy tale lawns." She gazed at him directly, her jaw squared slightly. "Well, these children are the offspring of the Set. They inherit the town, and I'm hoping I can turn them around a little."

"What's the Set?"

"The local establishment . . . the people who own the town." She was getting tough, her hands were clenched in small fists on her hips. He'd liked her better ankle-deep in low tide. The negativism of grad students! Jesus, was that far behind him! Serious talks about society with a capital S and espresso till five in the morning. And now the new confrontations with young women who had the entire feminist movement behind them . . . forget it! He was just a corny middle-aged divorced man with a half-grown kid, settling down, doing his best, up at dawn. She's fifteen years younger, he thought. I'd have to shout over the generation gap, for Christ's sake. "I really better be getting back to my office now . . . it's bedlam."

She waved lightly. "Nice talking to you . . . see you Monday, Maia!" she called, turning easily and walking away with long-legged strides over the dune.

"See you Monday!" Maia called after her.

Daniel felt calm. Emptier, but calm. The air was suddenly

still. Maia took his hand, unaware of the vibrations that had passed over her head like a quick summer storm. Gone now. A radical grad student, for God's sake. After a whole miserable marriage and a drawn-out divorce by long distance, who needed that? He slammed the car door so hard that Maia looked at him. He started the engine roughly, and it flooded. Sighing with impatience, he sat back, turned off the ignition, and gave the car a minute to rest. He still envisioned her, standing in the water, rolled up jeans, a gaggle of children pulling her round and round in the breezes. . . . Damn! The engine finally started. He jerked away from the shoreline, as if fleeing for his life.

"This is where Janie's mom saw the UFO!" Maia announced excitedly.

"What?"

"Right over there on that field! That's where Mrs. Garner *saw* it!" Maia pointed with one finger, clutching the jar with her arm.

Daniel looked at her. She had a saddle of freckles across her nose, and her glasses tilted down unevenly like his. Her mouth was feline, solemn, and sweet. "Hey!" he asked. "Did you have fun today?"

She looked back as the field passed her line of vision. "Janie said it had lights, very tiny ones. And lots of colors. Some colors we don't even have names for on our planet!" she said.

Daniel yawned as he drove. "If I were a visitor from outer space, I wouldn't pick Sheffield."

Maia looked at him seriously. "I thought you liked it here, Daddy."

"I do, I do. But you have to remember I'm not picky like I'd be if I were an alien."

She smiled. "Don't be silly."

Daniel turned toward town, and when they were stopped at the intersection light, he glanced at her. She seemed happy. "So, what's in the jar?"

"I named them."

"Okay, then *who's* in the jar?"

"This one's called Janie for my friend, and the big one is Laura . . ."

Passing Main Street, he had a surge of hunger. "Pizza?"

"Sure."

The counter man wiped their places, smiling at Maia, who held the jar tightly on her lap. Everyone smiled in Sheffield.

She must like that. He did. In the city, everyone frowned. Here, everyone said "Have a nice day!" as if they meant it. How could she not notice the difference?

"I'd like plain."

"Make mine with anchovies and peppers, please." He turned his attention to her. "How're you doing, kid? I mean is everyone treating you okay? . . . Well, I mean are you feeling at home yet?"

Maia looked down at the jar. "Sure, but Janie's my best friend, and she wasn't there today."

"Oh, I saw her this morning, she should be back Monday . . ."

"I hate Billy McGinnis. He pushed me into the mud when I had my sandals on."

"I'm sorry. Maia, what I meant was . . . you're not homesick or anything?"

Maia's eyes were faintly puzzled behind her glasses when she looked at him. "You're here," she said simply.

Daniel took a deep breath to counteract the small fear in his gut, fear of the fragility of children, of his huge responsibility. He bit into the pizza slice too soon and burned the roof of his mouth. He chewed silently. "Listen, honey," he said, remembering the morning. "The Doughertys asked me to a party at their house tomorrow night. . . . I was kind of wondering about getting a sitter. How do you feel about that?"

"What *for?*" Maia replied with indignation.

"Well . . . it's a new house and . . ."

"I'll be fine!" She gobbled her pizza. In between mouthfuls, she reassured him. "I never had a sitter in New York, and look at the crime rate there. You said it was really different here, didn't you? . . . And besides, I got lots of work to do." She now was doing her imitation of him. He marveled as she chewed and talked, looking harried, glasses slipping farther down her nose. "I want to run some experiments on these guys."

"I thought they were pets. You *named* them!"

"I won't hurt them. I just wanta try a couple of things."

He smiled. "I see . . ."

"Should take me till about midnight . . ." Her voice grew suddenly smaller. "You think you'll be home by then?"

Daniel kissed the part in her fine brown hair. "You want me to turn into a pumpkin or something? The latest eleven o'clock, okay?"

"Daddy, you're so silly, the coach was what turned into a

pumpkin, and there aren't any boys in that story except the prince. The prince stayed the same."

Daniel laughed, but he felt that old anxiety that the responsibility was too much. His marriage had been a fiasco, his early infatuation with urban life a mistake. Could there be something wrong with these trees and friendly people . . . something deeply wrong, that Laura hinted at?

"Hey, I know what . . . let's get a cone at that great Freeze Shoppe. Okay?" He swung off the stool and away from his thoughts.

She turned on the stool, eye to eye with him, wiping her mouth with the corner of her napkin, and nonchalantly, in a flat voice, she reminded him: "Sure, but they get it at the same place as Ye Olde Freeze on Lexington Avenue, you know." She jumped down.

He looked down at the top of her head with a pang of regret. Oh Maia, don't grow up so fast!

Wendy Dougherty leaned against the raw concrete wall of the rear library hallway, her bruised cheek touching the grainy surface; tears came to her eyes. Getting her mother to drive her there was about the biggest hassle anyone could imagine. Just 'cause she had to go into town twice, so what! So was it Wendy's fault that her father beat her up? The way her mother yelled at her, Wendy couldn't even think, she even had to go sit on the toilet and run the bathtub faucet just to cut out the noise. It was too much! First the fucking monkey and then her stupid father and then her fat-mouth mother. If it hadn't been for Chet, she would've flipped out long ago. She felt her swollen cheek. Oh my God, did she look like a slob. And she had spent the entire morning trying to get the roots of her hair to sort of blend in with the yellow-orange color that the lady in the drugstore said would *not* happen if she used Bright Lights. What a rip-off!

But she should've stayed home. She couldn't get her face together at all, and she looked weird. Thank God she didn't have pimples. But the big fat cheek and her *lips*! If she had stayed home, she could've explained everything to Chet when she was looking okay again. Tears started again. Chet wouldn't want her anymore. He'd say she grossed him out. Her heart caught as she looked into the main reading room. There was Chet at Miss Hill's desk. She saw his tight chinos first, then his muscular, T-shirted back, curved over the desk as he leaned over talking to the librarian. He thought Miss Hill was a case the way she kept getting all those books for him on whatever he told her he was interested in. Maybe it was the way he looked at her with those brown eyes that anyone would give their life for!

"Oh, Miss Hill, I always wanted to know more about pyramids, I mean like how those guys got the stones moved around, you know? I betcha they couldn't build one today . . . huh?" That's the way he put her on all the time. And sure enough, the next week Miss Hill would have a stack of books on her desk on whatever Chet asked about. And he would thank her like you couldn't believe, and he sort of meant it too sometimes, 'cause she really did try, the old cunt, he said. She was real nice to him. Chet even told Wendy once if he had a grandmother like Miss Hill he could be anything . . . an astronaut maybe or a lawyer, maybe even President. And then he launched right into his thing about how Wendy had all the advantages and was flunking out because she was really a dumb-assed broad. Sometimes he wouldn't stop being mean to her. He never hassled Jill Horgan that way. Jill was something else. Wendy'd felt like really gross next to Jill at the lab last night, and she'd really wished Jill and Scott Andrews hadn't come along. Now Jill was probably at Louie's Place with the other kids. Jill was real independent, and when Chet gave her a hard time, she's just go to Louie's Place. Wendy couldn't even go there, because her father would murder her if he found out . . . she wished Chet would be nicer. Didn't he know she'd do anything for him? Didn't he? Didn't last night at the lab prove anything?

She watched Chet's back as he leaned way over face to face with Miss Hill, doing a real number on her, nodding at whatever the old bitch said. Wendy forgot how awful she looked and went on in. She walked over to the magazine stand and riffled through the boring ones like *Saturday Review* and all that shit . . . there wasn't even a new *TV Guide*, just last week's *Time*. What a creepy place!

Wendy sat down loudly and coughed. The old man sitting next to her looked up. She knew by now he was old Mr. Harrison. He spent all day here. Wendy coughed again, this time without meaning to, and when Mr. Harrison looked slightly disgusted, she remembered to put her hand over her mouth. " 'Scuse me," she said. This place is an old age home, she thought.

She knew that Chet had heard her cough. She scraped her chair, but he didn't turn around. He signaled to her instead with his middle finger behind his ass. She would've maybe thought that was funny any other day, but not now, when who knew who was looking at her already. She blushed and looked down at the "People" section of *Time* till she felt like looking up again. Now Chet was pointing at the stairs as if she was some kind of trained dog.

She walked real fast over to Miss Hill. "Miss Hill, I can't find Hemingway."

The old witch looked like shocked or something, maybe it was all the bruises and stuff on Wendy.

"I can't find Hemingway," Wendy repeated, gritting her teeth, not looking at Chet.

"Come, child," Miss Hill said, leaving Chet standing at her desk.

Wendy didn't even look back at him. She went to the big card catalogue with Hill and watched the old lady take out the "H" drawer, slide out the oak board, and set it down. She tried to back off a bit 'cause Miss Hill was too close and her breath smelled like mold, but the old lady kept talking. Wendy sighed and sighed and kept saying yes, yes, yes, but Hill stuck to her like a spiderweb and leaned near her, whispering about the filing system.

What did Chet think when he saw her all beat up like that and looking gross? Did he hate her? Was he going to forgive her for not going right away to the stairs? Hill finally finished, thank God, and Wendy wrote the stuff on this slip like she was told, so Hill wouldn't get suspicious. Then she walked slowly to the stairs.

She started up to the second landing, her body hurting all over. She didn't know what to tell Chet. Where was he? Maybe he split . . . no, suddenly he was behind her. She felt him full length down her back, warm and already turned on, and his hands held her tits as she tried to tell him . . . "Listen," she began. But he pushed her gently up the stairs, staying close behind her. "Listen, Chet . . ." she tried again, but they had arrived at their favorite stack. "Ancient and Medieval History."

"You can hope nobody reads this shit," Chet had said a couple of months ago when they first found their place in the silent, musty stacks. Chet always said it would be really funny to see the expression on the face of some old fart who flicked the light on and found them at it in the corner. They'd left a blanket on the bottom shelf and nobody'd moved it. In the parking lot, back of the Lawsons' theater, someone was always shining a flashlight in your face; and the beach was the same story. So if you didn't have a car, you couldn't ask for a better place than this.

Before Chet grabbed her and took a real close look at her face, she tried to explain how she hurt all over, and what had happened after he left her last night. But he didn't listen, he just whispered that he wouldn't kiss her face if it hurt there and not to worry, and at first she winced with pain, but then on the blanket it wasn't bad and after a minute had passed, she couldn't feel anything but the heat inside her body and she felt like screaming with pleasure when he unzipped his chinos and thrush inside her . . . "Shhh . . ." he said. "Shhh. . . take it easy baby . . ."

Later, when Chet was lying next to her, he asked her if her father had beat her up when she got home. And she felt so good, so carried away from everything that made her feel rotten all day, that she told him the truth. She told him she got beat up for telling her old man about the lab.

The way Chet looked at her, she knew she should've kept her mouth shut. "First that fucking monkey and then my father punching me and now you . . ." she said, beginning to cry. Before he'd said he was real *proud* of her—after all, she and Jill and Scott went in with the monkeys and he never got past the first room.

He grabbed her and shook her a little. "Wendy, you are gonna get me in big trouble, you know? If I get busted, I stay there, man. Not like you. I ain't got a father who controls the press in the whole friggin' town, you know?"

And off he went into his entire Chet-versus-the-establishment speech. Wendy kept saying her father wouldn't ever say anything. He'd never print a word about it in the newspaper, the proof being there was nothing so far on the news even, and they must've found the spray paint and all that morning.

But Chet wouldn't listen. He pulled up his chinos and swung his silver Leo sign around on the chain around his neck, and he left her. She lay there alone and cold, listening to him run down the metal stairs.

*"Natural Products International."*

*"NPI, this is Chameleon control."*

*There was a click, a buzzing sound, then a man's voice. "Yes?"*

*"There was a break-in at the lab last night. McGinnis made a phone call to the police."*

*"What happened?"*

*"I haven't been able to determine that yet. McGinnis told the police that it was just some kids—routine vandalism."*

*"Who found the damage?"*

*"McGinnis. About six this morning."*

*"Has anyone but McGinnis seen the damage? What about the security guard, Jim Walters?"*

*"I don't know. He left early. The technicians were given the day off before they got inside. But the Perrinis went in to work."*

*"Follow up on Walters."*

*"Anything else?"*

*"I want to know if the P3 was involved in any way. Stay on top of it."*

*There was a click.*

It was early evening. Louise Garner watched Paul McGinnis adjust his tie in front of the mirror on the medicine cabinet. When he tilted his head like that, the geometry of his face was accentuated; the strong jaw, the perfect, straight nose, the thin mocking lips. He caught her watching him and closed his eyes briefly. She had noticed that habit of his long ago. He would shut his eyes, barely more than a blink, and make people disappear. Erase them, so that when he opened his eyes, they would no longer intrude on his consciousness. She'd thought he would never do that to her.

"Is there anything you want to tell me, Paul?"

She heard her voice, soft and tentative, and knew she was getting soft around the edges like the voice. She was less sure of herself and of reality. It had happened before, so she recognized the onset. ". . . Paul? I'm sorry . . ."

"For what?"

"I'm sorry I asked, but really I . . ." she sniffed. Her nose was turning pink and she knew he hated that. She smelled the after-shave lotion and wondered if Janie ever noticed it. She make a note to hide the bottle. "I think you owe me an answer . . ." she made herself say, instantly regretting it when she saw his shoulders stiffen. "Paul, I'm always saying the wrong things . . . but I'd like to know what's wrong."

McGinnis walked into her bedroom, sat down on the edge of her unmade bed, and put his shoes on with a shoehorn, flexing his toes. "Wasn't my performance up to par?" he asked mockingly.

She sat by him. "You seemed . . . distracted. Is it what happened in the lab?"

"I don't know what you're talking about."

"Why aren't you pressing charges?"

"You don't press charges for simple vandalism, Louise. Always turns out to be rotten public relations, and they never find the kids anyway. Who cares? Nothing terrible happened."

Louise walked in front of him and placed her hands on his shoulders, looking into his eyes. "Paul, I've been your secretary for quite a while . . ."

"Since first we fucked."

She felt the words as a slap, and tears of helplessness came to her eyes. "Paul, what really happened this morning? Why did the technicians leave so suddenly? What was that all about?" Her voice trembled slightly.

"I simply took advantage of the interruption to hold a work conference with the Perrinis. We didn't need the technicians."

"Paul . . . you know you can't manage entirely alone," Louise said.

"Who do you think you are, Louise?" he said very quietly.

She flushed at his tone. "Your fucking secretary. Isn't that what you said?"

"I'll tell you who you are," he continued just as quietly. "You are nobody. And as long as you stay nobody, you're fine. But if you try any more of that confidante shit with me, you'll wind up out of work."

She stared at him, her anger mounting over her timidity, her voice defiant. "You wouldn't dare fire me."

"Was that a threat?"

Louise swallowed. "I don't give a shit what you call it. Just get out of here and leave me alone."

"Shhh . . . you'll wake Janie, remember?" he said softly, as if she were quite insane.

Was she? She had to be, following the bastard down the stairs, out of habit, all the way to the kitchen door.

"I'm sorry I said that, Paul, I only wanted to help . . ."

He turned at the screen door. "See you Monday," he said.

The hinges on the screen door squeaked. "No," she said too loudly. "Tomorrow night at the Doughertys'—your birthday, remember?" She looked at the still, huge trees around the back of the house she couldn't afford, and at the tennis court, in disrepair since Harvey's death. Why couldn't she find the strength to sell the house, give up her job, and move away from Paul, from Sheffield . . . start a new life for Janie and for herself? Silence. Just the sound of gravel as Paul McGinnis walked down the back path, screened from the neighbors by a tall hedge. A private relationship, and even if everyone in town knew, he kept up the pretense and parked three roads down. Long ago, when they used to still laugh together, he said the town thought it was old lady Bridges he was after. In those days he had to reassure her because of Harvey, and because he still cared enough to bother. He used to say that if there was any gossip, it was about old Bridges, the rocking-chair wonder. Different days. What had gone so wrong? She was getting flabby. Her will to free herself of the whole situation dissolved at the sight of Paul turning for a moment at the end of the path. He glanced at her, his eyes impenetrable, and threw his jacket over one shoulder. He looked so cool in the heat.

"Mommy?"

She heard the voice from the upstairs. "Mommy?" Janie was waking up from her nap. Did she still have a fever? She went to the sink to get some cold water for her and her evening dose of antibiotic. First she would take care of her little girl, and then somehow, she would try to reorder her life . . . maybe in the morning.

# Saturday, August fourth,

cooled when the sun went down, but there was still no breeze. Barbara Dougherty had prayed for a break in the heat wave so she could serve hot buttered corn, but no such luck. And too hot for aspic. She walked around the living room, trying to smile, anxiously counting heads.

George Taylor, whose company was about to transfer him for the eleventh time in fifteen years, grabbed Barbara, buried his face in her neck, and said, "Sexy broad, when are you coming away with me?"

It was going well.

The room was a natural for a large crowd, she thought, like a summer ski lodge. Voices and laughter rose comfortably up over the taped pop music to the beamed cathedral ceiling. She could begin to relax a bit. "Where did you get those luscious crudités?" Jenny Hollis asked.

"Christy's."

"Christy's?" squealed Jenny. "God, who can afford it? For a farm stand they have prices like Tiffany's . . . I'm just going to have to wait for their tag sale!"

It was going to be fine. Bouquets of coral tea roses, irises, snap dragon, and sweet william on every highly polished end table were sure to keep everyone from noticing the bleached-out plaid on Jack's rocker and the dull chintz on all that twenty-year-old reproduction early-American furniture. The room was better with lots of people. The Set was clustered around her new modular white couch in the center of the room. Even Pam Vail had said it was handsome. Being in the Set was a permanent position, but staying on its lowest rung took so much effort sometimes. It *was* exciting though, being picked to host Paul's birthday party even if it did mean they couldn't buy the outdoor electric grill that summer.

Groups of people now stood elbow to elbow on the pale sweep of carpet. Men in red or blue linen jackets, women in flower prints, their shoulders bare, hair lustrous. Squinting slightly, she decided her home did look glamorous. She only hoped Jack had the Polaroid loaded and didn't get too drunk.

The bell rang. She wondered if it was the Perrinis, whoever they were. It took some nerve for even Paul McGinnis to call her at virtually the last minute and ask that they be tacked on to the guest list.

Daniel Lieberman stood in a spill of yellow bug light on the Doughertys' front porch, casting a jaundiced look at the knee-high black jockey statue while he waited for someone to hear the chime over the noise of the crowd.

"Sorry to be late, Mrs. Dougherty," he began as she opened the door.

"*Barbara*, please! Don't be silly, you're not late. Not at all . . ."

He wiped his feet on the green mat with the plastic daisy one more time, seeing the interior plush white carpeting that stretched out over the floor of the front vestibule and up the wide staircase straight ahead. "I had to finish up the dinner dishes and get Maia ready for bed," he explained.

"Oh, but we won't sit down for ages!" Barbara said adjusting the neckline of her flowered chiffon dress. Her makeup was smooth now, and she smiled up at him pertly. "*Do* come meet everyone."

Daniel paused at the foot of the stairs and rubbed the back of his curly light brown hair, with a tentative look at the mass of new neighbors on his right. He felt more than a little reluctant to dive into the throng. Through the outside sliding-glass wall of the large living room he saw candlelight, torches, spotlighted trees, and the flames of a barbecue pit. Inside were all his patients' parents, whose names he did not know; people who Laura had called "the Set."

"How's Wendy?" he asked.

"Good as new!" Barbara replied cheerfully, pointing to the far end of the room, where Wendy stood, her back to them, serving canapés. "*There* she is, helping out!"

Daniel nodded, noticing Wendy's adolescent rear end tightly encased in pink slacks; a middle-aged friend of her parents was furtively watching it as she moved in a desultory fashion from guest to guest. Suddenly Wendy turned so that he could see her face. She seemed almost good as new, and maybe even improved. Her closed, hostile expression had been replaced by a mild, almost shy look—a controlled puzzlement . . .

"You remember my son, Roy?" Barbara was saying. "Well

*there* he is helping too, and he's only ten. . . . Remember I had him to your office last week?" she said, waving at a freckle-faced child.

"Sure, he's in camp with Maia . . . listen, you think it's all right to leave Maia alone in the house?" he asked, filled with sudden anxiety. "I left your telephone number . . ."

"It's Sheffield! Lord, I leave my door unlocked all the time. Everyone does."

"No kidding . . . well, I guess I'll have to get used to all this safety . . ."

Barbara took his arm and walked him toward a group of guests. "Absolutely do not give a second thought to leaving her by herself. But if you ever need sitters, I have a couple of names for you . . . and there's no reason why you should have to do dishes with your busy schedule. I bet you don't have anyone to clean house, either?"

A slim, expensive-looking woman blocked their path, smiling. Her hair was black silk, as was her shirt. Her harem pants were the color of her lipstick, and she was deeply tanned. "You need a mother's helper, you poor man. I'm Greta. Greta McGinnis." She smiled radiantly now, as if that were a punchline, and held out a slim hand with red lacquered nails.

"*You're* not a mother's helper . . ." Daniel said, grinning broadly.

"Not at the moment," she teased, her eyes sweeping over him. "But I have lists of them, *lists*. You come over and we'll look at my lists," she said in such a parody of blatant suggestiveness that he laughed with her. Yet he found himself imagining the texture of her silk blouse and the touch of her skin . . . he barely noticed the man who appeared behind her. Striding a tennis player's comfortable walk, he had arrived quickly and silently, as if in sneakers. Daniel looked down involuntarily at the man's feet. No, it was loafers, with red and green Gucci stripes. His gaze lifted to the handsome square-jawed face, the gray eyes . . . the man was several inches taller than he, and trim. Very trim.

"Paul McGinnis. Welcome to Sheffield, Doctor . . ."

"Lieberman. Call me Daniel," he said. It felt as if they'd just cut a ceremonial ribbon when McGinnis shook his hand.

"You've met my wife?" McGinnis asked.

Greta McGinnis had stopped smiling just a little. "Oh yes," she breathed. "Just now; and I want you to know poor Dr. Lieberman's been absolutely put upon, doing *dishes* and that sort of thing. I think he should get a mother's helper or . . . something," she finished with only half-suppressed mischievousness.

"Dinner dishes! Liberation, let me count the ways!" A big, noisy man lumbered over, throwing his left arm around McGinnis, who recoiled slightly. The man pumped Daniel's hand. "Jack Dougherty! The little woman just told me you were late 'cause you got piled up with household chores. Look at me, talking! I'm in charge of the coals or I would've been at the door myself." Dougherty managed to hit all the consonants hard enough to spray Daniel liberally.

Daniel caught himself staring at the prominent purple veins that laced the man's nose. Jack Dougherty had small eyes like Wendy's and a rather beefy face, reminiscent of a football player gone to seed. The power was still there, the thick arms, but a paunch hung over his belt.

"I'm glad you made it, Doctor! Always good to have one of you in the house, eh?" he laughed loudly, patting Daniel on the shoulder. "Did you meet everybody yet? Hey, *everybody!*" he roared.

Hands reached out at him from all directions. Daniel smiled uneasily and plunged into the Set. They seemed so pleased he was there, reaching for him, patting him. Was he welcome, or was he dinner?

Dr. Joseph Perrini drove to the Doughertys' while his wife, Rosalind, looked silently out the car window. Their oval faces, oddly similar, focused on the passing scenery.

"If McGinnis thinks to ingratiate himself, he going to be surprised," Rosalind said finally, as they neared the party.

"I am tired of your speaking for both of us!" he snapped.

She turned to him. "It's a sloppy operation, Joseph, and it always has been. It's about time something was done about it."

A policeman waved them to the end of a long line of parked cars.

Joseph Perrini pulled the emergency brake up hard. "You've been really quite difficult lately," he said. "Finicky, on edge . . . are you tired?"

Rosalind pursed her lips angrily and spoke in her grating voice. "I just don't look the other way. You were there last month when those idiots from Radionuclide Disposal spilled an entire canister of waste next to the parking area."

"For heaven's sake, Rosalind. It wasn't Hiroshima, was it? You only react this way because you dislike McGinnis."

"He's a liar," she said furiously. "It's a sloppy operation. How do we know what happened Thursday night, Joseph? How did that monkey die? It was perfectly healthy on Thursday afternoon . . . and why no autopsy on a treated animal? Why would he incinerate it? I don't believe him at all."

Joseph Perrini sighed audibly. "You will not make a scene, I hope."

She looked at him in the dark car and did not speak.

His voice rose strongly and became threatening. "I am warning you for the last time: there will be no scene. You will not verbalize your opinions. I am not going to allow you to upset my work, my life, by your temperamental differences with McGinnis. This is only one project. I will not permit you to jeopardize the next and the next . . ."

She got out of the car and slammed the door. Finally she nodded to him. "I'll be silent for now," she said.

Shirley Lawson, ever on the prowl, sidled over to Pam and Charles Vail, who stood near the big stone fireplace. Shirley, a short woman with a nimbus of lamb's wool perm and a large turquoise Indian necklace clanking against her billiard-green caftan, gave Pam Vail's arm a squeeze. "Darling!" she exclaimed. "I was hunting for you. And Charles, of course. You know that next week is the midsummer benefit for the Sheffield Players' Theater and . . ."

Pam Vail's eyes glazed over with disinterest, and her jaw quivered with a trace of a suppressed yawn. That was her normal expression. She seemed always about to sink into a narcoleptic stupor. If she hadn't been so beautiful, the Set might have considered her boredom unattractive. But her flawless skin, glossy auburn hair, and disdainful hazel cats' eyes were all perfect; her features were marred only by a slightly pouting mouth.

". . . and so it's very, very, important this season that you and Charles not only save the date but make a real effort to get everybody there . . . even that new Dr. Liverstein."

"He's Jewish?" asked Pam, waking up.

"Lieberman, Shirley. . . . She means the new pediatrician, Pam, the one we brought Cindy to last week," Vail informed his wife with a warning look. "He took over for Dr. Cameron . . . we use him, Shirley."

"How nice . . ." Shirley said. "Howard and I send Amy and

Allen to him also . . . but anyway, what I meant was wouldn't it be nice to include him. He *is* from New York—probably has tons of exposure to the theater and cultural events . . ."

"I think Cameron said he was from Brooklyn," Vail interrupted.

"Brooklyn," Pam repeated, making the word sound like a terminal disease.

"Well *anyway*, let's include him at the benefit, and Charles, I really need you to make a rousing speech, and Pam, I want an instant opinion: Champagne or sangria?"

Charles Vail was a large, pleasant-looking, portly man with thinning ash-colored hair, considerably older than his wife. He seemed to have decided that his role was to guard her, adjust her ivory silk blouse as it kept falling open, revealing most of her small, high breasts, and make sure she wasn't overheard uttering any sentiments that would offend the more liberal investors at his bank.

"More than happy to make a speech, Shirley. More than happy. And by the way, I have some good news. McGinnis has just made a substantial contribution to the Arts Council this month, and at the last Council meeting we all decided that most of it will be earmarked for the community theater . . ."

"Oh, my dears!" said Shirley, clasping her hands to her chest. "What wonderful news . . . did you hear that, Ralph darling?!" she breathed to a man she knew would always be just behind her.

Ralph Jeffreys smiled widely. He was slim and middle-aged, with several chains of gold dangling onto his peach-colored turtleneck silk-knit shirt. "Terrific!" he said.

"Definitely champagne! That settles it . . . scratch the sangría, Ralph," Shirley said, smiling radiantly at Vail. "In fact that calls for a drink right now. Make us some vodka tonics, Ralph, would you. There's a darling . . ." She watched him tenderly as he glided to the large pine-planked bar that stretched diagonally across one corner of the room. "I don't know what I'd do without him. He's my major-domo."

Vail smiled tolerantly. "I thought this summer he was general manager of the Sheffield Players'."

"That too!" Shirley said.

"Oh Jesus, some asshole just goosed me," Greta complained *sotto voce* as she led Daniel Lieberman by the arm, away from a large swarm of neighbors. She turned near the pine bar with some amusement in her eyes and an enticing smile. "Now seriously, Dr. Lieberman, you just can't go on being a housewife . . ." she said, touching his arm with her fingertips. She smelled of Coppertone and jasmine. "I absolutely insist you come over and see my lists. Stop by tomorrow first thing. That means noon. There's the bar, you'll need it!"

Quickly, she disengaged her arm and slipped out the patio doors toward a large table where Barbara was setting up the salad. Daniel stared after her, smiling a moment.

Alone for the first time, he glanced briefly around. He noticed that in the center of the room on an angular white couch sat an odd-looking pale couple in dark, foreign-looking clothing. They stood out among the roses and flower prints like crows in a poppy field. Their faces, identically adorned with horn-rimmed glasses, seemed very familiar to him, as if he'd seen them somewhere before . . . in black and white, on television or in the news . . .

"Doc! Let me get you something to drink!" Dougherty bellowed at him.

Startled by the interruption, he turned abruptly. "Coke . . . who are those people on the couch, Jack?"

"Those people . . . oh, those people are the Perrinis, and that guy talking to them is Dr. Howard Lawson, Shirley Lawson's husband."

Daniel hadn't even noticed the lanky, bland-looking man sitting near the couple. "Perrini?" he mused aloud.

"Yes. Dr. Joseph Perrini and Dr. Roaslind Perrini, you know them?"

Daniel shook his head. "No, I don't think so . . ."

"They're not in your field," Dougherty said, punching him in the arm cheerfully. "Besides, they don't make housecalls. Can I put a little something in your Coke, Doc?"

Daniel held his hand up, smiling.

"Hey look," Dougherty went on, pointing to Wendy. "We've even got our own kids working tonight."

Wendy neared them now, placidly serving a tray on canapés with an odd, slightly confused expression on her face. She was squinting with concentration. The swelling had gone down, and the traces of scrapes were covered with Clearasil, so that from any reasonable distance a viewer would have assumed pimples.

"You met my daughter yet?" Dougherty asked.

"She . . . was in yesterday morning with your wife."

"Oh . . .?"

Daniel looked at Jack Dougherty, suprised. "I'm glad to see her looking fine. That was a pretty bad fall."

"Well, that's what I mean!" Dougherty said, his gruff voice covering his embarrassment. "These kids leave their stuff all over the stairs . . . just drop it behind them! What the hell do they care?" he blustered. "What was that you wanted? Coke?"

It was nine twenty on the grandfather clock near the stairs. Howard Lawson edged near Daniel, clinkling a gin and tonic in one hand.

"Are you in practice in Sheffield, Dr. Lawson?" Daniel asked politely.

"No, I'm with McGinnis Pharmaceutical Labs."

Daniel looked at the lanky man with the crew cut and black-rimmed glasses and at the small secret smile that seemed fixed in place. "Sorry, I heard 'doctor'—I assumed . . ."

"I'm a Ph.D. biologist, not an M.D.," Lawson interrupted.

Shirley, sensing tension, moved in front of her husband. "Is it true," she asked with theatrical intensity, "that every child in Sheffield came down with strep the same week you moved here?"

"It wasn't all of them, dear, only the Set," Lawson cut in with his quiet voice and secretive smile.

"Pay *no* attention to him," Shirley said firmly. Her perm bobbed, and her embarrassment caused her words to tumble out even faster than usual. "Nobody thinks there's a clique in Sheffield except Howard. He has a thing about it and he just goes on and on."

Lawson rubbed the top of his crew cut slowly and stared at Daniel through his black-rimmed glasses. He did not seem inclined to speak.

"What kind of work are you in at the lab, Howard?" Daniel asked politely.

"A little of this, a little of that. I'm a molecular biologist; recently I've gotten into genetic engineering, like everyone else."

Daniel looked puzzled. "I didn't know your lab was . . . I mean, didn't you say pharmaceuticals?"

"All molecular now . . . the cutting edge of pharmaceutical research. I'm sure you've read about the DNA recombinant work on insulin . . ."

"Yes . . . but . . ." Daniel stared. "Isn't that pretty hazardous stuff to be going on in a place like this? This is a well-populated area . . ."

Lawson interrupted, openly annoyed. "You people don't want nuclear plants, you don't want recombinant research, but you want all the benefits of the latest technology. I should think an M.D.. . . ."

"Hi!" Roy Dougherty tapped Daniel's arm, carefully balancing a tray of large shrimp.

"Hi," Daniel said, relieved to see the freckled, pug-nosed child; a nice kid he now remembered from his office. "How're you doing?"

"Fine. Want one of these things? They're dead. My sister's coming around with the other stuff on her tray if you hate shrimp."

Lawson reached for one and Daniel speared another with a toothpick, glad to chew in silent diversion. But Lawson had been overheard.

A bearlike, broad-shouldered man with a round beard came over. "Sam Benedict. Laura's father," the man said. "You must be Daniel Lieberman."

They shook hands warmly. "My kid is president of the local fan club for your daughter," Daniel said.

Sam Benedict was grinning warmly as he puffed on his pipe. "I'm sure the feeling is mutual. . . . I hope you're not taking any of this nonsense from Lawson here. He'd have you believe that if you want a clean, safe environment, it means you're a relic from the last century . . . that's the line, isn't it, Howard, horse and buggies or the great god progress?"

Lawson's smile remained fixed. "Worse that that. You know very well that our country has had more handicapping of important scientific research than any other. . . . We had the lead, but it's people like you who are holding us back. We're constantly wasting our efforts fighting the lunatic fringe."

Benedict took the insult silently and puffed on his pipe. Finally, he spoke with quiet intensity. "I'll tell you something. I will fight the degenerate values in this town to my last breath. . . . The Town Council allows an army base to run cockamamy tests near the beach for a price . . . then refuses to accept federal funding to save our only salt marsh . . . and now they think we're going to sit here in bovine bliss while you lab people switch genetic material from one species to another without even knowing what the consequences will be!"

"Come on, Benedict. We know what we're doing."

"Sure. You're creating recombinant monstrosities. You don't have to be an environmentalist to be worried. You just have to be awake."

Charles Vail cut in front of Sam and reached out to shake Daniel Lieberman's hand. For a moment he eclipsed the party with his bulk, like a shadow thrust between himself and his neighbors. Daniel was aware of manicured fingernails, soft, cared-for skin, and a dark blue silk jacket that brushed his wrist.

Introducing himself, he said, "You've met my daughter, Cindy, Doctor . . . Now Sam, I don't think you want to air all our dirty linen in front of new neighbors."

Benedict looked quizzically at Vail. "Why not? It's not my wash . . . it's your mess."

"The entire lab issue was settled three years ago," Charles Vail said in his avuncular tone. "Let's just get on with the growth and development of our town."

Benedict puffed his pipe thoughtfully. "I know the word 'development' is really big with you people this summer. I understand a shopping center is going up on the salt marsh right next to the hotel. Of course you will than succeed in causing our entire beach to erode in a few years. That's growth for you."

"Sam," Charles Vail began warningly. "We all have beachfront property to protect."

"Not for long," said Benedict. "Because the salt marsh is all that's holding the sand in place. But we were talking about the lab. How can you possibly justify a P3 facility, even if it does increase our scientific upper-middle-income population? That's beyond any sane reasoning."

"Excuse me," a cold voice broke in. McGinnis's gray eyes held Sam Benedict's own and did not waver. "Sam, I know you enjoy being our gadfly, but if you're going on again about the lab, the entire issue is hypothetical. A moot point. Sorry. The P3 has been inactive for over a year."

"Happy birthday, Paul," Sam Benedict said quietly.

Ralph Jeffreys, major-domo, cornered Jean-Claude Santé, who was on his way toward Pam Vail. Jean-Claude stood dejectedly listening to Ralph, gazing wistfully over his wife Angelique's head toward Pam's plummeting neckline. The Santés were an impeccable couple. Their elegant accents, their well-groomed neat figures and excellent taste in clothes gave them an unreal perfection, like figures on a wedding cake.

"Listen," Ralph said to Jean-Claude. "I stopped in Chez Claude last week for lunch and our posters weren't up. We need those Players' posters up this season!"

Jean-Claude backed away slightly. His handsome face held a diplomatic smile, but he gave Angelique a slightly frantic look. She shrugged. "Some one of the help must have taken them down . . ." he answered unconvincingly.

Jeffreys ignored that. "Any tourists staying at your hotel or stopping by for lunch in your restaurant would think Sheffield was a culturally deprived area! By the way, the chocolate mousse was *thin*."

"I am so sorry, Mr. Jeffreys," Angelique took over in her bell-like precise voice. "We shall make certain that your posters are put up at the front desk and in the entrance to the restaurant."

"Terrific!" Ralph said. "You do that and I'll trade you a mousse recipe, black velvet, redolent with bitter chocolate, that'll put Chez Claude on the map!"

Jean-Claude brushed past Ralph murmuring excuses, and with ill-concealed eagerness made a beeline for Pam. Angelique watched him go to her, gazing sadly at his back.

"It's all in the whisk," Ralph was saying.

Louise Garner stood just inside the patio doors. Her dark, silver-streaked hair had been carefully upswept but was now falling down from the severe chignon, in rapidly increasing disarray, onto her shoulders. She brushed at it absently. She held a martini in a fat tumbler, clasping it with both hands like a child. She wasn't looking at anyone. When Daniel spoke to her, she gave a start. "Hi, Louise, I didn't see you till just now. How's Janie doing?"

"Oh . . . oh, she's better now, Dan, thank you."

"She's really a bright kid, you know. With a sensational imagination."

She looked at him distractedly with her dark blue eyes. "Thank you."

"She . . . was telling Maia that you two spotted a UFO near the beach," he said, laughing, trying to put her at ease. "Very specific she was, and very detailed descriptions . . ."

"What UFO in its right mind would land in this creepy dump?" Louise said dryly, lifting her glass. "Cheers."

She silently finished her drink.

"So . . . she'll be back in camp Monday?" he asked.

"I *did* see it," she said quietly. She swayed back on her heels slightly and then rocked forward. "I'm a pretty decent mother, you know?"

"Of course you are," Daniel said, hoping somebody would interrupt.

"I wouldn't drive my own daughter around with more than a couple of Valiums and maybe two drinks . . . that's the limit."

"Look, I'm sure you saw something."

"And Janie was sober. Did that occur to you?"

He took her arm and looked at her directly. "I never said you weren't sober. The first I heard of this was when Maia told me. I'm sorry I even mentioned it, but I had thought it was Janie's imagination."

"I'm sorry too," she said, locking more dark strands in her chignon as others tumbled out. Her nose was turning pinkish and her eyes teary. "It's just such an ancient sore subject around Sheffield. When I reported it, I thought they'd put me away for good. It was about the time Harvey died . . ."

Now he began to understand. Somehow it was connected to her loss. She looked so vulnerable, he thought.

"I was driving Janie home from a friend's house. She'd decided not to stay overnight. It was a bad time for us both . . . I went to pick her up and we were driving along when suddenly there was a brightness, a shape. It lifted up . . . God! I haven't spoken about this in years. I don't know how you got me started."

"Excuse me," said someone from a few yards away. "Can I get you some more ice, Louise?" McGinnis asked without moving toward them.

"Oh . . . yes, Paul," she replied softly and held her glass out to his. "Excuse me, please,"she said as she walked away from Daniel, her eyes riveted to McGinnis's.

Just then Wendy Dougherty came up with a tray of hors d'oeuvres and handed Daniel a cocktail napkin.

"Wendy . . . how're you doing?" he asked gently.

"Fine," she said to the floor.

"Thank you," he said, taking a meatball. "You're sure you're feeling all right?"

"Yeah," she said in a dull voice, and walked away, maybe too quickly, because she swayed slightly and was about to trip over her right foot when she righted herself near Louise Garner. Daniel watched as Louise leaned maternally toward

Wendy, giving her a hug and some advice. McGinnis was nowhere in sight now.

A familiar voice called his name. There was a knock on the glass door behind him.

He turned to see Laura. "Hello," he said, walking out onto the patio. Charcoal smoke and citronella burned the back of his throat. "I didn't know you were here."

"I'm not," she said, smiling at him. "At least not officially. I'm just with my parents, and they're here only because we happen to be neighbors."

He looked appreciatively at her laughing eyes and at the graceful flow of what seemed to be an old-fashioned gauzy white gown that she wore. He wondered if she thought of him as of her parents' generation, or even worse, a lech . . .

"A penny . . .?" she interrupted his thoughts.

"I was thinking that's a nice dress."

She pointed to the lacing ties down the camisole top. "It's a nightgown. I think it's about a hundred years old . . . well, tell me, what do you think of them?"

"Who?"

"The Set. All the doctors and lawyers and Indian chiefs at the potlatch . . . what do you think?"

"Oh. They seem all right," he said, shrugging lightly.

She was watching him closely. "Some of them are."

"I'm sure . . ." he said, hoping she would change the subject.

"I'm serious. Promise me," she said intensely, "that you won't turn into one of *them*."

"Laura," he said firmly, hating himself for sounding fatherly. "It's not all black and white, is it?"

She looked away quickly to the lawn beyond him. "You must think I'm a negative bitch or a souped-up radical or something . . ."

"I don't think that at all," he said slowly. His eyes held hers for a moment. "It's just that I'm new here. These people are the parents of the children I treat. And I'm hoping for Maia's sake that it's a decent town."

She smiled reassuringly. "Well, it's not all bad . . . just deceptive. And if you're very discerning and, of course, always listen to me, you'll be fine," she said lightly. She gave a swift glance at the crowd inside and then looked back at him. Her green eyes darkened. "But some of them really are evil," she said evenly.

Daniel lowered his gaze. He watched the circles of reflected candlelight bounce over her bare shoulders. His gaze trailed down to her sandaled feet. "Oh Laura," he said.

She pushed her hair back from her face, her jaw setting slightly with the determined look he remembered. "Well anyway, now you know why I stick to the kids."

"Could I drive you home later?" he asked impulsively. "We could talk."

"I just live a stone's throw from here," she said briskly. "I'll walk, thanks."

He pushed his glasses back on the bridge of his nose and wondered why he always was attracted to the most complex woman around; mercurial, this stranger; her signals confused him. But he remembered her on the beach, the squashed fedora over her flaxen hair . . . and he tried again. "Maybe tomorrow. I'll join your campers' picnic," he said quietly. "I think you invited me."

"Tomorrow's Sunday," she replied in a much gentler voice, and touched his arm softly.

He didn't hear Sam Benedict walk over. "Listen," Sam said to Laura, "I think your Mom and I have had as much horseshit as we . . . oh, hello, Daniel . . . well anyway, I think we're heading back home."

A tray hit the terrace bricks. Glasses and plates crashed to the ground, and canapés flew like hailstones. Someone screamed.

"Oh my God," said a voice near Daniel Lieberman. Wendy was sprawled on the floor, her legs extended out past the open glass doors and her head on the white carpet. Breaking into a run, Daniel moved toward her. She was ashen pale and now the makeup stood out oddly pink, like calamine lotion, on her face and neck. The sullen expression was gone as she relaxed into unconsciousness. She looked very, very young. Daniel gestured everyone back as he knelt near the girl. "Get back!" he heard someone say behind him. There was absolute silence. He checked her pulse and found it slightly elevated, and then he asked for his bag, holding his car keys out to the nearest guest. He made sure that her airway was unobstructed and lifted her eyelids to examine her pupils. Then Wendy opened her eyes. She looked around very slowly and seemed confused by what she saw. She gazed at Daniel, blinking and looking puzzled.

"It's all right, Wendy, you just fainted . . ." he began. But he stopped when he saw a frightened expression come over her face.

"It's all right," he continued, speaking soothingly. "You're home."

Wendy's eyes widened and she stared at him in disbelief as she sat up very carefully, her eyes never leaving his face. She began then to look around silently, with terror in her eyes and great caution in her movements. A small sound came from her lips, but no words.

"Stay quiet, Wendy," Daniel said. "Just stay still and you'll be fine . . ."

She did not seem to hear him. The party guests began to speak softly to each other and whisper, but did not move. Wendy crouched, darting looks at the crowd as if trying to find a route in between them to escape. She swallowed laboriously and began breathing in rapid panting gasps of fear. Daniel began to think of the differential diagnoses, automatically ticking off possibilities, as he readied himself for action. Subdural hematoma, temporal lobe epilepsy, drugs . . .

Suddenly Wendy moved away. She began to scream shrilly in piercing cries and started darting rapidly around the room like a trapped animal. The guests were totally immobilized. She ducked behind the pine bar and disappeared. The silence seemed to grow more intense. Daniel and Jack Dougherty began to walk toward her simultaneously, moving with slow strides. Suddenly she leaped up and with crazed speed began throwing bottles and glasses at Daniel and at her father. Grunting with effort, she hurled heavy fifths of vodka, quarts of Scotch, and large bottles of tonic water.

People crowded away hurriedly and moved out to the patio, where tables stood ready with dinner and candles. They talked to each other anxiously, watching, moving out of range. The sound of their voices rose, their eyes were fixed on Wendy and the two men walking toward her. She threw glasses with such force that they smashed into tiny fragments on impact. Daniel noticed that her strength was far greater than he imagined. Her arms were not very strong, yet she now hurled glasses like a pitching machine, never slowing down. She continued making noises, sweating and screaming loudly again and again.

As Daniel edged toward her, he noticed that McGinnis, on the patio, was staring intensely at the girl, with an unreadable gaze. Under a spotlighted tree, the Perrinis looked at each other and spoke, then turned and began to walk away across the dark lawn. Howard Lawson stared, first at Wendy and then at the Perrinis, his odd, fixed smile still in place. In the shadows were the Benedicts, the Vails, and several other couples—the Taylors, Greta, guests who had all been lively and vivacious a moment ago. Now they all stood like lawn statues.

Ralph Jeffreys came out of the bathroom to the sound of screams and looked around with shock at the nearby walls. They were stained with Scotch and tomato juice that dripped down onto the white carpeting and splattered onto the chintz upholstery. Water from overturned flower vases dripped on tables. Glass was everywhere. A broken lamp lay on the ruined floor.

Jeffreys's arrival caught Wendy's attention long enough for Jack Dougherty to grab her arm. Because of his bulk he was able to hold her. Wendy's eyes were streaming with tears, and her hair was soaked with sweat. A terrible wailing sound began in her chest. Daniel cursed himself for not going through with skull X-rays. Dougherty looked bewildered, terrified. Was this the man who had beaten Wendy? Why the sudden onset of this wild behavior? It could be migraine . . . severe migraine could present itself this way. And temporal lobe epilepsy was something he would have to rule out. Or it could be a slow kind of encephalitis; schizophrenic break . . . even a brain tumor, although that was less likely. As he moved toward Wendy, he could hear far off now the sound of an ambulance siren. One of the guests had called the hospital. He looked around the shambles of a room. At its center, Barbara was reassembling the canapés on the tray. Compulsively, she picked them up one by one amid the shattered glass. Daniel wondered at her behavior, but was not suprised. People did strange things under stress. She didn't look at Wendy. What if the bruises were unrelated, coincidental; if indeed Wendy had ingested something deliberately—or if something was present in the canapés? . . . But then what of the other guests? What if someone had put a drug in only the food that Wendy ate . . . unlikely, but then so was Wendy's strange behavior. "Don't throw that food away," he said to Barbara.

Startled, Barbara looked up. Standing there in the midst of the ruined living room, with the neatly assembled tray, she began to cry softly; her doll-like face crumpled and her shoulders heaved spasmodically. Laura came to her side immediately from the patio and put her arms around her, taking the tray from her and sitting her down on the couch till the ambulance came.

After Chief Ned McLoughlin got the call that Wendy Dougherty had freaked out, he drank his Alka-Seltzer on the rocks slowly, knowing that it had started. August was a sure thing for the heat, humidity, and out-of-the-woodwork behavior that he had known, deep down, was on its way. Each summer there were more complaints, flashers, vandalism, nuisance calls, and general small police-blotter stuff than anyone would've predicted. So far this summer had been ominously quiet. Now suddenly there was vandalism and Wendy Dougherty on an acid trip . . . he didn't have to be there to know. And he knew also that out of this evening would come eruptions from the teen-age community; rotten, middle-of-the-night stuff that only adolescents had the energy for. God knows he didn't. He wanted to rest. He wanted to live out the rest of his days in his own relatively peaceful community several miles from Sheffield. Years ago his wife had complained bitterly that he was serving a community they couldn't affort to live in. But later, when he finally got to be chief and his salary made the move possible, she wouldn't budge. She clung fiercely to the town where they'd raised their sons, and to all their neighbors, and whenever he talked about the move, whe began polishing the furniture. God bless her. His sons were independent and resourceful, alive to the possibilities of ordinary adventure . . . not like some of the kids he saw in Sheffield . . . last summer he had driven by the beach and seen a good size crowd of boys the age of this sons, lying around on the sand. They had all taped adhesive on their backs in the shape of swastikas and allowed themselves time to tan around the symbols. As late as Labor Day the marks were still there, faded but indelible as tattoos.

Never yet had he been able to jail a vandal in Sheffield, because whenever he got close to a conviction, the parents would give their children alibis, tell him it was all worked out at home, or the vandalized place would refuse to press charges. Lord knows they were all into drugs and eventually there had to be a Wendy, but they were all so "cool," these parents and kids, always working out their "differences" and trying to "communicate." And the parents crossed the generation gap by joining the kids on uppers, downers, or whatever was being dealt down at the school parking lot or the Main Street head shop.

Maybe it was having his investigation squelched that galled him so much. He felt a repressed fury that his men had been sat on that way by McGinnis. Who did McGinnis think he was? Didn't he want police protection? McLoughlin was incensed even more by the phone call from the First Selectman's office. He didn't like being told to leave an investigation alone. Furthermore, why didn't McGinnis want to solve the crime, petty as vandalism was. Why didn't he press charges?

Yes, he could tell from the gnawing at his stomach that something had started. He looked at the note on his desk again. The Horgans had called earlier to say they were worried about Jill. Not that they wanted to file a missing person's report, just that she wasn't anywhere to be found. Her clothes were in her room, and she wasn't a runaway type. But her date had come to pick her up, and she wasn't there. She hadn't been home for dinner.

Yes, it was starting all right.

"Can't you give her something *please*, Dr. Lieberman?" Barbara Dougherty begged.

The parents stepped closer to the cart in the treatment room, where Daniel Lieberman bent over Wendy, and with the help of two nurses, was strapping her securely down. Wendy continued to writhe, her eyes closed, sweat dripping down her forehead and onto the white sheet beneath her head.

"I can't give her anything at the moment," Daniel said, "much as I'd like to. I don't want to medicate her before I know what's wrong with her."

He finished checking Wendy's vital signs. Her breathing, pulse, blood pressure, temperature were within normal limits. Wendy's eyes opened tentatively, registering fear; then she squeezed them shut and shook her head back and forth, nostrils dilated, her neck arched way back on the cart.

"Mr. and Mrs. Dougherty? Won't you come with me now? There are a few forms to fill out . . ." said a young nurse entering the treatment room. She stood by the doors and waited while Barbara turned back to gaze at Wendy. "The desk is just outside . . ." she added gently.

Daniel breathed a sigh of relief when they left. "I'm sending her for skull films," he told the senior Emergency Ward nurse on duty. Walking over to the nurses' station, he sat down at a desk and began to write orders. "Let's get on the X-rays immediately," he said. "And I want a CBC, differential, sed rate, blood glucose, BUN, and electrolytes as soon as possible, and get me a couple of extra tubes while you're at it; not heparinized." He handed papers to the nurse, who immediately buzzed the intercom for the orderly while the other nurse began preparing materials on a cart for blood collection.

Suddenly Wendy was very still, and he got up to recheck her vital signs. Again they were normal. With the nurse helping him, both of them wary of the moment she would tense and begin to writhe again, they worked quickly. Deftly inserting the needle in a small vein, he released the tourniquet, and in rapid succession, he pressed the other end of the needle onto one vacu-tube after another. The nurse moved the cart out of reach of Wendy's arm and took the blood samples away. Just then the orderly appeared at the far door to wheel Wendy down the hall.

"Nurse, " Daniel said to the younger women, "you'll go with them, won't you? I think they'll need your help."

"What *have* we got here?" the orderly asked the nurse as they walked Wendy out. The nurse rolled her eyes heavenward as an answer.

Daniel sat down to finish writing orders. "What's the extension for admissions?" he asked the operator, who connected him. "This is Doctor Lieberman. I have a patient here in Emergency named Wendy Dougherty. I'm admitting her. You have a private bed for her? . . . Medical . . . yes. She's in X-ray now. And she'll need round-the-clock-nursing. Can you get me a night special? Good. . . . All right, I'll be sending her up in a little while."

While Daniel spoke, a doctor with prematurely gray hair and a narrow, almost gaunt face entered, followed by an Indian resident.

"Hi, Larry," Daniel said as he hung up, standing to greet the doctor.

"Hi, Dan, I heard you were here," Larry Roberts said quietly. "I'd like you to meet Dr. Singh."

"How do you do?" the resident said with a slight British-Indian accent.

"Nice to meet you, Dr. Singh. Good to see *you* again, Larry."

Dr. Roberts smiled tightly. "Dr. Singh is a family-practice resident here at the General. . . . I don't know whether Cameron explained all this, but we open our offices to the family-practice resident, and he assists us in daily routine as he observes . . ."

"Whew, I wish I'd known that last week!" Daniel interrupted, running his right hand over the back of his neck.

"Well Dr. Singh was with me all last week and the one prior to that. I'm sure it was busy for both of us."

Caught by the bitter edge in Roberts's voice, Daniel looked directly at him; the naked envy in his eyes took Daniel by surprise. "Of course it was," he said evenly. "A busy couple of weeks."

"Was that Wendy Dougherty we just saw on her way to X-ray?" Roberts asked.

"Yes, Daniel said looking up, wondering if the Doughertys had ever been with Larry Roberts and not Cameron. Cameron had told him that several people had left the man, found him wanting in personal concern. But surely Dr. Cameron, the senior of the two, had always cared for the children of the Set. "Have you ever treated Wendy?" Daniel asked Roberts directly.

"She was never my patient, if that's what you mean. I saw her years ago when I was covering for Cameron, but I don't recall her history."

"Oh. Well I'm just going to call Cameron now, if you'll excuse me . . ."

Roberts raised his eyebrows slightly as if rebuffed. "Well I suppose you *might* catch him home. It's Saturday night. He used to go to concerts regularly on Saturdays when I covered for him, as I remember."

Daniel began dialing. "You should have been at the Doughertys' party tonight when Wendy took sick. What an evening!"

Roberts looked surprised. "You were there when it happened?"

"Yes. Would you excuse me, Larry? I hope Cameron's home."

"Oh, we're off! Dr. Singh, are you coming?" Larry Roberts said abruptly.

As they left, Daniel heard the welcome sound of Cameron's voice at the other end of the line. "Dr. Cameron. It's Lieberman here. I'm in the Emergency Ward at the General with Wendy Dougherty."

"Oh. What happened?"

"I wish I could answer that. I was at a party at her parents'; she was in the room, perfectly normal, then briefly unconscious, and after that, violent. I've just admitted her. Can you give me any special background?"

"Anything show up yet?"

"No. I did see her yesterday morning at my office. Brought in with bruises, contusions, mostly about the face—not the head. All superficial. And the neurological was completely negative . . . there was never any loss of consciousness. I didn't have skull films taken."

"I hear some worry in your voice, Daniel, but I wouldn't have had them taken either under those circumstances. I wouldn't be surprised if the father punched her around a bit. He's been known to hit his wife, and the family's not . . . well, it just isn't a healthy emotional setup. Wendy can be very provocative. How old is she now . . . twelve?"

"Fourteen. I wanted to call you yesterday about her, but I was so busy finishing up paper work on the strep epidemic. Miss Brown's been out sick all week and the files are a mess."

"Well all I can tell you is the family is unstable, and I know they tried some psychological counseling a few years back . . ."

"I may need to pursue that. But what I need now is a neurological consultant . . ."

Daniel heard a pause as Dr. Cameron apparently checked in his book. Then, "Do you know A Dr. Graham Hodson? 856-9836. Fine background. Good medical judgment. Did you get the number?"

"Yes. Thanks very much. Will he come out in the morning, do you think?"

"Oh yes. He's good about weekends and lives close by. Is Roberts there, and that family resident . . ."

"Singh . . . yes."

"Ah . . . well the young resident can be helpful if you need more hands. He's a pain in the neck if you don't."

That wasn't what Cameron wanted to tell him. He had heard the brief pause and change of voice. Was it to warn him to not be too frank with Roberts?

"I should be getting the blood work and X-rays back soon," Daniel said by way of good-bye. "I'll call you tomorrow and let you know how it's going."

"Good luck with Hodson. And let me know how you like him."

Daniel was leaving a message with Hodson's service when Wendy Dougherty was wheeled in, very still and pale. Again, he checked her vital signs. They were still normal. "Was she struggling much?" he asked.

"Yes, a great deal," the young nurse said. She handed him a large manila envelope with several X-rays inside.

Daniel pinned the films up on an illuminated viewing box and examined them. He sighed with relief. "That's what I thought . . . negative." Turning to the nurse, he said, "One more thing before we send her upstairs. Let's get a nasogastric tube. I want a sample of stomach contents. We'll need a few sterile bottles . . ." He went over to the sink to wash his hands.

Barbara Dougherty stuck her head in the door. "Can we come in now?" she asked.

"Give me a couple of minutes," Daniel said. The door closed. He turned to the nurse. "I don't think they need to watch this. I want samples before she gets restless again."

Wendy remained surprisingly still while the tube was threaded through her nose and down into her stomach.

Daniel noticed that her reactions were timed erratically and triggered by internal stimuli. He attached a large syringe and aspirated 20cc of stomach contents. He deposited the sample in a sterile jar and repeated the process a few times. Then he removed the nasogastric tube. "I'm sending these and some blood in to New York tomorrow for a toxic screen. Label them and put them in the refrigerator."

Daniel turned to look at the X-ray once more before taking them down.

"How's it going, Lieberman?" came Larry Roberts's voice behind him.

"Skull films are normal . . . nothing here," Daniel said evenly, putting the pictures in the envelope.

"How about the blood tests?" Roberts asked.

"I'm still waiting for them . . . would you excuse me now?" he said in what he hoped was not too curt a tone. "Nurse, let's get her to her room."

The young nurse skimmed through the chart quickly. "No medication, Doctor?"

"None."

"She'll be in Room 408," the nurse said.

Roberts left, nodding briefly to the Doughertys as Daniel crossed into the lobby. "We saw Wendy just now . . ." Barbara said softly.

The elevator doors opened, and they got in. "Doc, what's wrong with her?" Jack Dougherty asked.

"I don't know yet, but I've ruled out a couple of things. To start with, her temperature is normal so the chances are that nothing of an acute infectious nature, like meningitis, is involved. . . . I'll be doing tests, though, tonight and in the morning . . ."

The elevator doors opened and Barbara got out first, her face white.

"Her skull X-rays appear absolutely normal. The radiologist will check them further. There's also no indication of subdural bleeding . . . that's the sort of thing one might be concerned about after a fall," Daniel said, trying not to look directly at Jack Dougherty. "We will have to rule out the remote possibility of temporal lobe epilepsy . . ."

Barbara started to cry. "Will she . . . go into a coma?"

Dougherty patted her clumsily. "It's okay. She'll be okay. Listen to what he's saying, Barbara."

Wendy was already in bed in Room 408, now restrained across the midriff with a makeshift sheeting strap. The sides of the bed were raised to prevent her from falling, and her arms were strapped to the side bars with cloth ties. She was looking up at the ceiling and tossing her head back and forth. Near the head of the bed stood an attractive brunette nurse, smiling pleasantly and adjusting the top sheet as Wendy kicked it off. "I'm Miss Rivera," the nurse said.

"Dr. Lieberman, and the Doughertys," Daniel said to the nurse. "Could you go and check for me and see if the blood tests are back yet?" Then he turned to the parents. "Look, I have to ask you frankly: is there a possibility that Wendy was involved with drugs?"

Barbara sighed. "She never was . . ."

Daniel checked Wendy's pulse and breathing again. The same. "Is there any possibility that someone, even a guest at your party, could have slipped Wendy some kind of drug tonight?"

"In our house?" Barbara said in a whisper.

"Well, Wendy was working in the kitchen earlier . . . could a friend of hers have come to the kitchen door? Or maybe Wendy went out earlier this evening?" Daniel looked from parent to parent.

"The girl didn't leave the house," Jack Dougherty said curtly.

"You think it's drugs? Is that what this is?" Barbara whispered. "I've never seen anything like this . . ."

Miss Rivera came back with a small envelope. "Here's the report from downstairs," she said, handing Daniel the material.

Daniel looked through the colored slips. "Sed rate is normal . . . all the tests . . . all of them, normal." He looked up. "Is there anything that you can tell me about yesterday's bruises, anything at all that you may have forgotten . . ."

There was a silence, and Daniel felt a sudden partition drop between them. "Nothing," Barbara said, looking down at the vinyl beneath her feet.

If there was a speck of dust, she'd grab it, Daniel thought. Emptying ashtrays, arranging canapés, making small talk, it all pushed the panic away. "All right," he said. "Can you tell me whether Wendy ever complained of severe headaches?"

"No. My wife's the one with the headaches," Dougherty said harshly.

"There'll be a Dr. Hodson here in the morning, with your permission. Dr. Cameron recommended him as a neurological consultant. We should know more soon."

Barbara started to cry. "I'm afraid to go home . . . I'm afraid she'll go into a coma . . ."

"She'll be all right," Daniel said firmly. "If it's drugs, the effects will start to wear off soon. Now, why don't you go home and get some rest? She'll want to talk to you tomorrow, and you'll need some sleep."

Miss Rivera smiled a generous smile and took Barbara's hands in hers. "I will be here all night," she said.

"You'll call us if . . . anything happens?" Barbara asked.

"Of course," Miss Rivera said. "I will watch Wendy very closely. Try not to worry."

"I have one other question," Daniel said. "Has there ever been anything like this before? A sudden change of mood recently . . . anything?"

Dougherty shook his head. "No, this is the first time, and I hope to God it's the last."

"Excuse me," said the attendant at the nursing station. "You have a call from Dr. Hodson . . ."

"Okay. Go home and get some sleep, the two of you. And if you remember anything, give me a call . . ." Daniel said going to the phone.

Hodson's voice was brisk as they reviewed the case and discussed the medication. Yes, Daniel assured him, he had considered all the obvious metabolic diseases. And yes, all the blood work had come back normal. He described the girl's behavior.

"I'll tell you what, Lieberman," Hodson said finally. "I'll be over there about eight or so. I'd like an echo encephalogram.

I'd like to be there when it's done. Before we do a lumbar puncture, I want to make certain everything's in the midline, that there's no subdural . . ."

"I'll arrange that," Daniel said, trying to visualize the man from his voice. He was compact, not tall, and had a clipped mustache . . .

"And we'll need a sleep EEG afterward. So it's just as well if she is up most of the night."

"I don't think Wendy's going to sleep at all," Daniel said, thinking of the struggling, terrified girl.

*"Natural Products International," a female voice said into the receiver.*

*"NPI. This is Chameleon control."*

*A click, a buzz, then, "Yes?"*

*"We have a potentially serious situation."*

*"What is it?"*

*"The door to the P3 was forced. Walters says kids got in . . ."*

*"How many?"*

*"He thinks three or four."*

*"He saw the damage?"*

*"Yes."*

*"Then we'll have to deal with him."*

It was past two o'clock when Daniel Lieberman finally got home, a small house near the road on the outskirts of a large estate: "Just the right size. You don't even have to paint," the real-estate agent had said. He felt very guilty. Leaving the Doughertys' party with the ambulance, he had nearly thrown his keys at Laura. It had been a familiar, almost too natural gesture, based on the rationale that she was the only adult Maia knew and trusted in Sheffield and that it might be a long night. But he should have called. He could have spent a minute after he telephoned Cameron and Hodson. Now Laura would be sitting up waiting . . . he had just forgotten. It was the tension of the hospital, the parents, the strange illness, Wendy's tortured face . . .

He opened the door and walked quietly into the old house and up the stairs to his daughter's bedroom. Laura, still in the white gown she'd worn at the party, was asleep in a rocking chair near Maia's bed. Maia was also asleep, and in the crook of her arm rested the snail jar, tilted precariously toward the floor. They had forgotten to draw the curtains—

the window was open wide to let in the occasional breeze. Moonlight shone on the two peaceful faces. Daniel took the jar gently from Maia and set it down near her doll collection. Then he looked at Laura. Moonlight illuminated the smooth curve of her shoulder. She stirred and smiled in her sleep. He stood a moment, watching her.

He turned away and went to his own room, exhausted. There, he felt a sudden unaccountable restlessness. He paced awhile, then went downstairs to pour himself a brandy. Sipping it slowly, he peered out the living room window at the night. Finally he stretch out on the living room couch, eyes wide open, looking at the ceiling. He tried to pinpoint his anxiety—there was a bizarre quality to Wendy's case that left him uneasy. That was part of it. Something was wrong there. He tried to reconstruct the case as he tossed on the couch, his toe throbbing, his shirt plastered to the sofa cushions in the sticky heat. He reviewed the office visit . . . then his thoughts wandered to the party, all the new faces. Laura had said that some of them were evil . . . Laura.

He stayed awake till the first light of dawn. Then, for a brief time, he slept.

# Sunday, August fifth,

as Daniel entered Sheffield General Hospital early in the morning, a wave of nostalgia hit him. The city hospital where he'd done his residency and stayed on to practice had its own shopping-bag lady, and at the dilapidated entrance there had always been a bum to greet him with a "Hi, Doc!" No such welcoming committee here. In the lobby there were only a silent janitor cleaning fingerprints off the thick-glass entrance doors and a receptionist who looked as if someone wound her up every morning. The chrome and vinyl furniture looked unreal and unused in the cold light . . .

Graham Hodson matched his telephone voice exactly. He was a dapper man with a small brown mustache, a few inches shorter than Daniel. They stood near the open door to Room 408, conversing quietly, out of earshot of the girl in the bed.

"Has she had this changed level of alertness from the start?" Hodson was asking.

"Yes," Daniel said, looking through the door at Wendy. Pale and still, she might have been sleeping normally . . .

"As we discussed last night, I gave her some IM Valium. Thorazine was my first choice, but Valium is safer for now. She gave me quite a time a while ago, and I thought it wise to medicate her before we do the lumbar puncture. Otherwise, we'd have to hold her down and the pressure readings would be affected," Hodson said in a firm, brisk voice.

So she wasn't sleeping normally at all, just medicated and in between episodes. . . . "She's been behaving from the start as if reacting to visual phenomena."

Hodson nodded. "In a paranoid manner, wouldn't you say? And her pupils have been slightly dilated from the start, haven't they?"

"Yes." He looked at the reddened marks on Wendy's wrists, where, despite padding, they had chafed and rubbed from her restless tossing. "Also, her pulse has been on the high side of normal even though the blood work came back negative."

Hodson nodded. "Well. I completed the echo encephalogram and the sleep EEG and they were also negative. I think," he went on quickly, "now that you're here, Lieberman, Miss Rivera can set us up for an LP. Right, Miss Rivera?" he called through the doorway.

The nurse looked up, nodded and was off quickly, walking down the corridor. Hodson's tone set the pace for everyone. Daniel scanned the chart in his hand, noting all of Hodson's entries. "What do you think about the skull films?" he asked.

"Well, there's absolutely no evidence of increased intracranial pressure there, and then of course, with the other results, subdural hematoma is pretty much ruled out, isn't it?" Hodson asked rhetorically.

"I wonder about those scratches . . ."

Hodson laughed dryly. "I'd like to see the other guy, as they say."

"Last night I thought her behavior and the bruises might be connected."

"I doubt it," Hodson said. "I think it's entirely coincidental. And of course there's very little chance of a tumor or temporal lobe epilepsy here either." He paused, musing, "You know, I've seen cases like this in the Army. A kind of battle fatigue. But under these circumstances, here in Sheffield, well, it's rather strange, isn't it?" Hodson ran his hand over his mustache, and looked at Daniel. "Drugs are the best bet, but there's something odd about that, too. I've seen prolonged bad trips, and they just don't give you this acute, toxic kind of response for such a continuous stretch."

"I haven't run across anything quite like this before either," Daniel said frankly.

Miss Rivera approached quickly. Her dark, pretty face was marked with fatigue. "The OR is ready for you."

"Good. I'll go ahead then. Send Wendy up, please," Hodson said, leaving.

Daniel looked at Miss Rivera while he dialed to have Wendy moved to a treatment room. She had done two shifts without sleep and it showed.

"Are you off soon?" he asked when he hung up.

"Yes," she said. "They couldn't find anyone from the registry for the four-to-eight, so I stayed. I just heard my relief is on the way. Then I'm off to the city . . ."

"New York?"

She looked at him amused, adjusting a comb in her dark hair. "You like that place?"

He grinned. "Yes, I like that place . . ."

"My parents live there. I'll visit them and then return for the late shift tonight. I think I'll sleep this afternoon," she said, and for the first time he heard the slight accent in her speech.

The orderly came for Wendy, and as he transferred her to a stretcher cart, Daniel remembered that he had to make arrangements for the toxic screen. He could get the results on amphetamines, opiates, and barbiturates locally. But he was after something more elaborate. He hesitated, then said to Miss Rivera, "This is a bit of an imposition, but could you possibly drop off a couple of Wendy's samples for me while you're in the city? I mean, only if you don't mind . . ."

"I don't mind at all. It's Sunday and I know how hard it is . . ."

"If you're sure . . ."

She smiled expansively to reassure him, her brown eyes warm.

"Thanks very much. I appreciate it!" he said looking at his watch and then dialing. "Now I'll see if I can arrange it."

"Hrrrrmmmph . . ." said a voice after seven rings.

"Jeez, am I glad to catch you home, Bill!" Daniel said, innocenty grinning. "I didn't wake you up, did I?"

"Hey man, I don't believe this! I thought you were moving to the same time zone." The voice was clear now. Daniel knew Bill Edwards was propped up on his elbows, smiling. He could see him, amusement creeping into his dark eyes, his black, handsome face cocked slightly to one side . . .

"Listen, Bill, I'm in a real hurry now and I gotta ask you a big favor. It's Sunday . . ."

A chortle. "You're telling me it's Sunday?! I *know* it's Sunday, and you know what else? The *Times* isn't here yet! So, schlemazel, what else is new?"

Daniel laughed out loud and suddenly felt lonely. "It's pretty important, Bill . . ."

"Speak to me."

"Okay. I have a very strange case here. Could be drugs. But it would have to be something very potent and long-lasting. Now the problem is, it's Sunday and I need a toxic screen for whatever they're dealing these days . . ."

"No wonder you called me! You need a friendly family biochemist, right? And you want me to wake up some other poor sucker who happens to work in my lab. Right? Right! Okay, when can you get me the stuff?"

Daniel imagined Bill sitting up on the edge of his bed now, totally alert, in the sunny bedroom of the same fifth-floor walkup they'd shared back in medical school. In those days they were heading in the same direction and planned to set up practice together. But then, in the early years, Bill got a fellowship at Cambridge in clinical biochemical research, and before Daniel knew it, Bill was telling him how he couldn't stand routinely treating kids for diseases whose biochemistry was mostly unknown—ass backwards, he said. At that point their careers had gone in different directions. . . . Now he'd be crossing the room, trailing the cord, opening a shutter and squinting out at Perry Street . . .

"Hey man, are you there?"

"Oh, sorry Bill. There's a Miss Rivera here who'll be driving into the city in a little while . . . I can give her your address."

A hearty laugh. "Terrific! Pretty?"

Daniel smiled at Miss Rivera, wondering if she had heard. "Yep, very . . ."

"Great. What time's she getting here? I'll get rid of Gloria."

"About two and a half hours?" he said, raising his eyebrows questioningly at Miss Rivera, who nodded yes.

"Okay. Tell you what. Send her right over to the lab. You do remember the address of your alma mater, don't you? Or is all that fresh air getting to you?" Bill said, laughing.

"Thanks a lot really."

"Don't make it too long between visits, huh?"

Wendy lay on her side on the operating table. Her hair was covered by a green cotton cap and her hospital gown fell forward, exposing a portion of her back. Dr. Singh, who had asked to participate, stood in front of the girl and talked soothingly to her. His presence and the Valium seemed to relax her.

Hodson slowed to a different rhythm now. He spoke quietly as he prepared for the lumbar puncture, always telling her what he was doing in a calm, firm voice, although the girl made no response.

The nurse handed gloves to Daniel and opened the package of sterile surgical instruments. The wrapping fell back, and Daniel arranged the sterile interior of cloth to shield the tray as Hodson palpated the area between the third and fourth lumbar vertebrae.

"I'm going to clean this now, Wendy," he said to her back as he swabbed the area with Betadine. Hodson then took his pair of sterile gloves and arranged a sterile drape over the girl's lower back. Through the hole in the drape, he again palpated the spine between L3 and L4. This time he made a mark with his gloved thumbnail on the midline. "That's it, Lieberman," he said. "Wendy, you'll feel a tiny pinprick. That's all," he said, injecting the procaine anesthetic subcutaneously.

A nurse adjusted Wendy's head so that her spine was straight at the neck and gently helped Dr. Singh hold her in the knee-chest position. Hodson pushed the long needle very slowly into the center of the spinal column, searching for the gap between the vertebrae. At regular intervals he stopped to withdraw the stylet that plugged the needle, looking for signs of fluid. "You notice, Singh," he remarked, "the needle is angled in a cephalic direction, and the bevel's *always* kept horizontal. We don't want to damage any nerves. . . . I'm through the dura now," he said, watching for the first drops of fluid. "Right. Here they come."

Hodson turned a stop valve on the needle assembly and attached the glass manometer that Daniel handed him from the tray. The three doctors watched the clear fluid rise.

"Pressure's normal," Hodson said, satisfied. "But we wait a few minutes to do it right." They waited silently. "Good," Hodson said. "Let's have a few sterile tubes now."

Daniel handed them over, and Hodson turned the little valve and collected the clear drops for cell count, culture, sugar, and protein determination.

"That does it," Hodson said as he disconnected the manometer, withdrew the needle, and took off his gloves almost in one motion.

Daniel followed him out of the room. Out in the corridor, Hodson took off his mask and sighed. "It behaves like something organic, doesn't it? But what? You might think of schizophrenia, but it probably would present itself like this. I've thought of some far out possibilities, but let's wait for more information . . ."

"I'm sending the gastric contents and blood sample to a special outfit in New York for a toxic screen. Maybe they'll isolate the culprit for us," Daniel said.

"You'll let me know how things are going," Hodson said. "I'm off now."

* * *

"Jesus, I just can't understand this," Ned McLoughlin said somberly to the patrolman next to him. The patrolman shook his head in agreement.

McLoughlin stood looking on silently as a stretcher took the body away. Scott Andrews had been a round-faced boy, not big for his age, not a good athlete, and maybe that's why he had hung around with older kids at Louie's Place. But he'd been a nice kid, polite, cooperative. He had mowed lawns for spending money, hadn't dropped out of school . . . McLoughlin was puzzled. The accident made no sense. Scott had been thrown in the air upon the impact of hitting the huge oak tree, landing in a heap, thirty feet away. The motorcycle had to have been doing at least sixty to make an impact like that. The oak tree was nowhere near the road. The cycle had been coming up the hill. It was still daylight.

"Why would he have veered like that?" McLoughlin asked, half to himself and half to the patrolman.

"Someone on his tail?" the officer volunteered.

"All the way to the tree?" McLoughlin asked sarcastically. "There are no skid marks, no oil slicks, no potholes, no debris or obstacles in the road, nothing . . ."

The patrolman shrugged. "Maybe he lost control of the steering."

McLoughlin shook his head. "He would've had plenty of time to slow down."

"Brakes?"

"Even without brakes—he was going uphill! This is a twenty mile zone, and he wasn't a crazy kid."

"Well, what do you think happened?"

"I don't know. For some reason, he steered left, speeded up, and aimed at that tree!"

McLoughlin swallowed and closed his eyes. How was he going to tell Scott's mother? It was such a freak—as if the driver had been pursued by something . . . He looked up and down the road again, at the oak, shaking his head slowly. One godawful month, and it was just beginning.

*Paul McGinnis watched between the thin slats of vertical blinds in his office as the man approached. In the clear sunlight he saw the chrome locks on the man's attaché case, the loose weave of his beige linen jacket. He could, whenever he closed his eyes, photographically reproduce every detail but the face. The face remained elusive—it was so extraordinarily characterless one forgot it immediately. He pulled the blinds shut tightly and turned to look at his digital wall clock: 9:03. He walked to his office door to greet the man at the threshold.*

*"Good to see you again, McGinnis," the man said, shaking hands, his eyes recording McGinnis's navy blazer and handsome, tanned face; then the meticulous office with the large, black-lacquered desk, the buff leather chairs. "I haven't been to the lab in some time now . . . well, let's not waste any time. I hear we may have a problem."*

*The welcoming smile, still faint on McGinnis's lips, faded. "Rosalind Perrini," he said sitting back in the Eames chair behind his wide desk. "She must have contacted you . . ."*

*The man tapped his fingers impatiently on his knee. He had hands as small as a child's, incongruous with his average-sized frame. McGinnis's eyes rested on the hands like a portrait camera. The man made no answer. "She was upset. We had some words on Friday morning. There had been some minor vandalism—but she made a stink," he continued in his metallic, dispassionate voice. "And then last night I was at a party at the local newspaper editor's home. His daughter had a severe seizure, bizarre behavior." McGinnis pressed his fingers on the desktop and gazed at his prints a second before erasing them with his thumb. "Naturally, it crossed my mind that the girl could have been involved in the vandalism . . ."*

*The man sat very alert. "The Perrinis were there?"*

*"Yes. So it wasn't Rosalind who contacted you . . . well, the irony was I'd invited them only to placate her after the blowup Friday morning." McGinnis stood and crossed slowly to the front of his desk, his hands in his pockets. "The likelihood is that it has nothing to do with us, that the girl is into drugs."*

*The man took a thin folder from his attaché case. "What's the girl's name?"*

*"Dougherty. Wendy Dougherty."*

*The man wrote a note on a pad of paper.*

*McGinnis closed his eyes for a split second, then, "When Rosalind saw the girl lose control that way, she must have had the same thoughts I did. I didn't speak with the Perrinis, but I saw Rosalind's face. I saw them arguing as they left."*

*"You don't think it was anything? The Dougherty girl, I mean."*

*McGinnis sat lightly on the front edge of his desk. "I came to the conclusion that it was a coincidence. An unrelated event."*

*"And if you're wrong?"*

*"Then there are others involved and we don't know who they are. And if we could find them, we couldn't find their contacts."*

*"Yes," the man said, lacing his small fingers together. "Well at any rate, it's not traceable. Am I correct?"*

*"That's the beauty of the recombinant DNA technique."*

*"For now," the man said, "we'll proceed as if the girl's problems are due to other sources. We won't be overly concerned unless there's another incident."*

*"What about the Perrinis?"*

*"I'll contact them immediately and transfer them to another project."*

*"On Friday morning at the lab, she threatened to make the situation public."*

*The man stood. "They'll be out of the country tomorrow. Besides, he'll shut her up. He always does."*

*"And Chameleon?"*

*"You don't need the Perrinis at this stage, do you? They've done their job, and you have competent technical assistance."*

*"There may be delays because of this interruption. If you want it operational for a one-man target, I need more time to adjust the infectivity. Otherwise we'll hit a much wider group." McGinnis's voice had a tense edge.*

*"No. You'll have to see to it that attenuation is complete by the projected delivery date."*

*McGinnis's eyes were emotionless as he regarded the man. "If Chameleon were to run past deadline, would you continue funding or cut us loose?"*

*"Come on. After investing two years, we're not about to walk away."*

*McGinnis walked to the window and turned to gaze steadily at the man. "I hope not. It's my guess that no other country, no matter how far advanced in recombinant work, will come up with this idea. It's totally unprecedented and makes a singularly elegant use of the new technology," he said evenly. "If you people abandon the Chameleon project, you'll lose the opportunity to use this on target after target. Each time a different effect. Never identical symptoms. You'll throw away for a few months, what amounts to a lead of several years."*

*The man smiled pleasantly and walked to the office door. "Don't worry about us, McGinnis, we've worked together before, you know we'll do our share. We'll handle the Perrinis.*

*And since the Dougherty incident was probably unrelated, I don't expect trouble. You just do your best, and I have every confidence the material will be ready before November."*

*They stood in the square front hall, dimly illuminated by the tinted-glass entrance doors. The man tapped his baby-sized index finger on McGinnis's lapel with casual but warning emphasis. "From now on, McGinnis, we'll be having some additional surveillance here, routine under these conditions." His face was pink-tinged in the daylight and his eyes were brown, not blue— He put his sunglasses on.*

*McGinnis watched the man's back as he walked to the gate. The sound of the limousine motor was barely audible. There was no other noise except for the cries of birds circling the empty grounds. McGinnis went back inside. His wall clock said 9:23. He took a small tape recorder from the closet floor in his office, rewound and pocketed the tape, and changed into his tennis whites. He left the laboratory carrying his Prince racket, walking briskly and soundlessly over the wide slate floors and out across the cropped green lawn.*

Daniel Lieberman, in T-shirt and jeans, leaned around the bucket seat of Laura's convertible to look at Maia in the back. "If you won't tell me what we're having for lunch, will you at least tell me where you're taking me?"

"Kroners' Pond," Maia shouted happily, her fine brown hair flying in the breeze.

"I don't know how you talked me into this, kid!" he said, laughing and then peacefully leaning back against the headrest. They had the roads to themselves and they drove in silence for a while. Daniel tried to clear his mind of worry about Wendy Dougherty and to manage to stay awake.

"Would you mind if I asked where Maia's mother is? If you do, don't answer," Laura asked suddenly, her eyes on the road.

"That's okay. The last postmark was from Brazil . . . she, well she got very liberated till finally she just took off, like that," he said, snapping his fingers. "With a drummer."

"Oh."

"She sent me a postcard about how since she was a different person she didn't see the point of coming home to be someone she wasn't."

"Postmarked Brazil?"

"Yeah, very cryptic that card. Small writing, big signature.

Didn't even look like her writing. Maybe the drummer wrote it. Or maybe she really is someone else."

"Sorry," Laura said, glancing at him candidly. "Really that's too bad, Daniel."

"Aren't you going to show my dad the garbage dump?" Maia said from the back seat.

Laura slowed down slightly, passing a few charred hills of plastic bags and cans. "Sorry, Maia," she called. "I didn't know we were doing that tour today."

"*What* a *dump*!" Daniel said loudly enough for Maia to hear.

"Their latest solution," Laura said in a wry voice, "is to mash it up, wrap it, and send it two towns away."

He smiled. "I guess the town that gets it won't be too happy."

Laura pointed past him. "That's McGinnis's lab over there."

The spectacular low-lying assemblage of modern buildings came into view; mirrored glass windows glinted like ice. Then it disappeared behind a luxuriant row of old hemlocks as they descended the hill.

"This all used to be a huge dairy farm. The silos are still standing. Wonderful soil!" She stopped herself, smiling. "I shouldn't get started on that. But the combination of ecology and childhood nostalgia is pretty heady. The Kroners' farm was a rural outpost here in Sheffield when I was a kid. Then, when the last of the Kroner boys went through college and on to city life, Paul . . ." She stopped herself again, but this time she reddened deeply. "Anyway, the McGinnis lab took over the site."

Daniel gazed at her silently for a moment as she drove. "How do you feel about Paul McGinnis?"

Her hands tightened slightly on the wheel, and she didn't answer for a moment. "I'll tell you, I'm not real fond of him, although at one time I thought I was," she said in a flat voice, her chin raised slightly.

He wasn't surprised. Paul was handsome, had an appeal he didn't have to work at, a charm he could turn on anytime. And power. There were clearly Louise, and Greta. When, he wondered, had all this taken place? When had it ended? Or hadn't it? He recognized, with some dismay, the stirrings of involvement. Laura was watching the road. Suddenly she turned for a second and met his eyes. Her beauty was dazzling, like coming into full sunlight after darkness.

They curved along a dirt road now, rutted under their

wheels, spraying dust in the air like talcum, until they came to a stop under a large maple tree.

"Everybody out!" Laura said cheerfully, pulling up the brake. "Disregard the No Trespassing sign!"

"Really?" Daniel asked, looking at the chain fence. "I'm a city boy. I take these things very seriously. Muggers I can stand, but not watchdogs."

Laura was gathering the fishing rods from the trunk. "This is just a buffer zone. The lab's all the way over there, for Lord's sake. The creek may pass in back of the lab, but they don't *own* it, you know!"

"Sure, I know; it belongs to the People. But do the dogs know?" Daniel asked dubiously.

Laura smiled at him, her eyes sparkling, as she handed him the basket and the rods. "Maia, want to go fishing?" she asked.

"Yes!" Maia said.

Laura climbed agilely over the fence with Maia just behind, imitating her movements. Daniel, following last, stubbed his infected toe, repressed a yell, and limped behind them, cursing silently. They walked into a wooded area that grew increasingly dense with the jungle lushness of mid-summer. Insects hopped and buzzed, the air was heavy with the smell of honeysuckle. Soon they came to a rocky embankment and then a clearing, where a few old willows hung over a wide brook and the sun shone through the greenery. Daniel relaxed under a willow as Laura spread out a white chenille bedspread and opened the wicker basket.

"This is terrific fried chicken!" he said enthusiastically between mouthfuls.

"My mother had a surplus," Laura said. "She's somewhere between an obsessive-compulsive cook and a Jewish mother. Right now she's into canning and preserves."

Daniel laughed. "She must think we're holding you hostage. Did you explain?"

"Yes. And she said, 'I just happen to have a bunch of fried chicken falling out of the oven.' She's wonderful."

Daniel looked over at his daughter. "Poor Maia has to get along on my specialties, tunafish, hamburgers . . ."

"And Mrs. Paul's frozen fish sticks," Maia said matter-of-factly. "But mostly pizza."

Daniel winced. "Don't tell on your father."

Maia regarded Laura seriously. "He likes anchovies and I like plain. What do you like?"

"Sausage and mushroom," Laura answered, grinning. "What'd you think I was going to say, Daniel? Soy and mung bean?"

"Ginseng and granola." He felt absurdly happy.

After dessert, Maia began to climb the embankment near the willow, getting a worried "Take it easy" from Daniel.

"Only little kids keep moving in this kind of heat," Laura said, fastening her hair up with a barrette to cool her neck.

She was wearing a thin blue T-shirt, and as she lifted her long, slender arms, Daniel noticed that she wore no bra. She had the firm high breasts and leggy sexiness of a teen-ager. Again he sensed a fifteen-year gap between them, a gulf of time. Or was it his imagination? The memory of his ex-wife flitted by like a ghost, leaving a bitter feeling, draining his sense of well-being. He stood looking at the brook, admiring a few rocks jutting up in the center with the water bubbling by. There was a praying mantis on a nearby bush, undisturbed by his shadow. The restlessness passed.

He leaned againt the willow tree. "How far are you into graduate work?" he asked.

She looked up slightly startled. "Oh . . . well I've passed the qualifiers for my doctorate, but I haven't begun my dissertation," she said, and began energetically collecting plates.

He regarded her sudden burst of activity with interest and a little amusement. "How come?"

Laura shrugged. "You really want to know?"

"I'd like very much to hear."

She sat cross-legged, Indian style, and rubbed her palms on her blue jeans hesitantly. "I got a typical graduate student disease . . . I was overcome by a large wave of—what would you call it? A sense of futility. The probability that when it's finally all over I won't find a job. Or worse, I *would* find an academic job and sit there grinding out research papers that the world doesn't need, in order to win the tenure rat race. Either way, I lose. So finally I thought to myself: time out. Just for a while. To find out where I want to go."

"And have you found out?"

"Not yet. But in the meantime I thought I would do something tangible in my own town. If you can't get your act together where you were born, then forget it. So I'm trying a little consciousness raising."

"Anyone listening?"

She lay back, resting the back of her head on her hands,

and looked up at him. "They think I'm a little off the wall, you know."

Daniel looked at her closely as he asked, "Is Paul McGinnis the target of your campaign?"

"You bet. I'm after him. And not, as you're thinking, for purely personal reasons. I just don't want that P3 here in town."

Laura sat up, intensely gesticulating with her hands. "In 1976, the National Institute of Health set up guidelines for the construction of thoses gene-splicing labs so that none of the hazardous material could get out. At least that was the theory. But you see the NIH guidelines only affect projects funded by them, and besides, they depend totally on self-policing. I am just about as impressed with the scientific honor among McGinnis and company as I am with the local solution to the garbage problem. Anyway, even if everything were adhered to, there still are spills and carelessness. No complex system is ever one hundred percent accident-free. That P3 doesn't belong here."

"Does it make you feel better to know that it's not operative?"

"What?"

Daniel shrugged. "That's what McGinnis told your father last night. Said the P3 hasn't been operative for more than a year."

Laura gave him a curious look. "You don't believe that . . .?"

"Yeah, I do."

Laura went into immediate action scraping plates into a brown paper bag and sorting forks.

"Hey . . ." Daniel started.

"I told you, I'm not on a personal vendetta trip," she said without looking at him.

"Laura, are you sure?" She raised her head, her green eyes dark and resentful. "I'm sorry. That's something you must have asked yourself . . ."

She relaxed and impulsively reached for his hands, holding them within her own. They were silent. . . .

"Daddy!" Maia's scream suddenly cut through the stillness like a bullet. "Daddy! Come here!"

Daniel scrambled up the rocks. "Maia . . . where are you?" he asked, looking around.

"Here!" came her voice urgently, from just beyond a small ledge. He climbed over it and stared down at the sight that had made his daughter call out. Laura came up next to him. Near the edge of the brook lay a huge German shepherd, its head in the water. Maia ran up to them and encircled Laura's hips with her arms while Laura stroked her hair.

"Wait there," Daniel said, climbing down to the animal.

Insect voices drilled through the heat. The front paws hung limply in the water, and a few flies buzzed around the corpse. The dog's white-and-gray muzzle was underwater, some water weeds near the mouth. Dragonflies skimmed the surface of the brook nearby. A half-dozen bloated minnows floated belly-up in the quiet eddies next to the bank. Daniel lifted the dog's head out of the water and placed it on the grass. The short fur dripped in glistening points. Had it not been for the open, sightless eyes, the animal might have been asleep. Daniel stepped back.

"What happened to it, Daddy?" Maia's voice was shaky.

He looked up to the top of the ledge. "It looks real old, honey, I think it just . . . died of old age," he said quietly.

"Does it have a tag, Daniel?" Laura called.

"Yep, just a minute," he said. He reached down and turned the worn leather collar around the animal's neck till he could see the dull brass disk. "It says Hill . . . Goodridge Road?"

"Oh, she's the librarian," Laura said.

Daniel joined them, looking back down. "We'll have to contact the dog warden. And I guess I should tell Miss Hill. Are you okay, Maia?"

"Yup."

They walked back to the picnic site, Daniel cursing to himself at the interruption of his moment alone with Laura. "You didn't touch the dog, did you, Maia?"

"Nope."

Laura folded the bedspread and repacked the wicker basket. Silently, they headed back toward the car.

"Hey, Laura, won't the dog warden know we were trespassing?" Daniel asked as they climbed over the chain fence.

She smiled "Everybody picnics here. He won't care."

Daniel boosted Maia over with an extra hug. "Well, I guess the dog was really very old, had a heart attack, and died . . . that's what happened."

"Goodridge Road backs onto that property. That's how he got there . . . I wonder if that water's okay," Laura mused. "I hope they're not dumping waste."

He opened the car door for her. "Are we off to Goodridge?"

"Not if you want to see Miss Hill . . . she's at her desk. We'll have to go back to town."

Maia squeezed in between them while Laura started the car. "How old was it?" she asked.

Laura hugged her. "Over a hundred in human years," she said gently.

"At least!" Daniel added. "What do you mean she's at her desk?"

Laura swung the car around on the dirt road and headed toward town. "The library's open from ten to three on Sundays. Miss Hill pushed for it, fought the entire Town Council. She's quite a character, one of the original Yankee settlers. Her family used to own all of Goodridge and Kroners' farm, too. They sold it off early in this century . . ." She turned to him, grinning. "Does that history fascinate you?"

"Do I look unfascinated?"

"Sort of glazed over."

"Well, here I am trying to figure out how to break the news to this Miss Hill and you're telling me she came over on the *Mayflower*," he said, returning the grin.

"She won't bite you or get emotional, either," Laura said. "She's a tough old bird. I'll wait in the car while you and Maia go into the library."

Miss Hill was thin but sturdy, her dark clothes slightly loose, like chicken skin, and she looked cool and powdered even in her lacy cardigan sweater. Glasses hung around her neck on a black silk cord. When they arrived, she was writing intently on tabbed file cards. Daniel stood there looking down at her sparse yellow-gray hair till she looked up.

"Yes?"

"Miss Hill, I'm Dr. Lieberman, the new pediatrician in town?"

"What can I do for you? Need a library card?"

"You have a dog . . ." He paused, hating the moment.

"Toadie . . . something happen?" she asked, peering at him sharply like a bird, head slightly to one side.

"Yes, I'm afraid so . . . "

"Not run over . . ."

"No, ma'm. He got sick and fell into Kroners' Pond . . . he's dead, ma'm."

She blinked once. "Old age," she said. "He was seventeen. Did you call the dog warden?"

"Yes," Daniel said, surprised at her calmness.

"Well then I guess he'll get over there and call me later.

That's too bad about Toadie," she said, and sighed. "I was fond of him. A good dog. Well, it was only a matter of time. Thank you, Dr. Lieberman, for letting me know. Most kind of you," she said, and dismissed him by going back to her file cards.

He walked over to Maia, who was searching the shelves. "Let's go . . . okay?"

"Oh please, can't I stay here a little while? I haven't gotten a library card 'cause you haven't had time to take me . . ."

It was an innocent fact and there was no reproach intended. But he felt as though she had punched him in the stomach. "I guess you could stay till three o'clock. I have to go to the hospital for a little while."

"It's all right for me to stay by myself," she said.

"Maybe I can pick you up at three, then . . . that would be okay?"

"Fine."

"You're sure you can manage here without me or Laura?"

Maia smiled tolerantly. "Come on, Daddy."

"Okay," he nodded. There were many simple things he still didn't know about her. Things his wife had always taken care of, like exactly what age-level books she was reading these days, and whether she could count change accurately, and what her favorite color was. He was overwhelmed by the things he didn't know. He checked his watch. Just a little after two. That gave him hardly enough time to do anything he needed to do. He kissed her on the top of her head. "Meet me outside at three, okay?" But she didn't answer, because she was already sitting at the low, round table for children, absorbed in a book.

"Need a lift to the hospital?" Laura asked at the door.

"I was going to stop home and get my car . . . I have to be back here by three."

"You'll never make it. Hop in. I'd like to see Wendy too, if that's okay."

Daniel got into the convertible and looked at her. "I feel kind of strange with your driving me around, babysitting, cooking . . ."

"I do windows, too . . ." Laura said, the corners of her mouth turning up, as she whipped out to the Post Road.

Maia decided to look up "mud snails." She peered at the tall wooden file in the middle of the room and wondered if she would be able to reach the right drawer. She could ask Miss

Hill. But when she turned to look, Miss Hill wasn't at her desk, and she didn't see her in the reference section. She stood up and walked over to the card catalog. Without the Latin, she'd have to try categories. She was good at that. "Animals," no; "Shells"—can't reach that drawer. At only four foot one she was at a great disadvantage. Maybe they were listed under mud snails . . . Mud . . . Mud Snails. What luck, the "M" drawer was low enough to pull out. Yes, "Mud Snails," see: *Creatures of Shallow Waters*, by Gruen, John. The index number 551.8 was in the corner of the card. She copied it diligently, left-handed, on a small scrap of paper, with a blunted pencil. She looked around. Just a few grownups were reading at various tables. At the round table a young mother bent over a small child, pointing to a picture. Maia felt a sudden pang of sadness. She sighed. No Miss Hill, but there must be a directory.

She walked to the desk. She noticed that Miss Hill had left her glasses there, a black cord attached to them. Maia frowned, puzzled: why take them off? If you had a cord, didn't you just wear them around your neck? Surely Miss Hill would be back in a minute to get them.

She examined the map while she waited. She glanced at the big round clock. It was already two thirty-five. It might not be hard to find. The five hundreds were Level Three. She decided to go up there by herself.

Heading up the stairs, she noted the instruction at the landing: "Turn lights out when you leave the stack. Conserve energy." The first landing was lighted, so someone was there; she heard whispers, older kids. She went up to the next level, it was dark and the smell was stale and musty. She reached Level Three. It was so dark she had to feel the wall for the switch. She didn't like being there all alone, but she went ahead by herself and walked around the first metal section, checking the numbers until they matched the one on the slip. *Gruen*, she tried to concentrate. The books here were thinly stacked on dark green metal shelves. There were large spaces in between, and she could see the far wall now through a gap. She stood on a small stool. There was the book! She pulled it toward her, opening another gap and exposing several feet of wall beyond. She stared, and a scream stifled in her throat.

Through the space, she saw Miss Hill standing flat against the wall, palms pressed against it. The librarian was staring straight ahead, and on her face was a smile . . . but not an ordinary smile . . . her lips were stretched back over her teeth, pulled way back, as if Miss Hill had started smiling harder and harder until she couldn't stop. Her unwinking eyes glittered. Maia's heart thumped wildly.

"Miss Hill," she whispered, but the woman didn't move. Maia swallowed. Her stomach hurt with fear. She imagined that the fierce smile on the masklike face was growing; but the staring eyes . . . did they see her? Was Miss Hill going to grab her and choke her? She moved down from the stool very slowly and silently, but Miss Hill stood flat against the wall as if she were nailed to it, her smile frozen, horrible. She wouldn't come after her, would she? . . . Would she? *Would she?* Maia's breath came faster and faster, and now she screamed. She screamed again. But Miss Hill just stood there. Maia's screams echoed off the metal stairs and around the concrete stairwells as she ran wildly down.

Coming back from the hospital, Laura and Daniel were in a good mood. The dog had been forgotten, and things were looking better. Wendy had been sitting up, her hair brushed, fresh from a sponge bath, and wearing pajamas from home that said "I'm Number One" across the front. Daniel felt that she had recognized him. There was even a hint of her usual sullen expression when he asked if she felt better, although her nod was a little too zombielike—from the tranquilizer, probably. Still, it was good for a start. And she was drinking liquids and taking food. Even ate a pickle, Barbara had said. He wondered when she would answer questions.

"Were you ever a hostile teen-ager?" he asked Laura in the car on the way back.

"Of course I was," Laura said, so matter-of-fact that they both burst into laughter.

As they approached the rear of the library, a policeman stopped them. "No cars go through here . . ." he said.

Up ahead, they saw the back of a long, sleek rescue van, its red lights spinning.

Daniel ran forward, looking after the departing ambulance, and quickly searched the group of onlookers for his daughter's face.

"Daddy!" Maia called, reaching out her arms.

He picked her up. She curled into a ball, weeping on his shoulder. "Daddy, Daddy," she cried.

He looked in the direction of the siren. The onlookers began to disperse, and an elderly woman walked over to

him. "Poor little thing, she found her . . ." the woman said.
"What?"
"She found Miss Hill," the woman said, and walked away.
Maia shuddered against him. "She got very sick. She looked so crazy smiling like that. And she didn't blink her eyes . . . Why did she get sick?" she cried.
He held her tightly. "Let's go home," he said. "Let's get out of here," he said to Laura.

At home, Daniel went to the telephone immediately, and he dialed the hospital. "This is Dr. Lieberman. Is Dr. Singh there?"
"Just one moment, I'll page him."
There was a pause—then the gentle, accented voice: "Singh here."
"Dr. Singh, this is Dr. Lieberman. Were you in Emergency when Miss Hill was brought in?"
"Yes. I was there."
"Is she admitted?"
"No, no. They're sending her home."
"They're sending her home?" he repeated, relieved. "What was the matter?"
"I did not examine her. Her own doctor came. Dr. Stockton. He said she is excited so her pulse is high, but he says everything else is all right . . ."
"Oh, good . . ."
"Yes, they gave her a sedative and sent her home with her sister. Her sister told the doctor that she had received bad news this afternoon."
"What was she doing? How was she behaving? Dr. Singh, I'm sorry to bother you with this, but when I saw her a little while ago, she was perfectly normal . . . I'm afraid I was the one who brought the bad news."
"Uh . . . she was smiling."
"I think it is odd. I have seen this lady before in the library. Today her smile was most odd."
Daniel thanked him and hung up. He had an uneasy sense of déjà vu. Forget it, he thought. It comes in threes, his mother used to say. It never rains but it pours. Yet why did that stable, stoic lady go into emotional shock? And why hadn't he noticed it? He could have sworn that she had taken the news in stride—
"Soup's on." Laura's voice interrupted his thoughts. She stood in the doorway as if she lived there. Maia was by her

side, holding her hand. Bet it'd be a while before Maia stayed alone again, he thought. Laura belonged there somehow. Laura was definitely a special person, a whole involvement, maybe a lifetime. He wasn't sure he was ready to try again.

"Gazpacho," she said. "And the only thing that's ready beyond soup is a small salad . . ."

"And ice cream," Maia said.

The sun went down like a red beach ball, promising another hot morning. Chief McLoughlin headed up Park Street and saw Mr. Harrison squinting out at the sunset. "How're you today?" McLoughlin said out the window. He didn't get his usual answer from Mr. Harrison, so he slowed down the patrol car with a reflex action and looked in his side-view mirror. Mr. Harrison looked confused, puzzled by something in the empty sky. He stood there, his arms hanging limply at his sides.

Well, thought McLoughlin, the heat is too much for old people. The five-day heat wave had gotten everybody by now. Maybe even triggered the vandalism and the kids . . . but the poor old people, McLoughlin thought. Many didn't have air conditioning at home or air-conditioned places to visit during the day. Nobody had time for them. He always liked to have a few words with old Harrison, a ritual conversation that went: "How're you doing this evening, Mr. Harrison?"

"Oh, can't complain, lived through the day . . ."

"Take care. See you tomorrow . . ."

"Oh, we'll see, we'll see."

But today he hadn't answered.

McLoughlin didn't like it, so he turned the car to the right, went down a couple of blocks, and circled back up the hill again, squinting into the orange glow. Mr. Harrison wasn't there. He had apparently gone into the house. Well, it was probably the heat. McLoughlin called in on the patrol-car radio to check out any further information on the Horgan girl. There was none. Probably just went into the city for the weekend, he thought, and she'll be back home on Monday. He listened to the officers' report on the librarian, Miss Hill. Another elderly citizen. Not one he often said hello to. She was always in a hurry, and standoffish—but he often stopped and gave a lift to her sister; a different sort.

"What do you mean by shock?" he asked the officer who reported the outcome at the hospital over the car radio.

"I don't know," the officer said. "Seems that old dog found

dead at the Kroners' Pond was hers. The news must have upset her a lot, I guess."

McLoughlin thought about stopping by the Hills' house on Goodridge just to see if he could be of help, but he was worn down from the heat, the motorcycle accident, the long talk with Jill Horgan's parents, and of course the sight of Wendy. Years ago when he was a young cop, he remembered hearing talk about clusters; things happening that were related in time or place. And a lot of hypothetical talk about how they should be looked at, these clustered events, as if parts of a single fabric . . . a pattern. He had never really swallowed that theory . . . Say you got a rape on the beach and at the same time some guy beat up his wife downtown—were they connected? Triggered by what? Heat? Sunspots? Some other force? But even though he didn't believe clusters were anything but coincidence, he felt there would be more trouble coming over his car radio before the night was out.

Howard Lawson had absented himself politely after dinner, leaving the New York director to wander around the converted-barn theater with Shirley and Ralph. They turned on the work light over the stage, where they now sat on wooden chairs. The discussion became intense as the stage filled with foglike wisps of cigarette smoke drifting up to the work light.

"I can't tell you, Avery," Shirley said to the director, "how much it means to me that you agreed to give a seminar here."

Avery nodded. He took a drag on his Gitane. Shirley heard a slight sound outside that was familiar to her; it irritated her like ants at a picnic: a car had stopped in her theater parking lot again. The teen-agers embarrassed her. They interrupted rehearsals and serious works-in-progress . . . they left condoms behind. The police never did anything but smirk. She'd be damned if she would call the police again.

"How many people do you think will turn up for my talk?" Avery asked quietly.

Shirley looked at him, beaming. "Well, next Saturday is way off . . . time for Ralph to call everyone."

"Of course we'll post it in town and put an announcement in *The Sheffield News* . . ." Ralph said.

"And then I think, because you're a *very* special person, Avery, we ought to send a release to the *Times* . . ." Shirley added in her husky, rapid voice.

"What do you think, Shirl, fifty people?"

"At least!"

He nodded reflectively.

Shirley heard noises again in the lot and tuned them out, speaking over them clearly and loudly. "What will you speak about, Avery? I mean what shall we say in the press release? Do you have a title?"

He looked at her. "Say whatever you want to say, Shirl, and I'll talk about whatever the fuck I want to talk about when I'm talking. You know what I mean?"

Artists, Shirley thought, beaming at him tenderly, really are babies. She began to have a maternal warm feeling. She considered herself an earth mother, a giver of life and love to helpless, immature artists, exerting a control that was for their own good. Her children—or rather, Howard's son and daughter, Allen and Amy—never engendered this feeling.

Outside the Lawsons' Sheffield Players' Theater, in the corner of the small parking lot, near the woods, Chet sensed the change begin again. Earlier, he had attributed the weird feelings to nervousness. He didn't know how or why Ronnie Sawyer agreed to date with him. She was prettier than Wendy and an honor student, besides. But she bit the minute he asked, and even borrowed her father's Mercedes to meet him. Ronnie was sixteen, not stacked like Wendy, but at least you could talk to her. And that was really what he planned when he drove into the lot by the woods. After all, he couldn't park in front of her old man's house. Early on, after he'd fixed the flat, she'd let him take the wheel. When he'd leaned over the spare he'd felt real strange. There were a couple of colors in the hubcap that didn't belong. He'd blinked them back to chrome. Ronnie didn't want to tell her father about the flat. Now he sat at the wheel and kicked the tire iron where he'd left it on the floor.

It was a real high sitting behind the wheel of a Mercedes, and he had a sense of power and rightness, and extended it in a fantasy to Ronnie, whom he imagined as his wife. He usually liked to daydream like that, but suddenly he had this vision that his mind had moved over and was watching him from outside the windshield. He felt real shaky. Once he'd had that happen coming down from a bad trip, but it didn't last so long. Besides, he hadn't dropped anything in months. He was clean.

He didn't know where Wendy was and he didn't care, after that stupid broad opened her mouth like that to her father.

Tomorrow he would tell her who he dated over the weekend, who maybe he balled, and he'd watch her face. Ronnie was real bright, not like Wendy. She talked to him shyly and with respect. So Chet felt bad that he didn't feel like himself.

They sat on the front seat of the car in the darkness, speaking softly. How long had they been there? Had it been hours and hours? What time was it, he wondered. The car leather smelled new and Chet could feel the potential power of the steering wheel under his left hand. He slipped his other hand around Ronnie's shoulder, draped it there, very cool. Then he noticed that the texture of the wheel had changed, softened to something like wax, but in a second it changed back as he focused on it. He couldn't see very much after he turned off the headlights. Ronnie's shoulder yielded to his hand, and it was soft like velvet at first, and then it too changed, and the blouse fabric grew slimy, felt wet. He looked at her and tried to focus and will the texture to change back as the wheel had. But instead, the dark interior of the car brightened, almost as if lightning was flashing, and he saw that Ronnie was looking at him strangely. He said something to her, like "What's the matter?" but his words elongated as he spoke them and became a cry, or at least he heard them as a cry, and there was an echo under them that didn't stop. The words created an echo that lived by itself and got louder inside his head. The steering wheel began to melt quickly in his hand and that made him dizzy. He began to sweat. Breathing rapidly, he clutched Ronnie's shoulder but it had transformed to another substance entirely. It was like snakeskin to the touch, and he was scared to look at her. She was saying something to him, but her words were meeting the echo and making it worse; like he was under water and a waterfall ran over his head, all sounds pouring into it, volume increasing, no way to understand the words. Another flash of light. Colors changed. He could see way into the forest now, and there were leaves far away and he could see each vein of them, and blue light shone through them and through his hands. Now he could really see what it all was about.

He looked at Ronnie but she wasn't there. The girl who had been there wasn't there anymore, and he was holding on to something, a piece of some kind of creature like a snake, with markings like a rattler. And it was going to attack him. He heard the rattle. It was going to kill him. It was causing this sound, this change in his hands, and in the leaves . . . now, vivid colors flooded over its face and spilled down onto his hands and he squeezed the slime and pushed against the face, clawing it . . . he felt teeth on the pad of his thumb, but a snake like that could not kill him, not if he could see a hundred miles into the forest! He could escape by flying away. But now he felt paralyzed. The bite was doing it . . . poison was seeping through his arm. It was green, eating into his flesh. Now he felt the pain, acute and deadly, and he knew he would die soon, but this animal could not go free, so he would destroy it. He saw the huge serpent's mouth ready to devour him, and the rattle grew louder. He shook his head against the rushing sounds and picked up something heavy from the floor. Suddenly there was whiteness like a flashbulb glare and he saw that the animal lay still. And he saw the illuminated tire iron in his gigantic hand, and as he moved his arm back it all changed again and the designs of beads and stripes flew over her face. She moved and it was very black all around, except the animal was glowing like rubies and sapphires and he lifted up the heavy thing in his hands and hit at it, hit at it, struck it, and he could hear the sounds like shells breaking, meeting the rushing echoes. Light poured from the monster. Tears streamed down his face. To destroy an animal this size was superhuman, but so was he if he could fly, and maybe he could when the snake was down beneath his feet. He smashed it. It kept falling and rising. He smashed it and smashed it till there was nothing but darkness and the thing lay beneath his feet. Something released him and he breathed cool air and different darkness and the rushing changed to a humming and he walked above the ground into the translucent blue and orange leaves for many, many miles . . .

"It's them again . . ." Ralph Jeffreys said, hearing noises outside in the lot. "I'll go off and scare them away."

The visiting New York director looked around, owl-like. "What do they do out there, Shirley?"

"I've never looked," Shirley said, furious.

"They don't have drive-ins, huh?" said the director.

"Shirley, should I go out or call the cops?" Ralph asked.

"Oh go out, would you, darling? I can't stand the attitude of the police in this town. Here, take a flashlight."

The director looked at Ralph as he left. "It's too bad . . ."

Shirley stood and paced through the smoke. "I'm fed up here, that's what. Just fed up. Out here in the boonies!"

"Come back to the city, Shirl," Avery said solemnly.
"Ah, would that I could, darling, *would* that I could!"

Ralph stood in the lot and spotlighted the car with his flashlight. Nothing. No ignition started. He sighed impatiently and went to take a look. Maybe they had gone out to the woods or maybe . . . He looked through the window . . . the body was on the floor; shafts of dark hair clung to the upholstery. There was no face left; only shreds of skin and rags of muscle—hanging from the exposed and crushed fragments of bone. Dark blood was everywhere. He felt sick, but his fear in the dark held down the rising bile. Terrified, he ran back to the lit theater; by the time he got to the stage, he was in tears, and unintelligible. They looked at him, and he tried to speak but couldn't. Suddenly he vomited.

It was about ten o'clock Sunday night when Ned McLoughlin got the radio call he'd been expecting.

# Monday, August sixth,

began as quietly as the haze that muted the sun. The news hadn't yet come over the radio. Only a few people knew what had taken place the night before. The Lawsons' Sheffield Players' Theater lot was roped off, and the police technicians worked quietly. Most of Sheffield was still dreaming. Daniel Lieberman finished examining a newborn baby at the General; a healthy, eight-pound, normal boy. A nice way to begin the week. Then he sat on the edge of Wendy's bed and gazed at her pale face. He sat there as if in the presence of a sphinx, watching her for clues to whatever secret lay under the surface. Monday morning and she still behaved too quietly. There was barely a response when he tried to communicate with her. She seemed removed, far away. He had called in the psychiatrist that the Doughertys knew and was waiting for her arrival. What did Wendy know that she wouldn't or couldn't tell him? Would she speak to the psychiatrist? He wrote orders to begin gradual reduction of the Valium. It could be that the tranquilizer was making Wendy unresponsive . . .

Laura reached for her jeans on the corner ladder-backed chair of her attic room. Shades still covered the dormer windows, the air was cool; the light, blue. She got out of bed, pulled the patchwork quilt over her sheets, ducking the eaves by habit and looked around the small room, high up and solitary. She felt like a nun in a cloistered space and, suddenly sorry for herself, splashed her face with cold water. Then she stood at the too-low sink and leaned forward to examine herself critically in the mirror. Too pale, she thought—how ridiculous not to tan; boring, limp, ashen hair, a complete washout! She pulled her jeans on; even at twenty-six she could still pass for a teen-ager. She had a long waist; long, long legs; full, high breasts. Daniel liked all that, she knew. She twisted her head to one side and began to braid her hair, thinking of him, continuing her nice dream . . . his dark, sad eyes and his grin . . . the sensitive, expressive face, always changing when he looked at her. She wondered how it would feel to have him hold her . . . but she had been wrong before. She didn't want to be wrong again.

How had she gotten involved with Paul McGinnis anyway? Had it been his inaccessibility? A master technician at love-making, even programmed with expressions of tenderness, enough to fool anyone into thinking him human. Agility, timing, and beyond that, the power to convince her that at any moment his opaque gaze would unveil itself to her alone. Laura had waited for that moment when his aloofness would melt like magic, forgetting that she didn't believe in magic, forgetting even herself. Then, when he was everything to her, at the height of her addiction, of course he said good-bye. He'd accomplished his purpose. He owned her. That was as far as it interested him to go . . .

She quickly buttoned her work shirt and rolled up the sleeves. God, his magnetism had been astounding, and then finding out nothing human was there . . . nothing. How completely the magnetism had vanished. She had been amazed and horrified at herself. Where to go then? Her career, the world to which she fled from McGinnis, even that was poor judgment. It wasn't working out.

She leaned toward the mirror and pulled at her bangs, her green eyes filled with tears . . . certainly Lieberman seemed different. Why hadn't he arrived earlier? She jerked the watch off her oak dresser and slipped it on her wrist quickly, them pulled up the shades with an impatient tug, knowing she was about to get involved all over again.

First stop; Janie Garner. Laura pulled her van onto the circular gravel driveway and beeped once. She glanced out as she waited, at the patrol car, cruising slowly down High Street. She waved, puzzled. Her route never coincided with any patrol beat. Where was Janie? She was usually out front with paper bag in one hand and towel in the other. If Janie was late, Laura would be off schedule. Janie. Then Maia. Then loop around for Roy Dougherty. He should have been second, but Barbara couldn't sleep, couldn't get it together in the morning, and now with Wendy sick . . . so Roy was third. Then straight as an arrow up to Billy McGinnis. His young German governess with the raw-looking reddish skin and yellow hair would be there holding his shoulders, and she'd send him off like a mechanical toy, with a tap on his little backside. How could Paul have such an awkward, fragile little boy? Don't think. Then it would be down the hill en route to the beach, turning left for Amy and Allen Lawson, children of Howard's first wife. They both looked like Howard a bit, pathetically bony and somber, but their eyes were hopeful. Then Cindy Vail, waiting in her matching Florence Eiseman knit outfit like a poised, miniature adult. Her reddish hair braided and glossy, her pale eyes would look Laura over carefully before she took her slow walk to the van. The other children would move over instinctively. Billy would be pushed, too slow and clumsy to move fast, and a small fight would break out . . . enough daydreaming. Where was Janie? She beeped the horn. Why was that patrol car circling High Street?

Laura got out of the van and rang the bell on the white-pillared porch of the Georgian-style brick house. She rang twice, two muted chimes. Nothing. The house seemed deserted. The lawn was still trimmed by the neighbor's kids, but the gardening, which cast more time and money, was neglected now—the hedges were getting leggy and oddly shaped. Silence. Then Laura heard a small cough or a noise from out back. She quickly walked around the gravel path to the corner of the house, cool in the shadows of the large old trees that hung between her and the yellowing sky. There was a sudden rush of honeysuckle smell. And there was Janie.

"Janie?" Laura called.

The child stood rigid on the grass, like a stone angel, sneakers stained wet with dew, gazing fixedly ahead at something. Laura couldn't see. Laura quickly edged around the trees, shielded her eyes, and immediately saw what held Janie's attention. Louise Garner, a solitary figure in a pale blue silk nightgown, stumbled back and forth over the abandoned tennis court. With erratic movements, her arms lashed out at some adversary in an imaginary game. The clay court surface was pitted with neglect and a torn net hung down, partially rolled like a carpet at the center: near it, spindly daisies and thick weeds sprouted. Louise was so soaked with sweat that her skin looked oily in the sun. The thin blue gown clung to her body, and was filthy and ripped. She had apparently tripped several times and fallen onto the clay. Terra cotta powder overlying the court surface now streaked her face and neck, and coated her tangled strands of hair. Breathing rapidly from exertion and heat, she would stand very still and suddenly lunge out wildly as if at a deadly adversary. Then she would run back and forth, back and forth, on the ruined court.

Laura knelt by Janie. "How long have you been out here?" she whispered.

Silence. The child was transfixed by the sight of her mother's strange game. Her face was streaked with tears.

"Janie," Laura said gently, scanning the child's frightened eyes. "How long has Mommy been out there?"

Janie's round face began to crumple. "I got locked out . . . I . . ."

"It's okay. It's going to be all right."

"She was out here when I got downstairs. I can't get back in the house . . ."

"Don't worry, I'll do something right away. It'll be all right."

Janie finally took her eyes off the court and looked at Laura. "I called her and called her, but she won't answer me . . ." she said, and her voice broke. Her eyes filled with tears. "I left my towel in the house, but it's locked."

Laura lifted Janie up and hugged her. "I have a towel in the van," she said gently, carrying the child around to the driveway and lifting her onto the front seat. "Here's a Snoopy towel just for you . . . now wait here."

Janie looked at her questioningly.

"Mommy will be all right, Janie," she reassured the child, stroking her hair. "I'm going to try to help her. Now you stay right here and let me go and talk to her, okay?"

Janie nodded, and Laura quickly walked around the house and over the lawn to the court. As she neared, she approached more slowly. But she soon noticed the her presence didn't seem to affect Louise. The world in which Louise played her game was isolated, and Laura did not intrude there. Laura placed her hands firmly on Louise's shoulders and attempted to steer her off the court. "Come with me, Louise. Come, I want to help . . ."

Louise shook her off without so much as a recognition of her presence. Laura whispered encouragingly and again tried to struggle with her. The air was still and the sun burned brutally. Louise's arms were wet and difficult to grip and her movements were sudden; an attack or lunge began instantly, and Laura could only hold on to her for a few seconds before she slipped out of her grasp. As Laura held her, she heard the ragged, hoarse pants and gasps and her stomach contracted with a sudden fear that Louise would soon collapse from this exertion in the deadly heat. How long had she been out there? Laura asked her that, talked to her gently, soothingly, called her by name, but Louise didn't respond. Finally, breaking from Louise she ran to the back door to try the lock just to be sure. Janie was right. They were locked out, and she didn't want to break a window. She needed help. Couldn't get in the house to call an ambulance. The neighbors . . . no, they shouldn't see this. Louise had been through enough last time she was ill. The fastest would be to call for help from Daniel's house. Yes. Just a half mile. She walked quickly to the van with a glance back over her shoulder at Louise.

She started up the van. "Janie, Mommy will be all right, but I have to call the doctor. Do you know the name of Mommy's doctor?" she asked, whipping out onto the road.

Janie shook her head no and chewed on her towel.

Only a short distance . . . only a little way . . . she repeated to herself en route to Maia's. "Mommy will be all right," she said aloud, to convince herself and Janie. Maia was already on the road, on tiptoes, squinting at them through her glasses, smiling expectantly . . . "Maia. I have to use your phone. Is Daddy home?"

The child seemed to know instinctively that something was terribly wrong. "No." Maia said; immediately she flipped the chain with the key on it over her head and handed it to Laura.

Laura called for the ambulance from Daniel's front vestibule. She gave the details precisely, one slim hand on her forehead. Then, in a less steady voice, she begged, "Please don't use the siren if at all possible. There is no need to use the siren." She hung up and dialed Daniel. His number was printed on a board on the wall in big block letters, in an obvious underestimation of Maia's reading ability. The letters seemed to blur as Laura's eyes filled with tears again; the stupid letters seemed so tender and clumsy at the same time. She left a message with the answering service for him to go to Janie Garner's house. Yes. It was an emergency, she said. It wasn't until she hung up that she wondered why she had called him. No rationale at all, she decided, just those reassuring dumb block letters . . . she dialed Paul McGinnis then, wishing she didn't know the unlisted number by heart. Why call him? Well, Louise was his secretary and besides, she had no one else to take charge, to look after her. The fräulein answered.

"Billy will not go today to camp," the voice said.

"I'm calling about Mrs. Garner," Laura said coldly. "Just tell Dr. McGinnis that Mrs. Garner is at home and very, very, sick. I have called an ambulance. Just tell him right away." She hung up without even asking why Billy wasn't going to camp. She found that she was shaking. As she neared the van, she saw that Maia had her arm around Janie. There was nothing more for her to do. She would not go back now. The ambulance, the doctors, McGinnis, they'd take over. The children should not witness it. She would not go back. She would continue her normal route to the beach, wait there, and hold Janie on her lap till there was news . . .

McLoughlin slammed down the receiver and shouted into his intercom at the receptionist, "Don't put those newspaper guys through anymore. Just tell them they know as much as we do, goddamn vultures! And if any more townspeople call in, just tell them to use their common sense, for God's sake. They shouldn't wander around deserted places and they should lock their doors! What am I, the town babysitter? There's a lunatic somewhere in the area . . . excuse me, make that alleged phychopathic killer . . . let them use their common sense, hear me?"

A sigh. "Yes, Chief . . ."

"Sorry," he said in a mellower tone. "Just handle it, but get them off my back, okay?" McLoughlin sipped his Alka-Seltzer-on-the-rocks and resignedly flipped the switch up again. "Look, I'm sorry I yelled . . . I'm going back down to the parking lot . . . I'll be there if you need me."

Never, even in his imagination, had McLoughlin seen a corpse as battered as this one. He'd obtained identification through the registration in the glove compartment and then, worse still, he'd had to confirm it through the parents. He had expected something, yes, but not this. The deluge of calls was inevitable after the news broke, but he hadn't slept, couldn't hold his food down, and his nerves were on edge. He drove slowly to the lot, looking at the peaceful-seeming town; each neat hedge now a potential hiding place, each solitary acre vulnerable . . . and as he pulled into view of the technicians in the lot, he prayed one more time that this murderer had come from far away and by now was captured or dead in some distant place, that lightning would only strike once in Sheffield.

* * *

Daniel was surprised by Laura's message at the General. He raced to his car, wondering if Janie was sick or hurt. He pulled into Louise Garner's gravel driveway with a lurch, sprinted up the wide front steps, bag in hand, and rang the bell.

The door opened and Paul McGinnis stood there looking slightly puzzled. "Hello, Lieberman . . . What are you . . .?"

"Is something wrong?" Daniel interrupted. "I got a message to get here as soon as possible."

There was a slight pause, then McGinnis's expression relaxed into slight amusement. "Ah . . ." he said laconically, "must have been Laura calling . . . was it?"

"Yes."

"You must have thought it was Janie. Well, everything's fine now. It's all been taken care of," McGinnis said, smiling genially. "Laura is a bit of an alarmist . . ."

"What happened?" Daniel asked. He was getting annoyed. McGinnis was making him feel like an intruder.

"Janie is at camp. It was her mother who was ill. But Louise is fine now. She's resting comfortably."

Daniel nodded, puzzled, as he watch McGinnis set the lock to "open" on the inside doorknob and then close the door behind him. "What happened?" he asked with a small stubborn edge to his voice.

McGinnis put his hands in his blazer pocket and crossed the pillar near Daniel, forcing him to turn around. "Well, she was quite exhausted," he said slowly. "Laura apparently sent for an ambulance and it came, but Louise's doctor and I agreed that there was no need to move her. She'll be fine."

Daniel looked at the easy smile with growing impatience. "Exactly what was the matter with her?"

Paul McGinnis ushered him down the steps, over to the shade of a large oak, speaking confidentially and quietly. "She's apparently suffered another breakdown . . . I guess you have no way of knowing, unless perhaps Laura Benedict told you, but you see Louise hasn't been well for some time now. You may have noticed at the party she was drinking rather more than she should . . . she can't drink at all, you know."

Daniel felt he was being patronized, and he didn't like McGinnis's mocking expression whenever he said Laura's name. "I don't know anything about Louise Garner."

Leaning against the broad tree trunk, McGinnis looked out at the road. "She's unstable. Since her husband died she's been more or less my concern. Harvey Garner worked with me, you see. Well, since his death she's been my employee. That is, after she recovered from her breakdown. I'm afraid this won't be her last, either . . ."

Daniel stared at the handsome profile—the voice sounded like a film narration. McGinnis seemed devoid of any emotional connection to his words. He turned suddenly, thrusting his hands deeper in his pockets, and then, as if reading Daniel's mind, said directly, "I may seem rather distant to you, but believe me, I'm deeply concerned about Louise."

"Where's Janie?" Daniel asked.

"She's gone with Laura. I've left a message to have her brought to my house after camp. When her mother is better in a day or two, I'll bring her home."

"A day or two?"

"Yes. I believe Louise will be all right by then, with rest," McGinnis said with a glance at the upstairs window. "I guess you think I'm an optimist, saying a day to two? I'm a scientist like yourself. Mental breaks have patterns, and I've seen this one coming. I know how it goes."

"Doesn't she have any relatives who could take care of the child?"

"No. No one. Since Harvey died, Louise has been on her own." McGinnis looked off into the distance again. "She has only me."

"Would you like me to help you with Louise?"

McGinnis's stare removed the last trace of pretended intimacy. "That's not necessary. Louise was examined by her own doctor, as I said, and he gave her a tranquilizer. Now that she's resting quietly, I don't see the need for more disturbance . . . do you?"

Daniel Lieberman was being dismissed graciously but firmly. He turned toward his car, stubbing his infected toe on a white painted border rock. He'd be damned if he'd yell. "I'll call Louise later then," he said.

As if sensing his hostility, McGinnis patted him on the shoulder. "Thank you for helping us out."

Daniel said nothing. He got into his car and started the engine, glad that this one time the Volks didn't give him a hard time. Someday, he knew, the engine would die for good. He pulled smoothly out of the driveway and glanced in his rearview mirror: Paul McGinnis was watching his departure, standing there like a sentry.

* * *

McGinnis turned as soon as Lieberman was around the corner, quickly reset the lock and closed the door. He stood for a moment looking at the telephone in Louise's living room and began to walk toward it. Stopping, he stood a moment more. He picked up the receiver to dial and then, apparently changing his mind, he replaced the receiver and walked to the kitchen. He stood at the large messy sink and washed his hands methodically, knocking to one side last night's dinner pots and dishes. He opened his attaché case on the kitchen counter and took out a hypodermic needle and syringe. He assembled and filled the syringe from a vial. Holding it carefully at his side, he mounted the steps. He paused for only a second at the doorway of Louise's bedroom. She was crouched in a corner, still perspiring heavily in her stained, ripped gown. McGinnis walked to her, but as his shadow loomed above, it did not affect her concentrated gaze. She did not seem to notice him. McGinnis knelt by her side, he lifted the flounce of silk ruffle at her shoulder. He held her firmly, efficiently, as he injected the contents of the syringe into her upper arm.

Daniel made the necessary house calls, then left a message for Larry Roberts to cover for him, and headed for the beach. He switched on the car radio; at the sound of some noxious music, he turned the dial. Now the station was local and the newscaster's voice was clear:

". . . the body of sixteen-year-old Ronnie Sawyer was found late last night, brutally beaten to death in the front seat of an abandoned car in the parking lot of the Sheffield Players' Theater on the property of Dr. and Mrs. Howard Lawson. The victim was the daughter of Mr. and Mrs. Roger Sawyer. Mr. Sawyer is an industrialist who recently moved to Sheffield. The Sawyers have two other children. The parents are not available for comment. At this time, no suspect has been apprehended. We have no word yet from the Police Department as to whether there was a sexual assault involved and nothing as to the identity of the suspect. The police have made a special number available to anyone who may have information leading to the arrest . . ."

Jesus Christ, Daniel thought bewildered.

When he got to the beach, he jogged quickly from his car over the rim of grass to the sand, searching anxiously for Laura and the children. Tourists strolled near the striped umbrellas near the hotel. A few teen-agers lay near each other on reed mats. No campers. There were a few mothers near a group of toddlers. He kept walking. Finally he saw them. They were up on a small hill under a large old cedar. Janie was on Laura's knees and Maia close by her side. The others sat nearby in the shade of the trees, watching as Laura held up a glass tube. As he approached, the children started down the beach in twos toward the Sound, each carrying a small plastic cup. Laura watched them intently, giving him a small wave. Maia reached up to kiss him and he hugged her.

"I went to your house, Janie," he said quickly, kneeling near her and ruffling her hair. "Your mother is resting and feeling a lot better, and by tomorrow we hope she'll be all right . . ."

Janie nodded her head slowly, affirmatively. Maia smiled and took her hand, and they started down to the water. Daniel sat down next to Laura and looked out tensely toward the Sound.

"Most of the parents didn't send their kids today because of the news," Laura said quietly, not taking her eyes off the children.

"I just heard on the radio . . . unbelievable."

"We were scheduled to go on a walk through the woods . . . can you imagine? I have to confess I'm scared," Laura said, folding her arms over her knees, giving him a short look, and then gazing back at the children. "The Santés asked us to come in for lunch . . . Shirley Lawson is in bed and Howard stayed home with Allen and Amy. It's very frightening around here, you know, we're just not prepared for it. Each house is so isolated, no place really feels safe. But tell me what happened with Louise before the kids get back. You told Janie she's better? Is she really?"

"I didn't see her. McGinnis was there and told me she was better." He paused with a sidelong glance in her direction. "You called him?"

"Yes . . . when I saw her like that, I didn't know what to do . . ."

"Why'd you call me?"

"I wanted you to see her. Well, I don't know, I just thought you should see her."

"Well since I didn't maybe you'd better fill me in. Where did you find her and what was she doing?"

Laura described the scene on the tennis court vividly. "I've never seen anything like it," she concluded. "Except maybe the way Wendy acted at the party Saturday. That bizarre. But this was different. Louise was totally in her own world. She didn't even see me. She didn't throw anything at me, or hit me. She just went on with this imaginary battle."

"McGinnis said she's been sick before," Daniel said slowly.

"Yes . . . she was very depressed after her husband died. She was even hospitalized for a short time, still . . ."

"At the party Saturday night, Louise told me she had seen a UFO. She was really drunk."

Laura looked at him, her green eyes wide and intent. "She isn't insane, though. I mean you don't believe she is . . . do you?"

He shrugged. "The UFO incident must have been some sort of hallucination, and she still clearly believes it. I think she's very unstable."

"But not insane," she insisted.

"No . . ." he said, and rested against the tree contemplatively. "Was Sheffield really a peaceful community like the real-estate agent said—I mean, before I got here?"

"I guess . . ."

"You know if this were a ship, they'd throw me overboard like Jonah . . ." he said with a half smile, his eyes sad.

"I don't think there's been a homicide in town since I was born."

He had stopped smiling and appeared to be thinking intently.

"But," she went on, looking at him curiously, "maybe what happened to Wendy and this morning, Louise . . . maybe these things happen all the time behind closed doors—and we just happened to be there, you know?"

He half heard her. "Sure," he said in an unconvinced voice. "Like the library . . ."

Laura turned to reply, but he had already gotten to his feet. "Listen, take Maia home with you," he said abruptly, "and I'll catch up with you later, okay?"

Miss Hill squinted at the light through the slit in the chained front door. She undid the lock only after Daniel had handed her his identification.

"What a day to go around, Doctor! What a day you picked! Did you hear the news on the radio?"

"Yes," he said. "Terrible." He looked at her with relief. She looked herself again. Not quite as spartan as in the library, but the slippers and the flowered wrap she wore softened some of the puritanical quality.

She waited, looking at him with some curiosity, as if it were the first time she'd seen him. "One can't be too careful, even here in Sheffield . . ." she said politely.

"But we did meet, Miss Hill," he reminded her gently. "Remember, I'm Dr. Lieberman . . . I came to the library to tell you about your dog?"

She put her hand up to shield her eyes. The hall behind her was very dark and filled with oak furniture; an end table, an umbrella stand. "Oh yes, poor Toadie, it was simply awful," she said. Her voice was matter-of-fact, flat; New England as chowder.

"I just wanted to tell you that I was very sorry I upset you so much," he said, shifting his weight uncomfortably. "And, well I am really glad you're feeling better."

Miss Hill leaned against the door, folding her arms over her chest. "Well . . . she was very very old, you know. Seventeen."

Daniel felt his fear melt slowly away. He was standing on a normal front porch with a nice old lady, chatting. What had he expected anyway? People and dogs got old. The world wasn't falling apart. He cocked his head to one side. "I . . . thought it was a 'he' . . . your dog . . . I thought you called it a 'he.' "

"Toadie? Oh no. We called her Toad Hall because we like the name. But Toadie was a 'she' . . . we were going to have her put to sleep, poor thing. That's how old she was," Miss Hill said, and shook her head sadly. "And they insisted on doing an autopsy. Public health something or other. I could have told them nothing was wrong with Toadie but old age . . . but they went and did it anyway."

"I'm sorry . . ."

"Naturally, they found nothing. I could have told them as much. Well, Dr. Lieberman, I think it was very kind of you to come all the way out here to inquire about Toadie. I'd ask you to come in for some cold water, but I expect you're in a hurry, and then my sister is sleeping at the moment."

He smile."Well, I'm glad you're up and about. My daughter, she was the one in the library . . . well I felt responsible, hitting you like that with such sudden news . . ."

She touched her sparse hair. "Well I'm just fine now, just fine."

Daniel nodded and looked up at the wall behind Miss Hill as she opened the door wider to go inside. He noticed for the first time a round federal antique mirror edged with brass stars, with a polished convex glass. It hung opposite the entry, and the curved mirror surface reflected in miniature the interior of the front parlor to the right of the vestibule. The room was filled with more dark wood, bric-a-brac, and bookcases. And there, reflected in the center of the curved glass, was a woman lying on a chaise. The woman was nearly identical in features and age to Miss Hill on the porch. The fear returned with a rush.

"Miss Hill . . .?"

"Yes?" she answered sweetly. That was it. Too sweetly. The wrinkles netting her face took a different turn at the mouth, and the corners of the eyes were not quite the same. Even the sparse yellow-gray hair was fuller, softer, and she wore lavender perfume . . .

"Miss Hill, how is your sister?"

A wary look came into her eyes. "Resting," she said. "I told you . . ."

" Miss Hill, we've never met before, have we? It's your sister . . ."

She turned away abruptly. "You might as well come in," she said in a resigned voice. "Come in, Doctor. My twin sister. She's the librarian. She's the one you wanted to see." She led him through the vestibule to the parlor, and then she turned and looked at him pleadingly. "I'm sorry, Dr. Lieberman, but I don't want her taken back to the hospital. I want her home. People our age go to the hospital and don't come back . . ."

Daniel's eyes grew accustomed to the darkness. On the chaise near the heavily draped window of the front parlor lay the other Miss Hill, like an oversized rag doll. Her eyes were open and her face slightly contorted in an odd expression, like a smile, but not quite. He felt his heart pounding: it was so strange a look.

The sister wrung her hands. "I think it was the shock about Toadie, I really do. I talk to her, but she . . ."

He knelt by the chaise and looked at Miss Hill. Her pulse was normal, or perhaps slightly elevated. Her breathing was regular.

"What did your doctor give you when he released her?"

The sister handed a bottle to Daniel. "I gave her these. I still give them to her. She is eating and drinking liquid when I give it to her. The doctor called to ask that. I didn't tell him how she was behaving."

Daniel looked at the old woman's eyes. They were unblinking. Her face was rigid and her expression reminiscent of what Maia had said: "Smiling fiercely." Now just a ghost of that, but still he knew what his daughter meant. Like a mask, she had said. Miss Hill was not sleeping, but she was awake. That, the sister was quite accurate about; she was not awake. She was catatonic. As often as he'd seen it, he'd never get used to that behavior. It jolted him, so deathlike, petrified, so totally withdrawn. "I'm going to write down my telephone number for you in case you need me . . ."

"I'm sure she'll be up and about soon," the sister said as she tucked and smoothed the lap robe around Miss Hill's legs.

He stood watching her futile busy gestures. "I hope so. Promise me you'll call your doctor is she isn't better by tomorrow . . ."

"Tomorrow?"

"Yes," he said firmly.

She sighed. "I promise."

"And if there are any changes today, call him right away. Call me too, please."

She took the paper he handed her. "I will. You are a very kind man, Dr. Lieberman."

Kind, he thought, what's kind? The woman belongs in a hospital.

He wondered, as he drove off, what Miss Hill saw behind those unblinking eyes. She had been a quiet, functioning librarian, a voice in the Town Council, an old stoic . . . Could she have been unstable? . . . his mind began to race: A sudden madness. Was there a link between Miss Hill and Louise and Wendy? Calm down, he said to himself. Statistically, when you're dealing with large numbers of events, there are bound to be coincidences. But he'd been here only two weeks and there had been three cases of bizarre behavior. In the city, he'd see maybe two clinical cases like this in a few months, and that was New York, for God's sake. Then another thing tugged at his mind. Why didn't McGinnis want him to see Louise—standing there like a sentry in front of her house. He pulled up for a moment at the side of the road and switched the radio on to hear the local news:

". . . no break yet in the Sawyer case. Police now believe the girl was not driving the vehicle, but was escorted by a date. The car belonging to Mr. Sawyer was found parked in a theater parking lot by the woods known locally as a lovers' lane. Police now speculate that the killer may have been known to the girl. No word yet on the mystery date. The girl was last seen leaving her parents' home alone in the family car about eight o'clock yesterday evening. Again, the police have a number for any information . . ."

Automatically, Daniel swung the car around and headed back to the Garner house. He turned into the driveway slowly and got out of the Volkswagen, thinking of how he would explain his return to McGinnis. He couldn't even satisfactorily explain to himself why he had come back. He rang the bell and waited. Nothing. No footsteps. He rang again. He waited several minutes, surprised, walked out back and gazed at the tennis court in silence. The house seemed vacant. He glanced up at an upstairs window and thought he saw a curtain move. It was no more movement than the shudder of a leaf, but it reverberated in his mind—and suddenly he had a sense of something sinister there in the stillness. Confused, he got back into his car and drove until he found a public telephone on the roadside. McGinnis was not at the lab, the receptionist said. No, she didn't know where he could be reached. Daniel tried the General—Mrs. Garner had not been admitted, they said. He began to dial again, thought better of it, went to the car, and drove straight up the Hill like an arrow.

Well, he had stood on front porches today, he thought, but none quite like this. He looked at the enormous expanse of white stone in front of him, and at the tall windows through which he saw an empty house, and beyond, through the large glass doors at the rear, out back to the topiary garden flanked by acres and acres of green. Nobody home. He walked out back to a tall labyrinth of hedges and called out Paul McGinnis's name like a challenge. Nothing. "McGinnis!" he called again loudly, feeling anger mounting.

"Over here," came a female voice. He recognized it at once. He walked toward it hesitantly and was met at the hedge by two sleek black Dobermans. "Come *here*, Hansel. Come over here, Gretel, come on!" the voice commanded, and the enormous dogs disappeared. I should leave, thought Daniel, right now, I should leave . . . but instead he followed the dogs around the hedge.

Greta was lying face down on a chaise near a pool cut like a natural mountain lagoon. Rocks and fieldstone jutted out at the water's edge. Behind the patio stood acres of woodland and on the fringe of that, near the poolside, a white cabana. She propped her chin on her hands and smiled at him. "I said noon . . . noon, yesterday. You're late."

"I was—looking for your husband."

Greta shaded her eyes with one hand and examined his earnest expression with delight. "I haven't seen him in years . . ." she said sweetly.

"Right," Daniel said quickly in a flat voice, noticing that there was no strap across her tanned back, just the bottom of her blue bikini. "I didn't mean to bother you."

Greta arched her lithe body up like a cat, stretching backwards, the palms of her hands pressing on the chaise. Her breasts rose up toward him, perfect and tanned as the rest of her, just pale pink at the nipples. "You're not bothering *me* . . ."

He felt a flush of heat at his groin. "I'm looking for . . ."

"My husband. You said that. Well the thing is, he's never available." She looked up at him with an innocent expression on her face. "While I, on the other hand, am always available. Can I be of some help?" She sat cross-legged now, facing him, one slender tanned leg raised slightly toward his chin.

He looked at his shoes. If he made a sudden move, the Dobermans would undoubtedly attack him. "You know you shouldn't really be out here today by yourself . . . you've heard the news on the radio?"

She rose slowly and walked toward him, smiling her brilliant smile. "Oh, my dogs will protect me, that is if I need protection. But now that you're here . . ."

"I really have to go."

She exuded Coppertone, and her long black hair brushed his shoulder. "I am Circe," she said sweetly, gesturing to the pool. "And this is my Bay of Pigs . . . oh dear, I'm afraid I'm embarrassing you. I thought you were used to bodies . . ."

"Mostly toddlers," said Daniel Lieberman helplessly, and then laughed. Her dark eyes and scarlet mouth were irresistible.

There was amusement behind her eyes as she took his hand. "How about a swim . . . you must be so warm," she said teasingly, looking over her shoulder as she led him over the flagstones.

"I haven't time right now, really," he said, but continued to walk behind her, watching her sleek back, the shadowed hollows just above her bikini line . . . the dogs sat by the chaise, watching him. "I haven't got a suit . . ."

"Borrow one of Paul's," she suggested, opening the cabana door.

The day blacked out quickly as she closed the door firmly

behind them. By the time he'd adjusted his vision, Greta was lying on a cushion dressing bench, altogether naked, with brightly striped cushions scattered all around her. She was watching him, one arm casually behind her head; she lifted the other and pointed at the far wall. "There's a suit hanging there, Dr. Lieberman," she said with a slight, mocking challenge in her voice.

Daniel had done his stint of empty sex after his wife left, and even now he remembered that the binge of one-night stands always left him lonelier . . . but she was quite beautiful, a dark, perfect body, lying there among the cushions. The long celibacy, the challenge in her voice—he undressed and reached for her.

He fitted his fingertips into the hollows just above the curve of her firm buttocks and felt her pliant, silken hips move under his palms. She pulled his hands to her taut nipples and he circled the satin skin with his thumb, with his tongue, until she moaned softly in his ear and he parted her thighs. She rose then, kneeling quickly, smiling; her black eyes open and shining in the semidarkness. She mounted him urgently and drove the rhythm as she rode above him, her body strong and supple, back arched slightly, until finally her chin tipped up, her glossy hair swung back, and she uttered a cry of delight. Then, as she leaned over him, her warm silken hair brushing his chest, he felt the taut muscles of her body gradually relax. She lay back next to him, smelling of jasmine, and spoke in her normal husky voice, half mockingly:

"Next time," she said, with an edge of the victor's challenge in her tone, "next time you be a delivery boy . . . you'll knock and I'll be sleeping. You'll call to me: 'Mrs. McGinnis, I've got something for you!' And then you'll open the door and . . ."

He listened to the first words, aroused by her warm breath in his ear, but as he tried to kiss her mouth, she turned her head away and continued speaking. He tuned out the words then and traced a slow, deliberate line down between her breasts, over her navel, to the perfect black triangle glistening with his own semen, and again he parted her thighs, exploring her with his fingers, and traced a moist line over her abdomen, her breasts, up to her chin. All the while he watched her face solemnly. Then he cupped her chin firmly in his hand. Her eyes widened slightly and he kissed her soft scarlet mouth insistently, and only when she finally gave him her tongue and moved longingly beneath him did he pinion her arms by the soft undersides above her head, watching as her eyes closed, and thrust inside her again, and again, and this time it was his match. He knew it as she arched her long neck back, her eyes closed very tightly, and as she thrashed under him, yielding herself to him completely. He knew as if a spectator to his own performance.

At the end she called his name, her voice sounding thin and lonely as a child's in the night.

She nestled near him subdued and soft. Her luminous eyes had lost their mocking glitter as she looked at him. He felt sorry for her and himself. They were complete strangers, passing an hour. He felt, along with the physical chill of separation, a familiar emptiness pervade his soul. "Hey—how about the swim?" he asked gently.

Out in the sunlight they dove like porpoises. She came up from the water close to him, wrapping her legs around his. Slick and wet, her hair streamed, glossy as licorice, behind her. "Wouldn't it be nice," she said softly, "if this were an island . . . why don't you make it your island? No one will bother us . . ."

He looked at her. "Your husband?"

"A piece of paper, years ago," she said quietly. There was no trace of bitterness in her voice.

"No one else?"

She looked playful again. "No one worth bothering with . . . oh occasionally I let someone in past Hansel and Gretel . . . in fact, I've tried most of the town."

He looked at her with a slight feeling of recoil and realized that it was in fact only a sport. She was completely amoral and scarcely seemed to realize the effect it had on him . . . or did she? Was she simply pushing him to accept her as she was? "Well . . ." he said, not knowing what to say, feeling her smooth skin against his as she dove nearby and came up next to him, her hands trailing behind, lingering for a moment over his thighs. She emerged with a mischievous smile.

"I did like that Italian man Paul sent on vacation . . ." she mused sweetly.

"Who was that?"

"Perrini, looked like an egg . . . the one with the albino wife . . ." She swam away. "He didn't look like much, but he was terrific!"

He tried to envision the pale middle-aged scientist in her dark arms. "Dr. Perrini? Paul *sent* him on vacation?"

"That's what he told me. In fact if Paul had known we

were making it, he probably would have sent *her* away by herself . . ." Greta got out of the pool with a shake of her head; glistening, she rolled on her back on the chaise and pulled on the bottom of her suit.

"Why do you wear it at all?" Daniel asked, sitting by her, touching the curve of her hip.

"I don't like overexposure . . ."

He smiled, then looked at her thoughtfully. "Is your husband really that powerful a guy, I mean that he can just send people away?"

Greta sat up on her elbows and looked at him incredulously. "You're putting me on?"

He shrugged.

"He owns everything. He owns everyone and everything . . ."

"Not me," Daniel Lieberman said dryly.

"You," she said lying back down. "He doesn't need you. You're nothing, except you have a nice prick. And it wouldn't interest him."

He looked at her. Her eyes were closed. "Thanks. You have a nice cunt," he said flatly. Then he was sorry, because he knew she was testing him, testing him . . . and she had won a round.

Volley, match, silence.

"Sorry. It was really good . . . I mean I enjoyed being with you," he said candidly.

"You're a kind man, Lieberman; don't ever get involved with him." She rolled over to get a cigarette, her voice breaking slightly.

*You're a kind man.* He recalled the old woman's face. The events of the day came careening back at him, crashing through the idyll. "I'm going to have to go," he said abruptly, reaching for his clothes.

"Go back to your friend at day camp, why don't you?"

He didn't like the tone in her voice. "Maybe I will," he said, standing. She had put on her mirrored glasses.

She lit another cigarette. "Isn't she frigid or dykey or something?"

He turned, baited. "I wouldn't know . . ."

"Well there's your answer. My God, the girl must be twenty-seven. I was married three times at her age!" Greta said in a casual voice.

"She's a nice person," he said defensively. "Don't you send your kid to camp?"

Angry silence. She exhaled smoke.

"Billy. Your son?" he goaded.

"Right," she said in a clipped voice, and rolled over with her back to him.

"Come to think of it, when he was sick someone brought him into my office, not you . . . the first time I saw you was at the Doughertys'. Don't you take care of him at all?"

"Go home to Laura, baby."

Suddenly his anger was spent. He was sorry that he had tried to hurt her. She didn't deserve it. "Look, I didn't mean . . . I'm sorry."

"We have a fräulein. Blonde, with pimples."

"That's who brought Billy . . ."

Greta sttod up impatiently. "How could you forget, yah? The face that blew up the Hindenburg."

Daniel looked at her silently. She seemed very agitated, covering her feelings with her half-mocking smile.

"She's in charge, you see. Paul thinks I'm inept and that I tend to say vulgar things, especially about him, and of course the motherfucker is right. Anyway, he would prefer his son to idolize him and to see me in public only. That's the deal. I get to play. He gets the kid. *Auf Wiedersehen, Herr Doktor!*"

On the other end of town, a half mile past Louie's Place, was a vacant lot; weeds high as fences shot up between litter and rocks. The lot was a constant annoyance to the few people who lived in a nearby cluster of houses just inside the border of Sheffield, in one of its least influential neighborhoods. The late afternoon sun glinted off the broken glass, and a thin curl of smoke rose where a few overturned cans of oily refuse had caught on fire. It was a very small fire at first, nearly hidden in the weeds. A sixteen-year-old boy named Gary West stood there in his nylon jogging shorts and his net racing shirt with the faded number. He watched the fire grow bigger, the flames licking at the brush around his feet. Gary was over six feet tall, good-looking and a good athlete. Just that week he had even managed to get Jill Horgan away from Chet; in fact she had promised on Friday night to date him pretty much steadily from then on. She was going to wear his ring. But then he hadn't seen her again after that. Not all weekend. Now he stood in the lot and gazed at the flames . . .

A shout. One of the neighbors. A bunch of shadows; a big crowd; they pulled at Gary and stamped the fire out near his feet. He didn't put up any resistance. What's the matter with you, they asked him. A normal healthy kid, a good athlete, not into any of the self-immolation protest crap, so what was the matter with him? Sleep it off, they said. When the police car came, they were angry. They insisted on seeing McLoughlin. When he arrived, they complained bitterly about the way the town kept the lot and refuse. Garbage and fires and kids could get hurt! Did the Town Council think they were animals? Why didn't they clean up this mess? They'd nearly lost a kid in the fire. "What was the kid's name?" the young officer asked with a glance at the chief.

Gary. Gary West, they answered. A nice, quiet boy.

# Tuesday, August seventh,

Wendy threw herself in jerking motions back and forth, trying to loosen her body from the strong grip of two attendants. "No no no nooo!" Wendy screamed. "No!" Her face was flushed and beads of sweat ran down her forehead, matting her hair, her eyes wide with fear. She kicked out hard at a tangle of bedclothes, then at one of the men. The telephone, glasses, and night table were overturned. The intravenous stand had smashed against a wall lamp that now swung back and forth on a thin cord. Shattered glass covered the floor. Daniel Lieberman stood with Hodson at the door and watched Wendy lunge and duck in the arms of the attendants. She threw herself forward, escaped the grip of one attendant, and held the bedrail, moaning. It was a replay of Saturday night.

Daniel shook his head, disbelieving. It was as if the clock had never gone forward, as if she had not been treated.

"When did you take her off medication?" Hodson asked.

"I began lowering the dosage yesterday, but I'll have to bring it up immediately."

Daniel wrote the orders on the chart.

He injected the struggling girl with IM Valium as she stood, holding fast, her knuckles white from her grasp, looking from face to face in horror. She arched her head back and began to moan that deep animal sound that he recalled from Saturday night. Her eyes rolled back. Then she vomited.

It took some time before Wendy was calm enough to be put back in bed; meanwhile, an orderly came in to mop the room, and Hodson and Lieberman stepped outside to the quiet corridor.

"I've seen recurrent attacks with drugs," Hosdon said, pacing slowly, "but not like this. Is that the way she was at the party?"

"Exactly," Daniel said. "We've been deluding ourselves. The tranquilizer was masking the symptoms. From a clinical point of view, she's worse."

"The nystagmus wasn't there before; neither was the tachycardia. It gives every indication of an acute toxic delirium," Hodson said. "I suppose we better get a CAT scan, although I doubt that it will tell us anything that we don't already know."

Daniel stared out into space, listening distractedly. Then, abruptly, he swung around to meet Hodson's gaze. "Look, Graham, can you stay here awhile? I just can't go into it now, but this is not the only case . . ."

"What!"

"I'd appreciate it if you'd stick around. I'll explain later," Daniel replied simply.

Hodson met his eyes silently for a second. "I'd be glad to," he said. Puzzled, he stood looking at Daniel Lieberman jog down the corridor.

"Bill? Listen, it's me. You have anything for me?"

"I was going to call you later . . ." Bill said, catching the edge in Daniel's voice. "I was waiting, because we keep coming up with negative results. We checked for the stuff that's being dealt . . . we got negative results on PCP. We did *Cannabis* derivatives, cocaine, LSD, the usual stimulants, and a few way-out specials. How far do you want us to take it?"

"Just keep going," Daniel said. "Bill, the kid is worse than she was on Saturday night, there's a damn fine neurologist here and he's baffled too. And besides . . ." He hesitated and looked up at the ceiling of the phone booth.

"Besides?"

"Bill? I know it's going to sound crazy, but after this kid got sick, well, there have been other cases of behavioral disorders. I don't mean they're all the same. In fact they're dissimilar. But in a broad category the symptoms are behavioral and all bizarre . . ."

"Tell me about the other cases . . ."

Daniel spoke quickly and described what he'd witnessed and heard, careful to qualify his statement by including possible explanations of each case—Miss Hill's reaction to bad news, Louise's history of instability . . .

"Hey," Bill interrupted. "You're giving me a lot of that 'on the one hand, but then on the other.' What's with you?"

"I don't know. I just don't know what I'm talking about, Bill! I know something is happening, but I don't know what it is. Maybe it's all coincidence, but I have a hunch it isn't."

"Listen to me," Bill insisted. "When there are several cases of a rare illness . . . or when a set of bizarre symptoms appears more than once, what do we assume first?"

Daniel looked up again at the embossed-metal ceiling and then out through the glass door, as if to make sure no one could overhear him. "Ordinarily, a contagious process or an unusual environmental influence," he replied.

"You have it."

"But nothing fits!"

Bill's voice warmed with concern. "Go with your hunch, Daniel. I can't imagine what it is either, but I'll help you find out."

Paul McGinnis stood near the outdoor pay phone at an Exxon station off the highway near Sheffield. He looked around him slowly. The place was nearly empty. There was only an old car with its hood up at the edge of the lot; near it, a puddle of brownish water trickled slowly into the weeds. Heat waves rose from the softening asphalt, and a fat attendant in a blue uniform stood about ten yards away from the telephone, near the gas pumps, drinking a diet cola. A shiny white Peugeot pulled up for gas and pulled out quickly again. When the car left, he turned to dial.

"NPI."

"Chameleon."

A buzz, then a click.

"It's definite now that there was contact," McGinnis said.

A silence followed.

". . . I still have no hard information on the primary contacts, but several people may have been exposed to a treated animal last Thursday. Wendy Dougherty's pretty definite. I couldn't confirm until my secretary became sick . . ."

"Louise Garner?"

It was an unfamiliar voice. A worried expression crossed McGinnis's face. "Yes."

But our records show that she was hospitalized a few years ago for acute anxiety."

"That was different. Besides, I treated her with the antidote and she's recovering."

"McGinnis, couldn't the teen-ager be on drugs?"

McGinnis looked out the glass of the booth, squinting

slightly. The voice was decidedly different. He stood for a moment, looking like a player who finds himself in a strange game, wondering what the rules are and what his position is to be . . .

"McGinnis?"

"Yes."

"You and Louise Garner are on intimate terms, aren't you?"

'. . . You're aware of the precautions I took."

"But it *is* possible that you were the carrier and that Garner is the only case."

"I don't understand what you're driving at."

"If Garner was an isolated case and the Dougherty girl's problems have nothing to do with us . . ."

"Even if Louise were the only case, the material was still out for a time. One way or another, we've breached containment."

There was a silence.

"Louise hasn't been in isolation, you know. There's no way of estimating the extent of . . ."

"McGinnis, listen. Compared to the importance of this project and its function in our organization, one case is nothing. You understand? If you have any confirmation of spread, you'll notify us and we'll take care of it."

"It's already too late for that," McGinnis said with an edge to his voice. "And by the way, there's a new pediatrician in town and the Dougherty girl is his patient. I'm under the impression that he's begun his own investigation."

"Lieberman?"

McGinnis closed his eyes for a split second. "Yes."

"203 Bridge Road, divorced, daughter Maia, age ten. You see, McGinnis, we're on top of the situation. We're arranging for a courier to pick up the product tomorrow . . . we'll continue attenuation in another lab for the time being. Obviously, you'll be involved. Meanwhile, your instructions are to rid the P3 of anything related to Chameleon; animals, notes, equipment. We want it totally cleaned out by tonight."

"But what will you do if this thing moves into the log phase of epidemic spread? Do you have a plan?"

There was silence.

"Do you have a plan?" McGinnis repeated.

"You have your instructions."

There was a click on the line.

McGinnis stood alone for moment, leaning on the door-frame of the telephone booth. Then he walked near the edge of the four-lane highway, looking out at the panorama, the cars hurtling by, streaks of metal, so fast that the drivers' faces melted into anonymity. Like the face of the man with the small hands. Like that new voice . . . and he, Paul McGinnis, was just one person in the enormous impersonal landscape.

Walter Hayes's office was carpeted with a huge pale Moroccan rug. Quiet ochers and muted terra cotta designs played on wall graphics that looked like ancient frescoes. The walls were a soft beige color, washed with indirect lighting. A sound-insulated ceiling lent quiet. The décor was at once modest and luxurious, professional and sympathetic, solid and neutral—Hayes's image.

"Come on in, Dr. Lieberman," Hayes said, smiling a cordial welcome. "Good to see you!"

Walter Hayes, a craggy-faced, handsome man of fifty-seven, sat smiling expectantly with a hopeful look in his eyes, as if wishing impossibly for good news or, at the most, a small, soluble problem with the air conditioning. He had been the administrator at the General for fifteen years, running fund-raising, public relations, daily operations, and the staff. He rose from his seat behind his desk, walking toward Daniel. "Dr. Lieberman, I believe you know Miss Pendleton, director of nursing?"

"Sure. 'Morning, Miss Pendleton," Daniel said, smiling.

Everyone called Miss Pendleton "J. Edgar" behind her back. She was a heavyset, middle-aged woman with a humorless, bulldog look. She acknowledged his smile with a twitch of her lips but her eyes said, "This had better be good." Daniel felt uneasy as he looked at the two faces. "I'm sorry to bother you on such short notice, Mr. Hayes," he began. "But I'm afraid we may have a serious problem here."

He noted that neither face reflected change, so alien was any real sense of crisis.

"Is this about a case of yours?"

"In part, yes, but it's not just a simple medical problem." Daniel picked up his notes and Wendy's chart and pushed his wire-framed glasses back on the bridge of his nose.

Hayes looked up as Graham Hodson knocked and abruptly entered. "Hiya, Graham," he said enthusiastically. "Glad you could stay for this; we were just getting started. By the way, I'm counting on you in the foursome next Sunday. We'll be teeing off at ten."

Daniel waited to reveal his notes till Hodson sat. "Dr. Hodson is neurological consultant on the Wendy Dougherty case. I'd like to fill you in on this one first. The patient, fourteen-and-a-half years old, was admitted Saturday evening at about ten, with the provisional diagnosis of seizure of unknown etiology." He went on describing the case in detail. Hayes listened patiently.

"So that bring us to this morning," Daniel concluded, "when she had another seizure. This one was considerably worse than the episode Saturday night."

Walter Hayes shifted his glance from Daniel's notes to Hodson. "What's your diagnosis, Graham?"

"We can't reach any conclusions yet. Damnedest thing I ever saw. Closest we can come is drugs, but that isn't satisfactory for a number of reasons."

Hayes looked back at Daniel. "Why exactly did you want to see me about this particular case, Dr. Lieberman?"

"I have a hunch that there may be more than one case like Wendy's in Sheffield."

Hayes's mouth tightened slightly as his social smile faded. "Here at the General?"

"Yes. And other places in town."

"Excuse me just a moment," said Hayes, dialing his intercom. "I'd like to get Dr. Nelson in on this. Miss Pendleton, perhaps you . . ."

"I'd like Miss Pendleton to stay," Daniel said. "I think she might have useful information for us. I believe there are at least two other cases related to Wendy's . . . one was Miss Hill, the librarian. I brought her some bad news on Sunday, and later, my daughter found her in the middle of some sort of seizure. Dr. Singh, the family-practice resident, was here in the afternoon when they brought her to Emergency."

Daniel was in the middle of describing his visit to Miss Hill's house when Dr. Nelson entered without knocking. An amiable, quiet man, level-headed and leaning to the conservative side of center, he'd served as Director of Medicine for four years and would probably continue for a long time to come. He had no enemies. He listened now, looking very solemn, as Daniel filled him in and then continued with his description of Miss Hill.

". . . at the time I didn't make a connection. Wendy seemed much better yesterday, and obviously I'm not treating Miss Hill . . ."

"She's Dr. Stockton's patient, I believe," Nelson said.

"Yes. It was a purely personal visit. As I mentioned earlier, my daughter was the person who had found Miss Hill sick in the library and I, well, I felt kind of responsible because of the dog."

"Dog?" Nelson asked.

"We had found her dog dead on Sunday and unfortunately were the ones to bring her the bad news. Shortly after that, she took ill and was brought here."

Nelson rubbed his right hand over the lower half of his face. "You mentioned another case?"

"Louise Garner."

Miss Pendleton broke in sharply. "I don't believe we have a patient here by that name."

"You don't." Daniel said, noting with admiration her fabled efficiency at work. The nurses said she kept files in her chins. "Mrs. Garner is at home, being treated by her own doctor. At least that's what Paul McGinnis told me yesterday."

Hayes's relaxed body straightened to attention at the sound of McGinnis's name. He swiveled abruptly to face Daniel. "Now, what exactly is this all about? You're losing me, Dr. Lieberman."

"I heard from a reliable witness yesterday that Louise Garner collapsed at her home and appeared to be hallucinating," Daniel explained. "Dr. McGinnis himself confirmed that she was sick. He referred to it as a 'breakdown,' to quote him. He told me she was being treated at home."

Hayes relaxed back into his casual-seeming posture and regarded Daniel for a long moment, then glanced around the room. "It goes without saying that our discussion here is confidential. Some of you may remember that Mrs. Garner was at one time hospitalized here at the General for a nervous disorder . . ."

"Excuse me, Mr. Hayes, wasn't that a few years ago?" Daniel asked.

"But the fact is that this woman has been mentally ill before . . ." Hayes said clearly.

"What exactly is your point about Hill and Garner?" Nelson asked Daniel. "What's the connection between their behavior and Wendy's?"

"Only that all three cases are behavioral, with similar elements; disorientation, hallucination, terror . . . All occurred within a few days of each other, all had a sudden onset . . . and frankly, I can't account for any of them with a satisfactory clinical explanation," he said rapidly. "I find it disturbing, to say the very least. If there are links between these cases, other people are in serious danger."

Daniel's last words were interrupted by a loud knock on the door and the simultaneous entrance of a heavyset man in a police uniform, the open jacket exposing a wrinkled cotten shirt stretched tight across his paunch; his holster in plain view.

" 'Morning, Ned," Hayes said, standing.

With a fast nod to Hayes and the others, Ned McLoughlin found Daniel Lieberman. "Dr. Lieberman? They told me you were here. I've been trying to catch up with you the last couple of days—now it's urgent. Excuse me, gentlemen, Miss Pendleton . . . I didn't mean to interrupt a conference, but I have some news for Dr. Lieberman and I'm afraid I only have a few minutes . . ."

"Anything new on the homicide, Ned?" asked Hayes.

"Yes," McLoughlin said. "Yes, in fact, I wanted to talk to Dr. Lieberman about a new development. We found our homicide suspect this morning; a Sheffield boy named Chet Gabrini. He's eighteen, so I can mention his name. His prints match those in the car—that's definite. He's had a couple of brushes with us before, nothing serious. I haven't seen the boy yet myself; they've got him hospitalized under guard up in Bridgeport." He turned toward Daniel. "Well the thing is Doctor Lieberman, from what they tell me, he's behaving very much like I hear Wendy Dougherty was . . . if it's all right with you, I'd like a more detailed rundown on Miss Dougherty's present condition before I proceed."

There was dead silence.

"Chief McLoughlin," Daniel said, "we were just talking about the possibility that there were other cases like Wendy's in town. I was explaining that Miss Hill seems to have been suffering from a behavioral disorder since Sunday and Mrs. Garner . . ."

"Just a minute, Lieberman!" Hayes interrupted.

"Let him finish!" Hodson snapped.

"Mrs. Garner collapsed yesterday with a similar nervous disorder."

"We sent a patrol car over to the Garner house," McLoughlin said, turning as he spoke to watch Walter Hayes's face. "McGinnis told the patrolman the Mrs. Garner had collapsed on the tennis court fron heat prostration. But our original telephone message states Mrs. Garner was out on the court in her nightclothes."

"That's right. That's right, she was," Daniel said. "Laura Benedict was there . . ."

"Just a minute! Hayes interrupted. "Now just *one* minute please. Let's not drag in every name in town. As we discussed earlier, nothing is to go beyond this office. Let's keep skeletons in their respective closets and consider first the good reputation of this hospital!"

Daniel stood. "Before, I was speaking of the possibility of exploring a link between three cases. Now we have news of a potential fourth!"

Nelson spoke up firmly, looking at the group somberly. "I must say, with all due respect, Dr. Lieberman, that what we have here is nothing that new. If the behavior of Wendy Dougherty and this teen-age boy is similar, chances are that drugs are involved. The same drugs. I must conclude, Chief McLoughlin, that you have a police matter on your hands, and possibly we have a routine medical problem."

"Certainly not one that involves the General," Hayes added.

Daniel looked from one to the other. "Dr. Nelson, I did consider that possibility on Saturday night and sent Wendy's blood samples into New York for a toxic screen. I've just heard that so far the results are negative for all drugs the kids are currently using." He glanced quickly at Hodson, knowing the information was new to him. "The preliminary reports were mailed out to us this morning."

"And then, of course, there's the persistence of rather violent symptoms in Wendy's case that makes it extraordinary," Hodson added in his clipped no-nonsense voice. "I don't know about these other cases, but the one at the General right now is damned peculiar!"

"You could get this sort of persistence with LSD, for example, couldn't you, Graham?" asked Nelson.

"It's possible, but I haven't seen it. The intensity of the recurrence here is what's so damned odd!"

"But you said you *could* get similar symptoms . . ." persisted Nelson.

"I said it was damned odd!" Hodson replied, clamping his mouth shut firmly under his small mustache, as if holding in something larger than irritation. "And I've seen plenty of teen-age drug abuse, you know."

Daniel looked around again at the orderly opulence of Hayes's office. They were not going to take it well, not going to deal with it . . . "There was no LSD in Wendy's blood," he added quietly.

"What exactly are you suggesting then, Dr. Lieberman?" Nelson asked in his measured careful voice.

Daniel shrugged slightly. "I don't know, I wish I did."

McLoughlin was looking at him keenly. "We sure have had a few unusual events here the last couple of days, folks."

"It seems to me, as it stands now, that there's a perfectly routine explanation for each of these events," said Hayes. "Certainly the coincidence of two adults in this community becoming ill the same weekend for obviously different and accountable reasons has *nothing* to do with this homicide suspect; and in turn, he may have nothing at all to do with Wendy Dougherty. She is our only concern. I can't stress that enough. Legally, we want to watch our step, don't we? Graham, we want to be very sure that the parents of this minor don't accuse us of sensationalism; or of linking their daughter to drugs and a homicide suspect just because her doctors haven't come up with a diagnosis yet."

"What kind of sensationalism are you talking about?" Hodson replied. "There are sound medical reasons to look into this problem. We aren't suggesting a press conference, damn it!"

"Sensationalism is starting the rumor that strange things are happening in Sheffield. We have one hysterical, previously hospitalized woman and one elderly citizen reacting to shocking news . . . a homicide suspect in some other county whom we have no reason to believe even *knows* our patient. Sensationalism is connecting these independent cases; making assumptions about totally unrelated events! That's what I mean by sensationalism," Hayes said in a rising voice. He sat straight-backed, and overtly angry.

Nelson shifted uncomfortably in his chair. "Excuse me, Graham. I feel that we probably do have an incident of drug abuse here; some new thing that perhaps the lab in New York hasn't hit yet, Dr. Lieberman . . . After all, we haven't seen everything yet, have we?"

"I'm sorry to disagree, Dr. Nelson, but it's odd for such a cluster of bizarre incidents to occur within a three-day period. And Miss Hill and Mrs. Garner are not teen-age junkies. It's also hard to believe that we have drugs here that a New York City lab hasn't dealt with," Daniel said.

McLoughlin nodded vigorously. "It's a cluster, folks. Face it. And we're all going to have to look at it that way. Now it *is* possible that one of these kids was playing a practical joke with an unusual and potent drug . . . I mean by that, maybe somehow it was passed to each of these people without their knowledge, by someone who may still be at large, in fact." He paced thoughtfully, holding everyone's attention. "Or perhaps these people were all in the same place at different times . . . a soda fountain. Or they used the same water cooler. There are a number of ways that a practical joke could be played with a toxic substance. By the way, I do have one more police matter that might be tied in here somehow. There's a seventeen-year-old girl—about the age of the homicide suspect, a little older than Wendy. She's been reported missing from her home." In the silence, he reached into his breast pocket and put a wallet-sized photograph on Walter Hayes's desk. "Her name's Jill Horgan. I thought I'd drop this off in case she shows up to visit Wendy, or if she turns up as a patient."

Miss Pendleton had become increasingly agitated during McLoughlin's pacing. Daniel thought at first that she was just turning and watching him, but then he saw that she kept referring back to her notes. She sighed. " I wouldn't have said anything at this time," she burst in, "but what with all you've been saying about these other cases and now . . . with Wendy involved. Well, I am having difficulty locating a nurse named Miss Rivera . . ."

Daniel felt the impact of the name like a bullet.

Pendleton continued, "Miss Rivera was on the Dougherty case Saturday evening. She was due in again Monday evening, but she didn't show up. I can't reach her by telephone. Nobody answers."

Chief McLoughlin tilted his head, catching Lieberman's eye, but addressed Miss Pendleton. "This Miss Rivera . . . she called in?"

"No. She had even said she might be back late Sunday evening. That was up to her. But it was definitely her responsibility either to turn up or call last night."

"Has she done this sort of thing before?" asked McLoughlin.

"No. In fact that's just it," said Miss Pendleton. "She's always been very reliable. An excellent nurse."

"I'd like her address and phone number," McLoughlin began, but Miss Pendleton already had the papers ready and handed them to him silently.

Hayes watched unhappily as the papers were transferred. "Let's not stampede into anything here,"he said. "Now, we certainly don't want any adverse publicity, Ned. Things are pretty difficult as it is . . . as an administrator, I can tell you good help is hard to come by. I'm afraid some of our people take occasional unannounced vacations."

"I asked Miss Rivera to deliver samples for me in New York, and she did. She was in New York on Sunday. And she didn't seem the type for unannounced vacations," Daniel said in a flat, stubborn voice. His mind had begun to race. "I believe we must consider the possibility that some kind of toxic substance may have been released to the environment—either by plan or accident. But now we must also consider an infectious process—although I've never heard of anything remotely like this, with a complete absence of the usual diagnostic indications of acute infection. The main point is, whatever it is, we'd better act quickly."

He felt the intense, frozen silence that followed; it was almost as if a partition had slid silently down, cutting him off from Hayes and Nelson. He turned toward McLoughlin, who nodded sympathetically as if to say he understood the feeling.

"I'll check out the information we have so far, and I'll look into possible practical jokers. It's open season now. I'll get back to you, Lieberman," the police chief said as he closed the office door behind him abruptly.

"Well, I hope we've been of some help, Dr. Lieberman. I'm afraid my schedule calls." Hayes's voice was polite, under tight control, his smile once again fixed in place. "I'll alert certain key members of our staff . . . off the record . . . to be on the lookout for any behavioral illness, and to have them notify Dr. Nelson if any shows up. Miss Pendleton will keep her eyes open, too. But *carefully*. This is as far as we can go at this time. Of course, we have to remember we all have a hospital to keep running."

This was how they were going to deal with the entire matter, Daniel thought, and with him. They had slid down the partition, and now they'd pretend they hadn't heard.

It was quiet up in the ICU on the floor above Hayes's office while the group below talked heatedly. At the start of a coffee break, a middle-aged nurse named Miss Manderson sat down at the station near the monitor, while the two regulars picked up their shoulder bags from a nook under the desk and went to wait for the elevator to the cafeteria. Miss Manderson was a timid woman—so unassuming that she'd been nicknamed "The Mouse."

The Mouse was always willing to help take on extra tasks; sitting in for other nurses who wanted to get some coffee or go to the lounge. She had volunteered to help move Wendy on the stretcher Sunday morning to the OR. No one had asked her; she just happened to be passing by and had helped with the IV stand. A sympathetic person, she had smoothed the young girl's matted hair and had talked to her quietly while they waited for the elevator.

Miss Manderson's quiet attentiveness made her perfect for the ICU, and she was often on duty there. Now she sat with a book open on her lap, temporarily alone in the unit. She looked out into space, her head tilted thoughtfully to one side.

Suddenly a buzzer began to sound. The monitor flashed the number of bed four. In it was a twenty-two-year-old woman who had undergone open heart surgery the day before. Next to the patient's bed an oscilloscope screen registered an erratic green line with sharp pulses of irregular activity. The buzzer sounded monotonously; a thin, dangerous sound that normally signaled an immediate set of precise responses from the nurses at the station. But Miss Manderson remained motionless. The buzzer continued like the drone of a huge mosquito, drilling through the silence of the unit. Seven minutes passed. The green line on the oscilloscope smoothed out and became flat; the buzzer continued. But Miss Manderson sat still, her head tilted, the book on her knees held open by the palm of her limp hand, a strange, distant expression in her quiet eyes.

*"NPI."*

*"Chameleon control."*

*A buzz, then a click. "Any problems?"*

*"All set. His receptionist let us in for repairs, but I doubt that she'll remember to tell him. There was an office full of kids."*

*"Have you finished monitoring the residence?"*

*"You want that completed today?"*

*"This morning. While the house is empty."*

*"All right."*

Ned McLoughlin's office was a spare, colorless room, devoid of any decoration other than a large American flag in one corner and one framed photograph of the nine-man force standing on the front steps of the clapboard police station. There was a window high on one wall, and a green metal desk cluttered with papers and books. The walls were lined with bulletin boards covered with town maps and notes.

"Dr. Lieberman, what can I do for you?"

Daniel spoke quietly. "I think it is likely that there are other cases . . ."

McLoughlin nodded, walked over and closed his door. "How will we identify them . . . these cases?"

"Maybe I could get a better idea from the police blotter . . .there may have been unusual occurrences."

McLoughlin unlocked the middle drawer of his desk and withdrew a rectangular pad. "Blotter only records arrests, charges, and so on. You want the daily log, complaints, nature of complaint, date, time, place, procedure . . . sit down. How far back do we go?"

"Last week."

McLoughlin flipped pages. "After Wendy Dougherty got sick . . . let's see. Well, there was a small fire, suspicious, but no property damage, no charges. A sixteen-year-old kid named Gary West was involved. Fact is, at the time it looked like the boy himself set the fire and stayed around to watch. But we can't be sure. There was a big crowd by the time I got there, and they were pretty riled up . . . oh, and Scott Andrews. But you must've heard about that on the news."

Daniel shook his head.

"Well, a kid about fifteen, on a motorcycle, went into a tree . . . he was killed. Weirdest accident I've seen to date." Ned McLoughlin closed the book, leaned back in his chair, and described what the police had found.

Daniel jotted notes. "So far it's all teen-agers, the missing girl, too," he said. "What's her name again?"

"Horgan, Jill Horgan . . . yeah, it struck me too, that there were kids involved in a number of incidents. I went over to Louie's to check it out, but I didn't get far."

"What's Louie's?"

"Louie's Place. That's where Jill Horgan and this boy Chet Gabrini used to hang out. Scott was there too, sometimes . . ."

"Wendy Dougherty too?" Daniel asked.

McLoughlin shrugged. "I doubt it. Place has sandwiches, a jukebox . . . and uppers, downers, whatever. You name it. Jack Dougherty'd never let his kid near there."

Daniel stood and began to pace. "I don't know. It's not just kids. It's possible Louise Garner, Miss Hill, and the nurse, Miss Rivera."

"You know," McLoughlin said with a grin, leaning forward, his arms on his desk, "I knew you'd show up here before the day was out, Lieberman. I knew it in Hayes's office. By the way, I have a couple of leads on Miss Rivera. Not much yet. This is a pretty small force, and I'm going to have to follow the trail to New York. That's where she was last seen, right?"

Daniel snapped his fingers. "Could I use your telephone? I'd like to try to get hold of the last person I know who saw her . . . maybe he can be of some use."

"Help yourself," McLoughlin said. He passed the small file he'd begun across his wide desk to Daniel Lieberman and then turned back to the ledger, riffling through the carbon copies of reports.

Daniel checked through the Rivera file while he dialed and waited for a response.

"Dr. Edwards, please."

"Daniel?"

"Bill, listen. I'm down at the police station checking out some information. You remember Miss Rivera, who delivered the samples . . ."

"Very foxy lady," Bill said.

"She seems to be missing. At least she hasn't called in and hasn't shown up around here . . ."

"Come on, Daniel, you think I'm hiding her?"

"All I've got on her is some information that she has an apartment in Connecticut, but it's unoccupied right now. Her parents are somewhere in Manhattan, and she was headed there on Sunday. Father's name is Juan."

"It had to be Juan, somewhere in Manhattan, right?"

". . . it's a pretty small department here in Sheffield. Bill, I have to know about Rivera soon."

"Gotcha. Juan Rivera, Manhattan, that's it?"

"Afraid so . . ."

"It'll take awhile. I'll keep you posted. Nothing positive on the blood tests, by the way. We've done a couple more now. How was the General's staff, cooperative?"

"Anything but."

"Figured. Don't let it get to you."

Daniel hung up and turned back to McLoughlin. "He'll work on it. Can we go back a bit . . . Let's try before Wendy got sick. Back to the beginning of last week."

"I've been looking—last Monday was one marital fight.

Tuesday, a couple of traffic violations, and one drunk and disorderly tourist on the beach. Wednesday, nothing. Thursday . . . oh, right. That shows up Friday morning. Last Thursday night some vandalism on the premises of the McGinnis Laboratories. Reported Friday morning at seven-ten. But McGinnis didn't press charges, and there was no entry."

"Can I take a look at the complete report?" Daniel asked.

McLoughlin pressed his intercom and asked his secretary for the filed cross reference on Complaint Number 5463. "It was kids, that's for sure. They do a lot of this spray painting, petty vandalism stuff. The high school is always covered with graffiti."

The secretary brought in the file, and McLoughlin handed it to Daniel. Daniel read the report with increasing excitement. "Says here that Lieutenant Johnson didn't actually enter the building . . . it was the special lab, the P3. The rear door to the P3 had been forced with some object not found on the premises . . . and there was paint all over the outside of the unit and the main building as well . . ." He looked up finally. "All you have here is McGinnis's word that there was no entry."

McLoughlin made a sour face. "That, and a call from the First Selectman's office not to take it any further. No reason to spread it out big and glossy if McGinnis wanted it kept quiet. A lot of townspeople work there . . . bad publicity for Sheffield, they said. And not worth our time and the taxpayers' money if the guy wouldn't press charges!"

Daniel let his breath out slowly. "Does he have a night watchman? There's no record of it . . ."

"No? That's strange," McLoughlin said, looking at the report carefully. "I'm sure Jimmy Walters is there nights . . . it *does* say the alarm system was off. I'll check this out with Jimmy."

Daniel pushed his glasses up on the bridge of his nose. "Here's what I think. I think maybe the kids, whoever they are, took something out of that lab. Some kind of stuff for a souvenir: possibly a toxin with properties like LSD, only more potent, more long lasting, and chemically different enough not to show up in the tests at Bill's lab . . ."

"And now they're spreading it around Sheffield . . ." McLoughlin rubbed his eyes tiredly and took an Alka-Seltzer out of his top drawer. He dropped it into a glass of water from a Thermos on his desk. "Want some?" he asked Daniel.

"No, thanks. Are you going to question McGinnis?"

McLoughlin grimaced. "I'd like to. But we have rules to follow. I have to rely on information he volunteers, unless I book him. Are you suggesting I arrest and question the town's leading citizen?"

Daniel shook his head slowly. "Not at the moment . . . "

At the edge of the water, the children sat wrapped in towels, their hair still wet, dripping over their bare shoulders. Billy McGinnis, Maia, Janie Garner, the Santé twins, Amy and Allen Lawson, and Roy Dougherty. All sat in a semicircle, with paper cups in their hands, listening. Laura, in a racing suit cut low on her back, long legs drawn up under her chin, was talking softly to them while seagulls walked by in their tipsy way, nibbling on cracker crumbs the children had dropped on a nearby sandcastle.

Laura skittered a flat, small stone into the shallows. "See it? How many rings can one stone make?"

All the heads turned attentively toward the water. Rings widened from the skipping stone. "See how many? The rings go on out forever from that one stone. That's the way it is when you do just one thing, it goes on getting bigger and bigger. Like making someone feel good. Or bad. . . it all seems so tiny when you do it, but it gets sooo big!" she said, spreading her arms and reaching out to pat two little wet heads. She grinned at the upheld cups in Billy's and Amy's hands. "Right. I nearly forgot. We have to toast each other with orange juice for being terrific! Have we been terrific all day?"

"Yes!"

"To us!" they said with exuberance. "To us!" Their clear, thin voices rose up.

Laura frowned suddenly as she poured the juice, counting heads and cups unconsciously. "Where's Cindy?"

They all looked around and Laura stood up, anxiously scanning the beach. Down at the water's edge, at the curve of beach near the hotel cove, was a ledge of rock. Next to it was an odd, dark shape that she could not resolve, and standing not far from it was Cindy Vail.

Drawing closer to the hotel property, where the guests sat reading under beach umbrellas, Cindy Vail finally understood the shape she had noticed all afternoon near the big climbing rock. It was a pile of moving mud snails, wet and iridescent. Her pale eyes coolly explored the shallows where more mud snails were arriving in long lines, the antenna of each rhythmically moving from side to side, slowly piling over each other as they reached the darkening mass. Satisfied, she turned to go when she saw Laura and the others heading her way. Pretending not to notice them, she turned back to the mysterious mass. The surface of living mud snails glistened and writhed intriguingly, and she approached more closely. At the shoreward end of the mass, a whitish lump protruded, and she walked over to inspect it as the group caught up with her. As they moved closer, they could all see it clearly. The lump was a bloated and discolored human foot.

"Car two . . . Green, twenty-one. Headquarters. We have a thirty-five. Standing by."

The PA blasted, "Headquarters. You have a signal thirty-five at Green, twenty-one."

McLoughlin pushed the intercom and shouted, "Tell him I'm on my way. Get an ambulance. Get everyone down there."

The communications-desk patrolman spoke into the transmitter as McLoughlin sprinted out, Lieberman following him.

"Headquarters, to cars five and three. You have a signal thirty-five at twenty-one Green . . . proceed to Green twenty-one at once . . . all cars proceed to Green twenty-one . . ."

Lieberman slammed the police-car door, and McLoughlin spoke to him quickly as they took off. "Town's divided into eight color sectors. That code described the incident and exact location. This one's a drowning at the cove." He started the siren as he rounded the corner. "First drowning in seven years!"

They arrived at the hotel shortly after the two other patrol cars and just ahead of the ambulance. Daniel Lieberman jumped out and immediately saw Jean-Claude and Angelique Santé standing near the hotel with the twins. There was a large crowd of adults. Searching the beach anxiously for Laura and the children, he spotted them far off, under the large cedar. He ran toward them. McLoughlin headed down to the edge of the water to join the crowd accumulated there, angrily shrugging off a couple of reporters. The ambulance waited by the beach wall for the stretcher team. McLoughlin moved the onlookers away and began to rope off the area, shouting orders on the bullhorn.

Daniel looked over the group as he hurriedly approached, hearing the bullhorn in the background. All the kids were there. Maia rushed into his arms. Laura was holding Cindy Vail. Daniel knelt, shaken, beside Maia and tried to catch his breath, looking questioningly at Laura.

"It was an adult," Laura said. "Maybe a guest at the hotel . . . I don't know. Cindy found the body. I think I'd better get them all home now." She emptied sand from Cindy's sneaker while eyeing Daniel anxiously.

"Stay here a minute!" he panted. "Maia, why don't you fold up that stuff, and Janie'll give you a hand. I have to talk to you," he said to Laura.

Laura set Cindy down gently. "Go on, Daniel . . ."

Daniel spoke quietly and quickly, explaining the events of the day—Wendy's worsened condition, the toxic screen, the conference, the information he'd just received at the police station. "And then, while I was there," he concluded, "we got this call. It looks to me like possibly another related incident."

"And now you think the toxin's from the P3?" Laura whispered.

Daniel nodded. Distracted, he glanced briefly at her bathing suit, its dampness making her nipples tautly visible under the thin fabric.

"I don't know what McLoughlin plans to do about it, Laura, but I figure he can't do much. It's all conjecture. He can't interrogate McGinnis without some pretext . . . I can't get any answers from McGinnis myself. When I went back to Louise Garner's yesterday morning, he wasn't there. Or he was avoiding me."

Laura looked down at her bare feet. "I could talk to him at the lab. . . . It's not something I look forward to."

Daniel swallowed, gazing wistfully at her mouth. She had never seemed as lovely to him as at that moment; her entire being soft, feminine and yet totally independent. His breath caught suddenly as she looked back at him. "I don't want you to do anything that will hurt you," he murmured.

McLoughlin was striding over the beach toward them. Laura glanced at the children. "I wasn't thinking about myself," she said. "I just don't know how effective I'd be as Mata Hari, that's all."

"Excuse me," McLoughlin said. "Miss Benedict, Dr. Lieberman? Can I have a word with you?"

The children greeted McLoughlin loudly. He smilingly

returned the hellos and then said quite firmly, "Kids, you better get yourselves ready. We're all going to have to leave the beach . . ." He turned away, and as he stopped smiling, he suddenly looked tired, queasy, and grim. "Listen, that body's been in there awhile. I can't get any positive I.D., so I'm heading over with the medical examiner to check it out. I'd take bets that it's the missing girl . . . and if so, well, Dr. Lieberman, that makes a possible group of six teen-agers and—" Ned McLoughlin scratched his head, nudging the police cap slightly to one side—"I hate to ask you this, Miss Benedict, but we have an idea that there may be a chemical toxin . . ."

"I know. Daniel just told me," she interrupted.

"Well, as I recall, you did some investigating of that P3 lab and got some interviews with Dr. McGinnis in *The Sheffield News*. He might talk to you again. I see his son is in your group . . ."'

All right. I'll try," Laura said abruptly. "But I can't promise anything."

She walked away from the two men and pulled a cotton sundress over her head briskly, folded a towel, and scanned the area quickly for leftover sneakers and litter. "Hurry up, kids," she said. "I've got to get them home first," she said to McLoughlin. Then she pulled on her fedora and looked over at Daniel. "Wish me luck!"

"Hold on a second, Miss Benedict. Why don't you come with me? I want to discuss this P3 business with you. We'll leave the van for Dr. Lieberman. You can pick up his car at the station, and one of my men will drive the kids home."

They neared a police car. McLoughlin gave some rapid instructions to the officers and then turned back to Daniel and Laura. "I overheard some of the hotel guests say they're leaving Sheffield," he said. "The homicide, the missing girl, the press . . . *The Sheffield News* offices are a zoo with out-of-town reporters. They're all over Main Street asking questions. But I have an awful hunch we've just seen the tip of the iceberg."

At McLoughlin's car, as Laura handed her keys to Daniel, the police chief took off his cap and spoke thoughtfully. "You know, Lieberman, maybe you could check out Louie's Place. The kids won't talk to anyone with a badge. Maybe they'll talk to you, because you're Wendy's doctor."

"I'll give it a try," Daniel said. He looked over at Maia who waved from inside a patrol car. "I'll be home soon," he called to her. Then he looked at Laura. "Hey . . . good luck," he said.

As Daniel Lieberman neared Louie's Place he noticed a few small fruit stands by the road and an abandoned auto parts shop. He passed some vacant-looking houses with collapsing porches, and then a lot filled with charred garbage and blackened sumac. He wondered if that was the site of the recent fire.

On his right was Louie's Place. The building itself was covered with brown-stained shingles. The name was written in an arc of white on the large downstairs window over which hung a torn, colorless awning. Upstairs were some yellowing cream-colored nylon curtains. Louie probably lives there, he thought. He considered whether to bring in his black bag, knowing he'd be about as welcome in the juice bar as in Hayes's office. Bring the bag in, he decided, McLoughlin was right.

He pulled open the screen door. There was a silence as he stepped in. Give them time to look me over, Daniel thought as he walked past the booths, keeping his expression as neutral as possible. He was used to dealing with city kids. How different were these? He glanced around deliberately. Not one met his gaze. A girl rubbed her nose with the back of her hand. A boy combed his hair. One yawned and pulled a moccasin on a bare foot. Another chewed on the end of a soda straw while staring out the window in obviously feigned abstraction.

Louie looked like a giant infant. He weighed about three hundred pounds and wore a bland expression on his childlike face, his lips pursed in a soundless whistle as he wiped a glass very slowly with a towel. A girl got up, flipped her shiny brown hair back, and stuck a quarter in the jukebox. There was a click and suddenly the place was blasted with rock sounds.

Daniel winced slightly and sat at the counter near Louie, who looked at him as if he'd just arrived from another planet.

"I'm Wendy Dougherty's doctor. My name's Daniel Lieberman," he said to Louie, loud enough for nearby kids to hear.

"Oh yeah?"

A shrill giggle from behind him. He half swiveled on his stool in the direction of the booths.

"I'm very worried about Wendy," Daniel continued. "We don't know what's the matter with her."

Louie looked sad at that news. He had mournful eyes like a basset hound, with folds of fat over them. "What's it got to do with me?"

"Nothing—nothing you did or anything like that."

Louie sat the glass down. "One bad kid, I get a reputation. The police are all over me asking questions about Chet. I can't understand it."

Daniel nodded. He knew the kids were listening and could feel the vibes through his back. Not bad. They sensed he was not a threat, saw Louie talking, and had their eyes on the black bag on the counter.

"I'm not a cop," Daniel said in between records, so they all could hear. "I didn't think you'd mind helping me out. It may save Wendy's life . . ."

"Sure," Louie said, looking around the room as if for agreement.

Daniel swiveled around in the direction of the earlier giggle. "We're having problems figuring out what's making Wendy sick," he said, with a general look at his audience. They were all paying attention. "We've called in a neurologist, and we've done every test we can think of from an electroencephalogram to toxic screens. And we aren't any farther along. All we know is that both Chet and Wendy are very sick, and this was one place they hung out. That doesn't mean they got it here—just that maybe you can tell me something that could put us on the right track."

"Wendy never hung out here, Doctor," said a sullen voice. The speaker was sitting near the giggler. She was about sixteen, with dark, curly hair and a hostile expression in her brown eyes. At her reply, the giggler broke up again, but this time she clamped her hand over her mouth and shook with silent laughter. The giggler had a narrow, acned face and stringy hair.

"What's funny?" Daniel asked quietly.

She shrugged.

"How about Scott Andrews? He hung around here, didn't he?"

They all looked at the tabletops, motionless as stone.

"And Jill? And Gary West? I think it's pretty obvious that we have a problem, and that there may be a relationship between these incidents." The kids began to look at each other nervously as he spoke. "Unfortunately, neither Chet nor Wendy can tell us anything right now. They'll have to count on you. Now, I happened to be there when Wendy got sick. It was a very bad scene. That was Saturday night. Does anyone know if Chet and Wendy were together on Saturday night?"

The boy near the window spoke. "Chet was with . . . um . . . some of us on Saturday night, and Wendy was home on the Hill."

"And you're sure they didn't get together somehow?"

The boy nodded. "Chet wanted to see Wendy Saturday night, you know? He wanted her to come with us. But she told him she had to help her folks and she couldn't get out."

"Well, if they didn't get together on Saturday night, did they meet before? Were they here Saturday afternoon?"

"Too much!" said the giggler. "She wouldn't ever come here, not her."

All I'm trying to find out is when Chet and Wendy were last seen together. How about Friday?"

"What do we win for the right answer, Doc?" asked the dark-haired girl hostilely.

"Okay, cut the crap!" Louie shouted, his voice suddenly as huge as his frame. "Now, tell Dr. Lieberman what you know or get the hell out!"

The giggler spoke quickly, in a high, nervous voice. "They used to meet at lots of different places, like the theater parking lot . . . um . . . mostly they met at the library. I think they were there on Friday."

"On Friday?" Daniel asked. A chill was working itself down his back. "Does anybody know for sure?"

Across the room a long-haired boy spoke up. "It had to be Friday afternoon, because they had this big fight and Chet came back here really pissed off."

"For sure," the girl sitting next to him added. "He said Wendy was in big trouble with him 'cause she told her dad about Thursday . . ." she stopped and looked down.

There was an intense silence. Daniel stood up. "I know all about the lab break-in," he said calmly. "I have nothing to do with the lab or the police, my interest is only medical . . ."

He swept the lot of them with his eyes. They were sitting looking blank, a few looked puzzled. He waited, then spoke.

"Okay. Let's let it go for now. I have to know about Friday . . . Wendy and Chet got together at the library . . . ?"

"It was like a good place, you know. To meet," the dark-haired girl said. "Wendy'd say she had to return a book or something, and her mother would drop her off."

"And Miss Hill, that old librarian, she thought Chet was like into reading, you know? It was like a terrific setup," the giggler said.

"All the time he was just waiting to get into Wendy's pants," said another boy.

"Shut up, punk!" Louie bellowed, coming out from behind the counter.

"He was just telling it like it was," the giggler said defensively.

"Yeah!" The dark-haired girl tossed her head defiantly. "They'd make it in the stacks. That's where they were Friday afternoon. Balling. And the reason Chet got so pissed off was 'cause he thought Wendy had guts. 'Cause of Thursday night. I mean that was the test. And Jill Horgan passed and so did Scott. But Friday afternoon Wendy just flunked his test, you know? That's how he wound up with Ronnie Sawyer on Sunday night, anyway, when he freaked out." She crushed her cigarette out emphatically. There was a silence.

Daniel passed his hands over his eyes, thinking fast. The two teen-agers had in fact been in contact with Miss Hill on Friday afternoon. But Miss Hill hadn't become sick till Sunday. Neither had Chet. Then what did the contact mean? It clearly wasn't Saturday night that marked the beginning of these episodes. It was Thursday night at the lab. Scott . . . Jill. A sudden intense feeling of dread passed over him.

"You okay, Doctor?" Louie asked.

"No . . . no, not really." Daniel walked past the rapt faces to the screen door. He could hear his own footsteps. The record in the jukebox had come to an end. So had the conversation. There was a physical link to Miss Hill. That was established now. But why the delay in the onset of her symptoms? He leaned back against the doorframe.

"What do you think is the matter with them?" someone asked.

Other voices joined, questioning from the silence.

"What's it called?"

"Are they worse or what?"

"You think Scott had the same thing?"

"Is it curable?"

He only half heard the barrage of questions and finally shook his head. "I don't know what's the matter with them, and I don't have answers yet for any of your questions . . . was there anyone else at the lab?"

Louie shook his head. "They tell me no, Doctor."

Daniel looked at each of them. "If any of you has anything, like a bottle of pills or something, that Chet gave you, something from the lab, you just bring it to my office. No questions asked. It's no toy. You may save a friend's life, or your own."

The group regarded him with anxious, unguarded expressions—a bunch of scared children, he thought—and the strange thing is, they don't really seem to be hiding anything. He turned, puzzled, with that persistent feeling of dread, and went to the van.

As Laura entered the McGinnis Pharmaceutical Lab, the sun was glinting blood red off its mirror-glass front. She nodded casually to departing technicians as she walked into the reception area.

It was just as she remembered it. On a round glass coffee table one square crystal vase held three perfect August roses. Low-slung Le Corbusier chairs, symmetrically arranged, rested on a charcoal slate floor. The environment was stark, the air conditioning up a notch too far. Laura shivered slightly in her gauzy sundress, took a deep breath, and walked quickly to the slate-topped counter that during office hours housed a receptionist. She crossed behind it, sat in the receptionist's chair, and pressed the intercom.

"Paul?" she said to the instrument. "It's Laura. Are you in your office?"

There was a twenty second silence. "I was," said McGinnis, his lithe figure suddenly appearing in a doorway. "Laura. How unexpected. I was rather in the middle of some work . . . what brings you here?" He walked toward her with a disarming smile.

Laura would have forgiven him anything for that smile a year ago. Her heart lurched momentarily with the recollection, but as she watched him look around the empty reception area, calculating his moves with the smile still playing on his mouth, she felt a sudden wave of anger. Passing, it left her calm and resolved. "I didn't know if you'd be busy."

"I'm sure we're both very busy people, Laura," he said in an amused tone, his smile slightly mocking. "It must be very important."

He was very close to her now. She felt nothing. This realization freed her and buoyed her. She gazed at him directly. "I was wondering if the kids who broke into the P3 last week took anything out with them?"

McGinnis closed his eyes briefly, for only a split second. That was his only change of expresssion. She remembered it at once. "But they didn't get in, Laura. Who told you about it?"

"Chief McLoughlin," she said evenly.

"Ah . . . yes." He sat deliberately in a Le Corbusier chair—to gain time, she thought. "Well, they painted our gate for us and so forth," he said, looking slightly bored. "The usual pranks. But they didn't get beyond the back door."

"But they tried to get in the P3?"

"Of course. After all, it's an oddity and much publicized—you've helped that along, haven't you? Anyway, I reported the entire incident to the police."

"How can you be certain they didn't get in?" shechallenged.

McGinnis held her gaze a moment. "Is there something you haven't told me that makes this very important, because I really do have to get back to work . . ."

"Something was taken from here, Paul. Maybe you haven't noticed it; whatever is missing."

"Like what?" McGinnis's eyes were ice gray.

"You tell me. It's your lab."

McGinnis looked at her long and hard, brushing her body with his eyes deliberately. He rose with the grace of a sleek animal. She felt naked and embarrassed, and then, realizing his purpose, pulled herself together. "Well?" she said sharply.

"Oh Laura, Laura," he said softly, "what am I going to do with you? You're really crazy . . ."

"Like Louise?"

He stared at her. "On the subject of P3 labs: this one is not operative now and has not been for a long time."

"I want to see it." Her voice was flat and calm.

"The tour was finished last summer, baby."

"I want to see it," she repeated stubbornly, feeling a hot blush spread over her face up to the hairline.

He started walking back to the door. "Come back next year."

Laura reached for the telephone on the reception desk. "I'm calling Chief McLoughlin."

McGinnis turned around, unsmiling. "There's nothing to tell him."

"I'm telling him you tried to rape me."

"In my own lab? You've got to be joking."

"He'll be here immediately if I call him. You'll be headlines . . ."

"And you'll be a town joke."

"I don't care, and you know it."

McGinnis stepped toward her to take the telephone away, stopped, and looked at her contemptuously. "Everyone knows why you persist in this rampage against me."

She slapped his face.

"Let's go," he said. "Although I don't suppose even an empty lab will satisfy you . . ."

They walked in silence over the close-cropped, perfect grass, around a large willow, to the side of the building, and down a path to the rear of the P3. The metal door looked new. He opened it with elaborate courtesy.

She walked in ahead of him without speaking.

The intense quiet was the most notable thing about the lab. The air was somewhat stale, and no sign of use disturbed the polished chrome and stainless steel of the kitchen. In the animal rooms, empty cages lined the racks. Immaculate. Only now, in the large room, she heard the overhead hum of the filter system. The lab benches had a few pieces of inactive equipment here and there, under dust covers. The glove boxes were empty. There was no sign of recent life. She felt stupid, defeated.

"This lab complex is absolutely sealed and insular, even when it's not in use. NIH guidelines are adhered to strictly. The air is filtered. You could stand at the open back door and not be in contact with the interior air, because of the negative pressure and the double doors . . ." McGinnis switched a hood on. "Safety hoods, sterile precautions, filters, rigid procedures, inspections . . . Sheffield has never been endangered by this lab, your emotional diatribes to the contrary."

"And you're sure they didn't get in?"

He closed his eyes for a split second and then glanced around the spotless lab. "There was no sign of entry, Laura. We do have an alarm system. And anyway, as you plainly see, there's nothing here. If the P3 were active, you wouldn't even be allowed inside . . ."

They were walking back through the animal rooms now. As he spoke, she saw it. It was a three-by-five card taped unobtrusively to one side of the cage rack. McGinnis's shoulder grazed her as he passed, and she realized that his height, nearly a head taller, had made him miss seeing it. In the three seconds that she had to glance furtively at the card, she read the word "August," typed on top, and then, underneath, the numerals 1 to 31. Probably a cage-cleaning schedule. The first two dates had been crossed off by pencil marks: August first and second. Her thoughts streaked like lightning. Those pencil marks, she realized instantly, were her only proof of recent activity in the P3. She wanted to examine it more carefully, but didn't dare.

"Could any one of your staff have left a toxic substance near the entranceway? Something delivered here and not put away—left outside? Something that should have been locked up?" Laura asked, to cover her pause.

McGinnis turned back to her with a puzzled look. "A toxin on the doorstep? In a basket perhaps?"

She leaned against the animal cages and looked at him nonchalantly, her green eyes all innocence.

"Laura, for the hundredth time, this is not Fort Detrick. I wish you'd be reasonable. It's so difficult having an intelligent conversation with an ecology fanatic . . . We don't specialize in mysterious compounds out of science fiction . . . just ordinary pharmaceutical work. Syringes and needles are about all we'd have that would interest kids, and they're locked up. And my technicians, while not environmentalists, are not morons. They don't leave things around outside empty buildings. Ready?"

She had managed to remove one side of the card without making any noticeable movements. Now the other side. She turned her head a bit. "What sort of monkeys are you people using these days? Endangered species?"

Suddenly, his face relaxed into a grin as he walked to her. "Now I begin to understand what you want."

She remembered too late, flushing deeply, the subject of their first conversation. She had challenged him on the use of illegally acquired animals . . . he must be thinking she was inviting him to reopen the relationship. She had the card in her hand now, behind her back. His arms reached toward her.

"I never can tell with you . . ." he said, and pressed his lips on hers.

She stood quite still. The contact with Paul's cool, thin lips was slightly distasteful and elicited none of the old response. He pulled away finally, turning from her with an abrupt, angry gesture. As he turned, she placed the card in her hat. "Did you enjoy that?" she asked him quietly, hoping that she had kept the triumph she was feeling out of her voice.

"I'm not into necrophilia," he replied, striding out of the facility ahead of her. He locked the door behind them.

She breathed the fresh air with relief. "At least two of the vandals who were on your property last Thursday are very sick," she said, watching him closely. "Both with bizarre behavioral symptoms."

"Who?"

"Wendy Dougherty and Chet Gabrini," she answered, watching his eyes as she paired the names. "There may be others as well . . ."

His expression stayed neutral. "I see . . . but who knows where else they all were, Ms. Benedict. You people are so short-sighted, you can't see past your own rhetoric."

He loped across the lawn and was gone.

It was dark. Maia had already fallen asleep. Daniel sat restlessly at his makeshift desk, trying to make notes on recent events. He got up to wash the dishes and stir the remains of overcooked spaghetti. For the hundredth time he wondered where Laura was. Then there was a familiar squeal of brakes, a huffing noise like an old horse! His Volks. A knock. Daniel dropped the plate on the counter and ran to the front door.

Laura was radiant, looking triumphant and pleased with herself. She had showered off the sand and changed her clothes. She wore a lavender silk shirt and white cotton slacks. "I brought back your car," she said, handing him the keys. "It rides like a camel."

"Dinner's a little more than *al dente*, do you mind?"

"What I really want is a vodka and tonic!"

Daniel raised his eyebrows slightly. "Come on, at least have a carrot stick with it."

She followed him into the kitchen. "What would you say if I told you that McGinnis was a liar and that the P3 was operative when those kids broke in there last Thursday?"

"Hold on," Daniel said, upset. Something about the triumphant, angry tone of her voice reminded him of his ex-wife packing up. "I already got the picture. You hate the guy. Just tell me what you found out—let's keep the personalities out of it."

She flushed and looked at him curiously. "I'm telling you McGinnis is a liar and the P3 was operative. Lawson was just afraid to contradict him in company, or he's in on it too!"

"In on what? Slow down . . . don't get paranoid. I don't care about McGinnis. Can't you just forget about him? It's over."

Laura looked at him for a moment and then took the three-by-five file card out of her hat and slapped it on the table like an ace. "This was on the cage rack. He didn't see me take it. I just knew the bastard was lying!"

Daniel inspected it silently, pushing his glasses back. When he saw the dates, he understood. He looked up at her glowing face and felt the electricity of her concentrated energy, and all at once his excitement about the card was submerged in a sudden wave of jealousy. Again he thought of his ex-wife . . .

"I don't know what was going on in there, but they sure cleaned it up fast. You still think I'm being too emotional?" Laura said, folding her legs under her on the chair.

"What took you so long? How'd you convince McGinnis to let you in the P3?"

He regretted his words as he said them. She stood, looking at him with an unfathomable expression in her deep green eyes. She started to speak, and he braced himself for the rebuke.

"Hey, Daniel—it's me, Laura. I stopped by to tell McLoughlin and change my clothes . . . she hurt you terribly, didn't she?" she said gently, coming to him, running her fingers softly through his curly hair as he held her tightly to him, his arms wrapped around her slim waist. Finally he stood, staring at her long and lovingly as she touched his eyes and the corners of his mouth, ran her fingers back and forth over his lips. She seemed to melt against him as they kissed, merging together, no barriers and nothing held back. Even as they at last separated slightly, they stood thigh against thigh, unwilling to part further. As he pulled his T-shirt over his head, he could feel her warm breath as she moved her lips against his chest. Then, as he reached to undo the tiny buttons of her thin silk blouse, he could feel the soft nakedness just beneath rise against his impatient fingers. She helped with the buttons, and he lifted the tissue-weight fabric, letting the shirt slide off her shoulders and fall like a whisper to the floor. He stood for a moment, watching her tenderly, gazing at the loveliness of her bare breasts; then he molded his hands around them, moved his mouth urgently over her till she shuddered against him. Breathless and trembling, she took his hand and led him silently up the stairs. He felt totally possessed by her, his body suffused with yearning as he followed her long-legged stride. She turned once to glance back at him, her mouth slightly open, her full lips soft, face flushed with exhilaration, and he felt joy.

# Wednesday, August eighth,

Daniel squinted up at the shadow-slatted ceiling of his bedroom, getting his bearings, then automatically reached for the ringing telephone. A warm shoulder was in the way.

" 'Morning," Laura whispered.

Her smiling eyes that turned down slightly at the corners reflected the wonder he felt—the surging feeling that made his breath catch. He slowly drew a long strand of hair over one of her breasts, stoking it into place with the back of his hand.

The continued ringing jarred him sharply. The service wasn't picking up. Someone was ringing through, or the service itself alerting him; an emergency.

"Dr. Lieberman," he said grudgingly to the receiver, his concentration divided unevenly between the telephone and Laura's leg as she ran her slim foot up his ankle, her knee moving up his thigh . . .

"Dr. Lieberman, will you accept a collect call from Dr. Edwards?"

"Sure . . . Bill?" Memory of the previous days' events surged back, and he pulled Laura closer, in an unconsciously protective gesture. "What's up?"

"I found Miss Rivera."

Daniel's stomach contracted. "Where?"

Laura lay rigidly attentive, her head resting on his chest.

"I'm at her parents' apartment on Ninety-seventh, off Amsterdam. She's right here in the room with me."

Daniel breathed again. "She's all right, then?"

"No," Bill said, lowering his voice slightly, "not exactly. She's not the lady I met on Sunday, in fact she's not what you'd call employable. She's sitting here about ten feet away from me in the kitchen. If I wave my hand in front of her eyes, she doesn't react . . . she's sitting out here on a wooden chair, hugging her knees like a kid, pupils slightly dilated, respiration okay, pulse on the high side of normal. Are you there?"

Daniel sat straight up, scarcely aware that Laura had moved to the foot of the bed and was watching him solemnly. "How long has she been like that? Do you know?"

"The story I got is that Sunday she was absolutely fine. Her sister said that she just was too tired to drive back to Connecticut and decided to stay over. Monday morning she complained of a headache, and as the day went on, she became less and less communicative. By Monday evening she was like this."

"What's the family doing about it?"

"They're taking care of her like a baby. She doesn't voluntarily do anything, so they dress her, feed her. Her fourteen-year-old sister is in charge of taking her down the hall to the bathroom. The sister times it so the neighbors won't notice. Oh, and another thing. She isn't talking, but every once in a while she says a few words to herself. Very simple words, in Spanish. The family's from Ponce originally and came here when she was six years old . . . the father thinks she's acting like she's back there in time, like a four-year-old."

"And they haven't taken her to the clinic?"

"Not yet. They believe that whatever's wrong with her is involved with Sheffield and overwork, and that it will clear up if she stays home and rests. The father doesn't want her to lose her job. He tried calling the General, but because of his English, he was disconnected several times and gave up."

Daniel passed his hands over his eyes and reached for his glasses on the night table. "It's possible that with any progression she'll stop eating entirely and will have to be fed intravenously. You'd better get her to a hospital. Convince them that she's physically sick."

The alarm clock sounded. Laura turned it off and silently walked into the bathroom.

"Physically sick with what, Daniel? You're suggesting that someone slipped her this toxin when she was on duty Sunday morning?"

"No . . ." Daniel stared into space a moment.

"What's wrong? You there?"

Whatever's going on here, we're dealing with long time lapses between contact and onset . . . I just found out that Wendy was in contact with Miss Hill last Friday, but Hill didn't get sick till Sunday. Rivera was fine when she walked out of the General on Sunday . . . fine when she saw you."

Bill let his breath out slowly. "Your're saying that we may

have something other than a simple toxin. Something contagious—is that what you're telling me?"

"I have a strong hunch that's so, yeah. That's what the pattern's beginning to look like, even with limited information. There's a delayed onset of about thirty-two to forty-eight hours."

Bill spoke softly into the receiver. "What else do you know that's making you so nervous?"

"Okay. Are you sitting down?"

"Shoot."

"I found out that last Thursday night there was vandalism at the site of a P3 lab here is Sheffield and the entrance door to the P3 was broken. The owner denies any entry, but then he also said the P3 was inactive—and now it turns out a project may have been in progress there. The entire thing was covered up, the lab was cleaned up, and there is nothing left to go by. But listen, Bill, the vandals included some of the kids who are now sick."

"Daniel, I'm going to get Miss Rivera to a hospital, put her in isolation, and I'll start tests. Maybe we've been looking for the wrong kind of things."

Daniel paced, the long telephone cord dragging behind him. "Bill, if it turns out this is a contagious illness, then we could be seeing the start of an epidemic right now. And whatever it is, you and I have been exposed to it."

"That little fact hasn't escaped my attention . . . but you were in contact with this kid Wendy on Sunday."

"Friday," Daniel said. "And Laura was with her as early as Saturday."

"And neither of you is sick, right? So let's not panic just yet."

Daniel noticed Laura standing and watching him from the bathroom doorway. He felt a new panicky stirring in his gut. "Bill, do you think we should try to bring the public-health people in on this right now, even if it's conjecture . . ."

"We don't have anything tangible to tell them yet," Bill interrupted.

Daniel pushed his glasses back on the bridge of his nose, thinking. "Bill, you have any thoughts on what we could be dealing with? Some kind of CNS virus they were culturing in the P3?"

"I haven't the foggiest. I'll work on it. And, Daniel, just in case one of us does flip out a little more than usual, we'd better keep in frequent contact . . . oh, and love to this Laura of whom you speak with such a funny tone in your voice. Talk to you later."

Laura was getting into her white slacks, picking her watch off the night table as if she'd always slept there.

Daniel hung up and looked at her anxious face. "You know about as much as I do, so let's not talk now," he said, moving toward her.

"We have about one minute," Laura whispered. "Daniel? Whatever happens, I'm glad I stayed, I'm glad we had last night . . ."

She opened the door silently and tiptoed downstairs to the front hall. He followed. At the door, she turned to him. Silently, he placed his hands gently on her shoulders, holding her away for a last look.

"Is there anything I can do?" she asked.

He shook his head. "I need a lot more answers, fast. I'm going to go after them now."

"Are we exposed?"

"Whatever it is, yes. But here we are, still functioning. I don't have any idea what it is yet."

Laura nodded, her eyes gentle. "Take care, Daniel," she said, touching her index finger to his lips.

Suddenly she was gone. The silence in the vestibule was overwhelming. Daniel concentrated, collecting his thoughts. Laura had been in contact with both Wendy and Louise Garner . . . he had been in earlier contact with Wendy and, by his timetable, should have begun to feel sick days ago. He wondered whether he would know he was sick and maintain control or be suddenly overwhelmed by the illness. Miss Rivera had complained of a headache and fatigue prior to onset. But Miss Hill . . .

Sitting at his desk, he made some careful notes. The total symptomology so far: paranoia, apparently hallucinatory experiences, violent behavior, withdrawal . . . regression. Each case different. Questions to be answered . . . Afterward, he carefully put the notes in his drawer, half aware of wondering who would find them after he'd gotten sick himself. How long did he have to find the answers?

Daniel woke his daughter, showered, dressed, and called for messages as she got ready for camp. When he gave her breakfast, he noticed Maia watched him silently over her glasses, drinking her orange juice. She continued to stare at him as he sat opposite her trying to behave in a normal manner. What had she overheard? They'd been so careful . . .

"Daddy?" she said finally. "What's wrong?"

"Nothing, why?"

She looked down at her plate delicately. "You poured orange juice on your cereal . . ."

"Oh . . ." Daniel said, looking distractedly at his bowl. Maia thought this was an ordinary day. Whe shouldn't she? He wished it were. He considered the pros and cons of getting her out of Sheffield immediately. "I have a lot on my mind today, honey. Anyway, it doesn't taste too bad, you should try it."

"Yuck," Maia said decisively.

*"Natural Products International."*

*"NPI. Chameleon control . . ."*

*There was a buzz, a click, then, "Yes?"*

*"Lieberman was talking to a Dr. Bill Edwards in Manhattan. He's spotted the connection."*

*"Right. You have anything more on Edwards?"*

*"Not yet."*

Daniel Lieberman stood at the receptionist's desk in the lab entrance hall, looking unhappy. "What time do you expect him?" he asked the young woman sitting there.

"He didn't say . . . he often plays a little tennis in the morning if nothing much is going on." She smiled, showing her perfect white teeth.

"All right. When he comes in, just let him know Dr. Lieberman is looking for him."

"I'll do that. I'm sure he'll get back to you," she said. "Have a good day!"

He swung around to leave and then saw Louise Garner, her silver-streaked hair pulled tightly back, wearing a tailored blouse and skirt, walk sedately through the area. She spotted him and smiled nervously.

Daniel could feel his heart pounding. "Hello, Louise," he said as calmly as he could.

"Dan! Oh, I was trying to telephone you," she said, her eyes misting and her nose turning slightly pink, giving her formal, groomed look a slight blurriness. "I don't know how to thank you and Laura for being so kind about Janie and everything."

"It's . . . how are you, Louise?"

She smiled and took his hand. "I'm really fine. Paul thought I should work this morning, just to, you know, get used to the sound of voices again and everything before I spring myself on Janie."

He continued to stare, astonished, and could not help it. "I'm glad you're feeling better . . . I'm really glad to see you."

She tucked a loose strand of hair up with her hand. "I'm afraid I just shouldn't mix tranquilizers and booze . . . I'll never do it again. I hope I didn't do anything notable, did I? I just blacked out. I mean I have no idea what I did . . ."

Daniel looked at her carefully. "Well Janie's going to be glad to see you! Have you seen Paul around?"

"Not this morning . . . can I give him a message for you when he comes in?"

"It's okay, Louise," he said reassuringly. "I'll hunt him down myself."

McGinnis's front door was opened slightly at the second long ring. Daniel looked at Billy's nursemaid through the half-opened door. Her unattractive face, usually reddish and raw-looking, was pale, her pimples vividly prominent. Her yellow hair was still uncombed.

"Yes?" she said.

"Is Dr. McGinnis at home?" he asked.

She blinked, then continued staring at him, just missing eye contact. She was concentrating hard, and the effort made her features tense and strange. "What?"

"Is Dr. McGinnis here?" Daniel repeated gently. "Are you feeling all right?"

"I am not well," she said. "I um . . . I think Billy's father is outside. He's not in the house." She closed the door quickly.

She was not feeling well. If his suspicions were correct, he'd have to add the new behavioral signs of distraction, disorientation . . . a milder form of this illness, perhaps. Or was he letting his imagination go too far? He strode over the huge lawn toward the sculpted, tall hedges out in back of the house. The Doberman, Hansel, appeared and sat down placidly observing him. Then Gretel slid by him like a shark, making him jump slightly.

"McGinnis!" he yelled angrily. "I want to see you! Where are you?" he shouted, his voice shattering the suburban quiet like a siren. "McGinnis, I'm bringing you some bad news!"

"He isn't here," Greta said firmly, appearing from behind the boxwood topiary on the path near him. She was dressed in tennis whites, mirror sunglasses perched on her head. "Oh, it's you. I thought it was a delivery boy."

"You're sure he's not here?" he asked challengingly. He was unaffected by her appearance, dazzling but too slick. Her hair pulled back in a pony tail made her sharp features appear quite brittle.

"Of course I'm sure he's not here. I was just having a lesson with my tennis pro. Don't just stand there glaring, Lieberman, come meet José."

"I don't have time, Greta. I'm looking for your husband. It's urgent. Have you seen him around or not? Your nursemaid seems to think he's out here."

"You talked to the Hun? I thought she was staying in bed today, sick. It's the first time she's ever told me she was sick. She doesn't believe in doctors. Thinks medicine is poison. Had to practically *force* her to give Billy his dosage. I only hope she followed it through. Anyway, she's wrong about Paul." She glanced at her watch. "He's probably en route to the lab now." She smiled her ingenuous smile suddenly. "I couldn't interest you in doubles, could I? We've only just begun."

"Greta, I have to ask you a couple of questions, dead serious."

"Okay."

"First of all, this nursemaid, when is her day off?"

"Lieberman, you *couldn't* . . . "

"I'm serious." His expression stopped her. "When was her last day off?"

Greta calculated slowly. "Usually she's off Saturdays, but because of the birthday party, I gave her Monday."

He sighed. Monday, and she was sick now. Today was Wednesday. "I know you dislike her and could care less, but have you any idea where she goes on her days off?"

"She has a boyfriend—one of those cycle whizzes who hang around Louie's Place. I think she gangbangs with his friends."

He stood up and began to pace. "One more question. Have you noticed anything unusual about Paul's behavior lately? Anything he said to you, or any conversation he's had with someone else . . . I know all this sounds a little vague, but I'm looking for any departure from his normal routine. Especially since late last week."

For the first time, she looked genuinely concerned. "That is a little vague . . ."

"Anything. Think about it."

"Well, nothing comes to mind right off the top . . . but I really promise to think about it and get back to you if anything does occur to me," she said slowly. Then, as if to shake off any possible taint of seriousness, she gave him a long predatory stare, like a construction worker at lunch break, and shook her head slowly. "I do wish you'd change your mind about doubles, Lieberman."

Dead ends. Symptoms without a known common cause. Nothing fit. There had to be answers somewhere. McGinnis would be a goddamn stone wall. Louise obviously didn't know anything. But maybe Howard Lawson? Was he involved? Shirley might be the way to Howard. She'd be shaken after last Sunday, and off guard. Maybe she knew about the lab. He stopped to telephone his office from a roadside pay phone, and finding no emergencies waiting, he instructed Miss Brown to get in touch with Larry Roberts immediately and tell him to cover. There was a weighty silence on the other end, and then Miss Brown informed him in a patient, hushed tone, that in case he had forgotten, Wednesday was Dr. Roberts's golf day. Didn't Dr. Lieberman know that *he* was covering for Dr. Roberts?

"Miss Brown, you'll have to call him at his club and get him off the course. Tell him I have an emergency on my hands. Maybe he already got nine holes in, so don't feel too bad." He hung up fast.

The Lawson driveway was lined with huge, flowering rhododendrons leading to the main house. The theater was far downhill, barely visible from the house, and the theater parking lot was hidden from his view. But the woods into which Chet Gabrini had disappeared stretched out into the distance. He stood staring at the trees and then down the hill toward the scene of the murder for a moment. He turned at a sudden metallic sound on his right. Behind the shrubs, the lanky figure of Howard Lawson was crouched over a flower bed.

"Good morning," Daniel said.

Lawson turned slightly, clippers in hand, and glanced casually up at him. "Hi," Lawson answered with his usual secretive, knowing smile, and he went on cutting zinnias as if Lieberman's presence were routine. "Shirley's out shopping. Even thespians have to eat."

Daniel forced himself to smile back. "Actually, I wanted to see you . . ."

"Mostly she sends Ralph, but he always gets the wrong brands. Anyway he's still in bed, upset."

"I was hoping to talk to *you*, Howard," Daniel repeated.

Lawson looked quizzical; he was thinking it over. "Yes? Well, here I am. I take some mornings off for gardening, but usually I'm at the lab. I suppose you really came here to see Shirley before tackling me . . . but let that pass."

" I was just over there myself," Daniel said, searching for an opening, a crack in the smooth facade.

Lawson sniffed the flowers. "Oh," he said, suddenly hostile and alert.

"I have some questions . . . maybe you have some answers."

Lawson cut another flower. He made no response.

Daniel searched his face. "Remember, Howard, when we were talking at the Doughertys' party, you and I, about the P3?"

"Correction. We were talking about genetic engineering. You asked me what I did, and I told you."

"You're right, of course, I remember we had some words about recombinance . . ."

"My work is done in the open part of the lab complex . . . that's the problem with you people. You hear about genetic engineering and immediately your mind goes to P3 security. We do all kinds of biological work in our operation, and only under specific conditions would we activate the P3. All the labs are a hundred percent safe for the work done in them," Lawson said mechanically.

The idea, Daniel decided, is not to engage this man in battle. He noted that despite his mild voice, Lawson's nostrils were dilated and pale with anger. "I never questioned your work or its safety. I gather that you don't work in the P3. But I wondered if the P3 has really been operative this past year?"

Lawson deliberately put the flowers one by one in a straw basket. He looked at Daniel and appeared to make a decision. "It's been operative as long as the Perrinis were here, maybe longer," he said in a bored voice. "Is this going to be an interrogation? Look, Lieberman, I'm just a fixture there. I went to MIT with Harvey Garner, so I've been at the lab since the beginning, four years before Paul took it over from Garner. They can't get rid of me, just keep me off projects . . . I'm a fixture. Nobody notices me."

"Is that so?"

"Absolutely. Don't you think I know what they say about me? What they say about Amy and Allen . . . that I did it by cloning," Lawson said in a thin monotone devoid of emotion.

"The fact is, nobody pays any attention to me at all, not there, not here . . . you ever see the film about the scientist who vanished? That's me."

Daniel sat down carefully on a flat rock. "That puts you in a very interesting position, Howard."

Lawson's thin face was guarded. "How's that?"

"Like a fly on the wall. I mean, obviously you have a concise, observant, trained, scientific mind. You're probably the only person to whom I could turn at this moment. I need information." Daniel held his breath, hoping that he had aroused in Lawson the right blend of self-pity and self-importance. "I guess the project you just mentioned that was still on last week is finished. You did say that the P3 was utilized till the Perrinis went on vacation?"

Lawson pointed a finger at Daniel as he spoke. "Correction. *You* said vacation."

"I stand corrected . . ."

Lawson crouched down near the ferns and examined their undersurfaces, pruning between them silently. "They might be on vacation now, but they won't be coming back here," he said finally.

Daniel knew he had to cover his excitement. To get information from Lawson he had to go at the man's pace and by his route. "McGinnis said they were coming back. What makes you sure they're not?" he asked carefully.

"I was friendly with them, you see. I even have their vacation address in Lausanne. We never talked about their work, if that's what you're hoping. Any industrial P3 project is automatically top secret. But . . . we did talk a lot about gardening." Again a silence, a secret smile.

I'm sitting on a rock talking to a total *meshugana*, Daniel thought, exasperated. "Gardening?" he said blandly.

"My hobby. His, too. And here's the thing. During one talk we had, Joseph Perrini said he was going to try lantana." Lawson looked up as if he had just said something extremely significant.

"I'm sorry," Daniel said. "I'm not a gardener. I don't understand."

"Well, lantana is a common flowering bushy plant that grows outdoors in tropical climates. In Sheffield, it's an *indoor* plant. And it won't grow in Lausanne, either." Lawson waved his trowel for emphasis. "Don't you see, Joseph Perrini planned to use lantana as an outdoor plant this coming season, so he *knew*, before he left on Monday night, exactly where he'd be planting this fall, and it wasn't here!"

So it wasn't just a botanical digression. "You're positive?"

"Yes. Especially because he was going to plant both lantana and tulip bulbs. Of course spring is possible . . . but the probability is early fall. I'd put money on it. By next month, Joseph Perrini plans to be somewhere where there are no frosts in the winter."

"I see . . ."

"And furthermore, I'd bet McGinnis knows all about it. To me it means that the NPI project is over and their work is finished."

Daniel pushed his glasses up. "What's NPI?" he asked, alert.

"Natural Products International. Some kind of outfit that makes biologicals," Lawson said casually.

"Wait a minute. Let me get this straight. The Perrinis were working in the P3 on a DNA recombinant project for a company that makes biologicals?"

Lawson looked surprised. "Why not?"

"What exactly is their specialty, do you know?"

"Plant genetics." Lawson looked back at his own garden. "They're famous for their work with plant DNA. Their leaving here indicates that the NPI project is either completed or dropped. These things leak. Another lab could figure out the status of our project just by the departure of the lead team. So I would suppose McGinnis wanted to make it seem temporary, just a summer vacation, not to call attention to anything final. That's why they left quietly. But they *did* leave very suddenly . . ."

"Do you have their address?"

Lawson reached into his back pocket for a thin wallet and pulled out a piece of paper. "Who knows if it's real, and who knows why you're pumping me about the P3. But that's all right. I like puzzles."

"I'll just copy it down," Daniel said, ignoring his last comment and jotting hurriedly before Lawson changed his mind.

"They won't tell you anything, you know. It's futile."

Daniel shrugged and smiled. "I can't lose trying. What do I know, Howard, I'm just a country doctor."

Lawson slipped into a hostile mood at Daniel's smile. "Yes, you are. But you made it into the Set, didn't you?"

Daniel handed back the paper gingerly. "I don't think so, Howard."

He replaced the paper in his wallet and put it in his back pocket. "Yes, yes you did," he said in a neutral tone. "I don't know why. Could be that you're a Jew. They don't have any."

Daniel's eyes widened slightly. "Quotas?"

"Sure. In the Set. But they like novelty, I suppose. A little exotica Why else would they include you?"

"And where do you fit into the Set, Howard? Are you exotic, too?"

Lawson looked at him blandly, unsmiling. "I told you, I'm invisible."

Paul McGinnis walked down Main Street hand in hand with his son, Billy, only slowing his stride when the child tripped trying to keep up with him. At the door of Ye Olde Freeze Shoppe, he handed Billy a dollar for an ice-cream cone.

"Could I have a double, Dad?" Billy asked nervously, never quite sure of this handsome giant who sometimes walked with him, sometimes talked with him, and then, for long stretches of time, seemed to forget he existed.

"Sure," McGinnis said, glancing at the thin body, the knobby knees. "As long as it doesn't spoil dinner."

Billy grinned. "Oh, it won't!" he said, and disappeared inside the store.

An ambulance roared by. McGinnis lifted his chin slightly, his eyes grew alert as he surveyed the street. There were two stores closed. One was a dress shop that might have closed early, but the other was a newspaper and stationery store that ought to have been open at this time. He looked at his watch. Billy came back with a double Rocky Road. They crossed the street and sat on the bench under the old elm. As Billy bent over the rapidly melting ice-cream cone, McGinnis stroked his son's hair distractedly, thinking about the siren and the news that he'd heard on the car radio that a body had washed up by the cove. He had done careful calculations of the possible rate of contagious spread, based on estimates of three or four contacts during the lab break-in last Thursday. He eyed with some unease the darkened stores and surveyed the street for any visible clue that an outbreak was in progress.

"Dad?" Billy looked up at him with a chocolate-streaked smile. "Thanks for the ice cream."

His concentration broken, McGinnis looked directly at his improbable son and heir. The boy was doing well at school, gifted in science, they reported, and a serious student. He still had time to grow, and perhaps that runty frame would fill out and he would someday stop being so uncoordinated. Children changed. McGinnis closed his eyes for a split second. "Glad you like it," he said stiffly.

"They're going to get Chocolate Crispy Swirl in next week . . ."

McGinnis leaned back, not listening, absently rubbing Billy's shoulders. If the recent events in town were the consequence of the break-in, the project was ruined. After so much work and just when they were about to reduce infectivity to the desired single target—that was the irony of it. And all through inexcusable carelessness. Human error. He could guess what NPI would now do with Chameleon—they would cut loose from the project and abandon Sheffield to its fate.

In his office at the bank, Charles Vail looked out and saw McGinnis and Billy under the old elm tree. Across the street, a man who passed himself off as just another out-of-town reporter stood at the counter in Ye Olde Freeze, just next to where Billy had placed his dollar. He watched McGinnis and the boy.

*"Hotel Chamberlain . . ."*

*"Parlez-vous anglais, monsieur?"* Daniel asked.

*"Pas du tout, monsieur!"*

So much for that. *"Je voudrais parler à Docteur Joseph Perrini ou Docteur Rosalind Perrini . . ."* Daniel said, hoping they would be back in their room. It was nearly dinnertime in Switzerland.

Silence. Crackle.

"Hello, hello?" said Daniel.

*"Oui. J'ai mal compris . . . à qui desirez-vous parler?"*

*"Je suis Docteur Lieberman. Docteur Perrini, est-il là?"*

"Dr. Lieberman?" The voice sounded dubious. A silence.

*"Oui . . ."*

Crackle.

*"Je regrette . . . un moment . . . un moment."*

Daniel sighed, waiting for the voice of Doctor Perrini—man or wife. He hadn't spoken to either of them at the party. How would he explain his call? What information could he get from them?

"Yes? Who is this, please?"

Another voice. This time heavily accented, but English-speaking, not Dr. Perrini; a French accent. Was his French so terrible that the clerk hadn't understood a simple request to speak to someone? "This is Dr. Daniel Lieberman. I am calling from the United States to speak with Dr. Joseph or Dr. Rosalind Perrini . . . are either of them available to come to the telephone?"

"I'm afraid that is impossible."

"It's urgent."

"Are you a relative or . . . what is your name again?"

Daniel bent over his desk, steeling himself against the annoying echo of his own voice and the officiousness of the other's. "I am Dr. Lieberman, a colleague of the Perrinis. I need to speak with them . . ."

"Dr. Lieberman . . . I am very sorry. *Je regrette, Docteur.* But the day before yesterday the Perrinis were in an automobile accident near here. They were both killed . . . the funeral arrangements are already made and someone has come for their . . . baggage and things already. This tragedy was in your newspapers, no?"

"No. No it wasn't."

"But these people, were they not famous in your country?"

"Yes, they were."

"Perhaps today it will be in the newspapers there, no?"

"Maybe so. Listen, thank you. I'm sorry."

"Is there anything else we can do?"

"No. *Merci beaucoup, monsieur.*"

Dead end. Cable under the sea or satellite through space. Whichever, this trail had led to a blind alley. The Perrinis were dead—two top geneticists and not one word in the paper. Someone had come to take their effects, and he should have asked who. . . .

He stared at the polished surface of his predecessor's mahogany desk. A sweep of his arm had rid it of notes, lollipops, junk mail, forms, and sample bottles. It had probably always been this neat when Cameron was around. Things had been different then. Summers past were never like this. Cameron would have been just as affected as Daniel by the events of the past week. Cameron would've said, the town's going crazy . . . but that was it, wasn't it? The town was going crazy!

On impulse he dialed *The Sheffield News*. He took several clean pieces of notepaper out of his drawer while he cradled the receiver under his chin.

The receptionist sounded harassed and told him Dougherty wasn't in.

"Can someone else help you?" she asked hurriedly.

"No . . . is there anyone else out sick? Is Jack Dougherty sick?"

"Yeah," she sighed. "He's sick and we're really shorthanded. Some kind of bug going around the office, I guess, of all times!"

"I'll call him at home," Daniel said, and hung up.

The telephone at the Doughertys' rang and rang . . . listening, Daniel remembered Barbara telling him in the hospital corridor how depressed Jack was and how he didn't even get out of bed. And he'd thought it was because of Wendy. Had the man been sick? When had it begun? He hung up and made a note. On a separate piece of paper he wrote, What is NPI? He scribbled other notes: incidents, times, names, questions . . .

There was a buzz on his intercom. "Dr. Edwards is on the phone," Miss Brown said.

He picked up the receiver quickly. "Bill? Anything?"

"Tests are coming up negative, negative, negative . . ."

"Okay, listen. I just found out that Joseph and Rosalind Perrini died in an automobile accident the day before yesterday in France. Maybe I overlooked their obituary, but I don't remember seeing anything on them. They were pretty famous in their field, right?"

"Right. Molecular geneticists. I haven't seen anything on them either, but what's the connection?"

"Turns out they were the lead team on this project at the P3. The project was for a company called NPI—Natural Products International, which markets biologicals, at least according to another scientist at the lab. Anyway, the Perrinis left Sheffield on Monday and now they're dead. So we need information on NPI—like who the hell are they, where are they based, and so forth. And what kind of work were the Perrinis involved in prior to coming to Sheffield . . ."

"I'll get on it . . . Daniel, did any more cases turn up?"

"I'm afraid so . . . and not all as obvious as the ones I told you about. I think these reactions are highly individual—there's a mild form, the only signs are a failure of concentration and slight disorientation. I think the thing is spreading like a forest fire, whatever the hell it is. . . ."

* * *

*"Natural Projects International."*

*"NPI. Chameleon control."*

*There was a buzz, a click, then, "Yes?"*

*"Lieberman spoke to Edwards again. The 212 telephone number is 555-2049. They mentioned the Perrinis and NPI, but Lieberman has no specific information."*

*"You'll have to watch Edwards closely."*

*"Should we intervene?"*

*"Only if it becomes absolutely necessary. Personally, I don't think he can get much farther. We've covered our tracks pretty well."*

Daniel was still at his desk accumulating notes. Louise Garner's recovery both encouraged and confused him. He was underlining the details of the case when his intercom buzzed.

"Chief McLoughlin here to see you, Dr. Lieberman." Miss Brown sounded surprised.

"Please send him in."

McLoughlin's broad shoulders filled the doorway as he entered, looking tired and defeated. He sat at the end of Daniel's desk. "Well . . . it turned out the body was the Horgan girl. The medical examiner said she'd been in the water since about last Saturday. Thought I'd stop by and let you know."

The two men looked at each other.

"Another murder?"

McLoughlin shook his head. "No. There was no injury before death; no blows to the head or bruises. She died by drowning, that's all . . . some kind of scratches on her. But the examiner said they're just surface stuff. Animal scratches, he thinks."

Daniel turned over the new information in his mind in silence, and McLoughlin waited for him to speak.

"Wendy has those scratches, too . . . early as Friday morning, when she first came to my office, she had them. Animal scratches. It was Saturday that Jill went into the water?"

"Yeah, that's pretty definite. We also know that she was a senior lifesaver; a real strong swimmer. . . ."

"That's it then . . . I think that Jill and Wendy both came in close contact with a frightened or angry animal at that lab Thursday night," Daniel said. "The scratches are good circumstantial evidence for that—Laura saw empty animal cages in the P3, and the file card was probably a cage-cleaning schedule. Some kind of treated test animals must have been in those cages on Thursday." He pushed his notes across the desk to McLoughlin and filled him in. "Now it looks to me like the cluster began one week ago with at least these two cases: two contacts at the P3 lab with a contagious agent."

"How about Scott Andrews?"

"Originally, I thought Wendy was the source of the whole thing, but I'm sure if Jill drowned Saturday—a good strong swimmer, well she must have experienced some mental change, something that rendered her incapable of normal functioning. She had no time to catch it from Wendy—had to be primary. And Scott. He must have experienced an hallucinatory episode to do what he did . . . that was early Sunday, the third primary case."

"How about Chet? He's caught it, too."

"Somehow he must not have made primary contact, because he didn't get sick till Sunday night. Wendy probably transmitted it to him on Friday afternoon and to Hill at the same time."

McLoughlin got up, scratched his head, and walked over to a chair at the side of the desk, thinking. "When I checked through Jill Horgan's movements prior to the missing person's complaint, I found out she'd been chased off the beach for necking with Gary West on Friday night . . . he was supposed to have been her date Saturday night, but she never showed up."

Daniel pointed to the notes excitedly. "Gary West had to have been exposed Friday night . . . I didn't know how till now. But it makes sense. He probably did set that fire on Sunday . . ."

McLoughlin and Daniel looked silently at each other for a moment.

"There must be a lot of people sick now if this is transmitted so readily," Daniel said.

McLoughlin sat in the chair near Daniel. "Do you still think it's possible that each of these people could have ingested something . . . you know, the practical-joker theory?"

Daniel took his glasses off and rubbed his eyes. He spoke carefully. "I'm afraid the answer is no. I see a typical pattern of epidemic spread. Pediatricians see it more than anyone else. Like the strep epidemic that's just ending now . . . and this sickness came from a microbiological lab, which means it can be anything—viral pathogens unknown to this region. I suppose anything can be cultured there. Only problem is that with all the oddball diseases described in the texts, nothing quite fits."

"Listen, Lieberman, I'm not a medical man. But I can bring McGinnis in for questioning if it'll serve any purpose."

"I doubt that at this point you can get any more information than Laura did. And you can't hold him on the file card, can you?"

McLoughlin was looking very angry. "You know that security guard I told you about? Jimmy Walters? We can't find him I mean, literally he's gone. I don't like the way this all feels; everything keeps slipping away. A clean lab a lot of lies people missing, and then these godawful things happening when you least expect them. What do you suggest as the next move? I'm not going to sit and wait for the next murder!"

Daniel looked at the papers. "Each of these people has made contacts. I'd like them found before they show up as statistics. I'd like to see the detective unit trace all Jill's, Wendy's and Scott's contacts from Thursday night on. I know we can't cure it yet—we don't even know what it is. But we can keep the sick isolated and tranquilized . . . wait a minute, I want to try this number again."

Daniel Lieberman dialed while McLoughlin watched him gravely.

"Hello?" Roy Dougherty answered.

"Hi, Roy, this is Dr. Lieberman. Your Mom or Dad home?"

There were TV sounds in the background. The boy's voice was hesitant. "They're both sleeping."

"Could you try to wake them? I have to talk to them," Daniel said with a quick look at McLoughlin.

"I can't wake them up. I already tried," Roy said.

Daniel's heart sank. "Listen, just stay put, okay? And don't worry. I'll send somebody to make sure they're all right."

He hung up and faced McLoughlin. "The Doughertys . . . we'd better get them to the hospital. My thinking is that if we're dealing with a contagious illness, your men are going to turn up clusters of cases around the guests at the party. Here's a list I made; I'm afraid it's sketchy. Also, people who frequent the library, Louie's Place . . . the hospital staff. And all these people's families."

McLoughlin let his breath out slowly like a whistle. "How're my officers going to avoid causing a major panic with this news? People get scared. Hell, I'm scared myself! I mean how is this thing spreading? What do I tell my men?"

"I don't know how it's transmitted. Maybe respiratory

contact. Maybe by mouth. I'm not sure. I can only tell you the thing has an incubation period of thiry-two to forty-eight hours and these strange symptoms. I'd tell the men to bring the sick to the hospital. And since they're going to be exposed, warn them about what they themselves might experience. If they do feel any disorientation, anything weird, they shouldn't drive. They should call for help. And their families should be told what to watch for, because I don't know how much warning the victims have. I just hope we have enough tranquilizer in town." Daniel reached into his desk drawer and took out a large bottle of yellow pills. "Here. For you and your men, just in case. Dosage is on the label. Take it at the first sign of anything wrong. Don't wait. It won't cure you, but it'll keep you from harming yourself or anyone else. And you'd better make arrangements to keep in regular touch with someone reliable from out of town. That's all we can do, Ned."

McLoughlin pocketed the pills. "I'll get in touch with Jim Denton, chief of police up in Norfolk." He started for the door and turned when halfway across the office. "Lieberman, I want to hear it from you again. When you say something like a respiratory infection, you mean a real medical illness? I mean is that what you're actually saying?"

Daniel nodded. "I mean a set of specific psychiatric symptoms that are being caused by a virus or bacterium!"

# Thursday, August ninth:

"I mean a set of specific symptoms caused by a virus or bacterium. I mean exactly what I've stated—an infectious illness!" Daniel repeated.

Sunlight came through the high windows of the antiseptic meeting room and filtered softly onto the eight persons at the brown Formica conference table. The sunlight picked out the bright white of the doctors' coats as they shifted uncomfortably in their seats.

"Dr. Lieberman," Hayes said, "please sit down and bear with us a bit longer. After all, you're presenting a rather revolutionary theory."

Daniel sat down and looked around the table unhappily. Hayes was at the far end. Nelson, looking unusually drawn and tired, was next to Hayes. Larry Roberts, in a white coat, assiduously avoided Daniel's eyes. Miss Pendleton sat rigidly erect, as if braced for more bad news.

The invited guest sat next to each other on the other long side. First, Mr. Majeski, the florid, pudgy Health officer from Sheffield County; Dr. Grace Thurson, a state epidemiologist, pinch-faced and impassive-looking; finally, Dr. Albert Sealy, a toxicologist from the Harvard School of Public Health, who was visiting Dr. Thurson's laboratory and had been invited to accompany her to Sheffield. He was smoking a pipe, watching all of them with a faintly bemusedexpression.

"After hearing Dr. Lieberman, I understand what's been happening to our phone lines this morning," Nelson said somberly. "Information's received dozens of calls. People wanting to know the name of the illness going around and if we have a vaccine for it. They've been calling it the 'crazy sickness.' All the callers have been quite panicky. Finally, I had to run off a position paper for the staff. Here's a copy for each of you, just pass them around. Now my business is medicine, not squelching rumors. I don't like this at all."

The Xeroxed pages went around the table, and Daniel

glanced at his copy briefly. He realized he had not one really strong ally here. It appeared that Hayes had not informed Hodson of the meeting. Singh was also missing. And he'd had to trade off McLoughlin's presence for the Health people. In fact it was only after the Doughertys had arrived by ambulance and after Daniel had made several calls that Hayes termed it "harassing" that Daniel had even gotten his conference, and now it was going badly. From the moment he had taped his chart to the portable blackboard, there had been general disagreement and disbelief.

"Any hypothesis," Larry Roberts said, "can be supported if you slightly distort the evidence. We've all been guilty of that at one time or another. But you've taken really extraordinary license. We all know that several of your 'cases' are phenomena attributable to alternative factors. We've even discussed possible etiologies of three of them. And your other hypothetical cases, including fatalities, mind you, haven't even been personally observed by you! One of these 'cases' occurred in Switzerland, no less! Yet there it is on your chart. You've merely drawn inferences, Lieberman, and that's not good enough."

Daniel rubbed his neck for a moment, then looked up at everyone. "Could we all agree," he said, his growing frustration under tight rein, "that many strange and some violent occurrences have taken place in Sheffield since last week? That, in fact, if you were to examine the police reports of a five-year period around here, you wouldn't find any equivalent to the nature of events of these last seven days?"

"Exactly what nature?" Dr. Thurson asked quietly. "Neither I nor Dr. Sealy are Sheffield residents, Dr. Lieberman."

"Just what's on this chart, Dr. Thurson," he answered rather abruptly, pointing to it. The chart gave detailed descriptions of the known cases, including the time from contact to onset, the nature of the symptoms, and prognosis.

"Could we agree for starters," Daniel repeated, "that this represents a cluster of very unusual events?"

Dr. Thurson's lips pursed slightly and her pale, lined face stared at him, stolid and unforgiving. Before he could mollify her, Miss Pendleton intervened.

"Of course," she said firmly. "I'm sure that Miss Rivera and Miss Manderson, two of my most reliable nurses, did not just coincidentally suffer breakdowns this past week."

Nelson nodded reluctantly. "I'd second that, and am personally very concerned about these developments. But where does this information take us, Dr. Lieberman?"

Daniel sighed with relief at what appeared a breakthrough. "Well for one thing, we know we've got a pattern, and although I can't prove my theory at present, I'm sure that we're dealing with an infectious illness. Not a chemical toxin. Until we can work it out, all new and recent patients with acute behavioral problems should be placed in isolation immediately. We should address ourselves, with all the help we can muster, to a full investigation of this illness, its entire epidemiology. We should be working out a treatment now. It's our job to categorize and control this disease. Also, I believe we should prepare ourselves for an imminent state of emergency."

Mr. Majeski smiled, politely nervous. "Dr. Lieberman, I'm not a medical man and you'll excuse me for saying this, but we don't know what we're looking *for*. Your advice could cause a panic. As Health officer, I must warn against spreading rumors, and ask everyone to avoid any hysteria-producing news in town at all costs."

Larry Roberts, who had been sitting with his chair tilted back, let the front legs bang on the floor. "I think you are being unnecessarily alarmist, Lieberman. I agree totally with Mr. Majeski. I only hope that you won't attract any further publicity for this notion, although it seems, from the switchboard, I'm a bit late." He got up and stood behind his chair, looking calmly at everyone in turn. "You've described a range of neurotic and psychotic symptoms with *no* clinical signs of infection whatsoever and attributed the entire hodgepodge to some mystery virus! I can hardly believe my ears! What do you think this is, a town in the Middle Ages with some form of mass mania?"

Dr. Albert Sealy smiled dryly at Roberts, moved his pipe to the side of his mouth, and made a few notes.

"Dr. Lieberman, is there any specific communicable disease that you think could conceivably produce this range of symptoms?" Nelson asked.

"Not one that I've come across," Daniel replied. "I've considered numerous possibilities, various forms of meningitis, encephalitis . . . and even a few rare African viruses. Keep in mind that anything can be cultured in a P3. It's set up for working with dangerous organisms. And let's not forget the recombinant work the lab was doing."

"Not this again. Dr. Lieberman. This is a total fantasy," Hayes interjected angrily.

"DNA recombinant research isn't fantasy. Mr. Hayes, and Paul McGinnis . . ."

"He told us there was nothing. . . ."

"Damn it, he was lying!" Daniel said loudly. "Whatever it is, it is progressing in wider and wider circles daily. Some of us in this room have been exposed . . ."

"Oh, come now," Larry Roberts said.

"Everyone who's had contact with Wendy is exposed!" Daniel continued. "Her parents are already sick with the same illness. All the guests at the party last Saturday night have been exposed, and visitors to the library . . ." My God! Maia, he thought, and then a vague thought intruded for a moment, formless, but significant . . . as his mind reached out to it, he was interrupted, and it disappeared.

"Go on, Dr. Lieberman," Nelson said abruptly.

Daniel blinked. "I—I believe you'll see more cases crop up near Louie's Place, yes. Also in the homes of the teen-agers. The staff of the General will develop cases, and obviously, homes and families of infected personnel. The police force is out now checking these contacts. Look, folks, I'm trying to present a realistic picture. I think we're heading fast into the log phase of an epidemic."

He tried to recapture the thought that had flitted by, but could not. What was it . . . damn!

"Well, Dr. Lieberman, you certainly don't need the help of our department for an epidemiological profile . . . you've done it yourself," Grace Thurson said coolly.

Hayes slapped the arm of his chair. "This is a lot of hocus pocus about viral substances from a lab! . . . Now, if you were to conjecture that a toxic material has somehow been released, as Chief McLoughlin himself suggested . . . maybe a pesticide tree spray or a contaminated water fountain. That's not unheard of. Even a water main to specific parts of town . . ." Hayes turned to Albert Sealy. "Tell us, Dr. Sealy, have you any thoughts on this situation from your vantage point?"

Sealy adjusted his pipe and leaned back. "Yes, yes I do . . . from a toxicological point of view, there's very interesting potential here. You may all recall the clusters of hysteria and lunacy in the Middle Ages, as Dr. Roberts pointed out before . . . originally attributed to the wrath of some patron saint, but eventually, of course, ergot poisoning turned out to be the cause of many of those epidemics . . . a simple fungus contaminant of rye, that's all. Acted like LSD."

"That's an excellent thought, Albert," Thurson said. "Are you suggesting that this may actually be what's happening?"

Sealy shrugged lightly, looking slightly amused. "There probably have been other outbreaks, maybe even Salem, Massachusetts, at the time of the witch trials, for all we know. But I'd say we have a marked resemblance to the medieval villages from what Dr. Lieberman has described. It would be good to pursue the thought. But my hunch is that these few cases are probably the extent of it, maybe a few customers of the same grocery store. I wouldn't recommend doing anything further unless you actually see a good healthy crop of cases. Then I'd look first to your rye flours and so forth . . . oh, by the way, did you have a church fair lately?"

"I don't think so," Majeski said, with a worried look on his round face. "Maybe we should embargo the bakery goods, but . . ."

"You're barking up the wrong tree!" Daniel said loudly.

"All right. All right. Then explain the absence of fever or of *any* abnormality in the blood work if we are dealing with an infectious illness," Nelson responded. "*That's* what I can't understand, Dr. Lieberman. How can you sit there and defend your theory in the face of your own tests!"

"The incubation periods, the clear time gaps between contact and onset . . . Miss Rivera was healthy Sunday morning. She was fine Sunday afternoon in New York when she delivered the blood samples for me . . . ."

"She delivered blood samples?" Thurson asked.

"Packed in Styrofoam and sealed. Don't get sidetracked on that. The point is she wasn't *in* Sheffield when she began presenting symptoms. Her contact was twenty-four hours prior to onset, at least. Same with Miss Hill and with Wendy. This is just not a toxic material, its behavior is that of a transmitted viral or bacterial illness."

"Excuse me, Dr. Lieberman . . . I wasn't getting sidetracked," Thurson said precisely. "I know you have developed a theory which you'd like accepted. But it's my job to question the details. There are alternatives . . . the packaging of this sample may have been contaminated, or Miss Rivera might have ingested a toxin and had hidden symptoms for a period of time before actually becoming overtly ill. Now, I don't want to be railroaded into accepting *any* unproven theory."

Daniel made a deliberate effort to restain his anger. "Dr.

Thurson, I understand and appreciate your caution, but just in case we are dealing with an epidemic of a new infectious disease, I think you should consider including my theory along with Dr. Sealy's and the Styrofoam packaging."

Before answering, Thurston wrote several lines on a pad. "How would you say it is being transmitted? And what shall we call it?"

"Maybe it's spreading via the respiratory route. But I don't know for sure. And it does not have a name, either. I think the 'crazy sickness' is inappropriate . . . but I'll tell you something, Dr. Thurson, the victims don't care if it has a name or number. It's here in Sheffield."

"Oh dear," Larry Roberts said. "According to you, we shall all soon be ranting screaming lunatics, jumping all over Main Street, disheveled. Sheffield will be Bedlam recreated."

Daniel stared at him a moment and then spoke very quietly. "I suppose that some people will become passive, some will withdraw, and many will even be partially functional. It's hard from these sample cases to know how each victim will react. So far, it seems unusually individualistic. Soon we'll be dealing with hundreds of cases, in and out of Sheffield. Then those of us still functioning will get a clearer picture." He picked a piece of lint off his khakis deliberately.

Nelson stood and crossed to the window, clearly upset. "Dr. Singh isn't here with us because at the moment he's sleeping. For those of you who don't know him, Dr. Singh is our family-practice resident and often sleeps here at the hospital . . . the point is, it appears to me that he's not sleeping normally, but actually has withdrawn in some odd way. He doesn't respond . . . I'm afraid he is also showing symptoms of this behavioral type, and I certainly agree with my colleague vis-à-vis the Dougherty cases and a few others. But my thinking remains that the causal agent is a toxin and that it will simply wear off. As soon as it does, one of the patients will tell us what happened. It's been only five days with Wendy. Only five days after all."

"And if it doesn't wear off? If it does irreversible brain damage? . . . And I hope Dr. Singh is in isolation," Daniel said as an afterthought. He glanced at his watch. He was stymied, and the conference might take all morning. "I think you should create a floor isolation unit immediately, warn the staff, watch incoming cases for any behavioral symptoms, and get epidemiological data on each case. Bring in additional staff, especially people experienced in infectious disease work. Call in the Center for Disease Control. Where's Hodson, by the way?" Daniel asked, hardly pausing for breath.

"He wasn't home and didn't return my call," said Hayes.

"What exactly did you want the state agency to do at this time?" Dr. Thurson asked Hayes, ignoring Daniel.

"I'd say wait and see. If it was a contaminant, it may be self-limiting."

"Dr. Thurson," Daniel interrupted, "we need your resources, your people, lab equipment, technical expertise. Possibly computer facilities."

"We'd be in harmony if you'd concede, as Chief McLoughlin did, that this is most likely the result of a practical joke . . ." Hayes said.

"But he changed his mind. Was that why he wasn't invited to this meeting?"

Hayes leaned forward, suddenly very angry. "Now don't put this on an adversary basis, Dr. Lieberman. If this is a medical problem then only medical people need confer on its solution. The Police Department has no place here except to investigate crimes."

"Maybe our town sanitarian could begin air and water sampling," Majeski volunteered. "But I'd agree the less the newspapers and police are involved, the better off we'll be. You can see how something like this would be treated in the press . . . because of that murder, we've gotten quite a reputation already. After this, not one summer resident would be left by tomorrow. And for *what?* What if you are one hundred percent wrong?"

Nelson looked upset. "It's just that we don't have anything concrete to go on, Dr. Lieberman. I'm not blaming you, but it's difficult for us to buy such a vague and strange picture . . ."

Grace Thurson smiled at Sealy. "Well, I will have to make a report . . . I could emphasize the toxin possibility and . . . what do you think, Albert?"

"Definitely. We could get a few wheels turning quietly. These things usually don't pan out, but . . ."

Graham Hodson woke up not knowing where he was. He felt dizzy, nauseated, and surreal, as if he were dreaming. The room was strange to him, and as he placed his feet on the floor, he felt a clammy sensation. He began immediately to attempt a differential on himself, automatically reaching for his wrist to take his own pulse. But the gesture, as it was carried out, lost meaning, and so he sat, hands crossed, wondering what . . . Suddenly he remembered in a lucid instant. A diagnosis. Yes, but no medical terms came to him as he searched his memory for the words that seemed to hover just beyond the reach of his conscious mind. He could not stand. Finally he managed, but felt weak. His head throbbed painfully as he walked by habit to the bathroom. For a clear instant, he thought he was only dreaming and not sick. It was all a dream: the waking, walking, amnesia, weakness . . . He went immediately to the sink to look in the mirror, expecting that this routine confrontation with his own image would awaken him.

Hodson saw what he imagined must be his face suspended in the center of the square silver surface. He recognized the clipped mustache. The features were familiar. But the image he gazed at was deeply cracked, like a ruined clay statue. One gaping fissure ran diagonally from cheekbone to upper lip, like a dueling scar. He could see a cross section of tissue along the edges, layers of epidermis, and the glistening fibroblasts beneath. He saw purplish, hairlike capillaries laced throughout the orange and yellow globules of fatty tissue. Then beyond the fissure he saw darkness: deep darkness like that of outer space. His head had cracked and emptied of contents. A second fissure ran down his forehead to his left eye, exposing bone which shone bluish and oysterlike from beneath. As he watched, mesmerized, another fissure slowly yawned open along the parietal suture of his skull, as if in a silent earthquake. Then, to his horror, he saw that there was nothing inside but a few bruised and fragmentary scraps of brain tissue, their disconnected dendrites swinging slowly to and fro in a cold breeze. Hodson fell to the floor of the bathroom, unconscious.

"I suppose they handle these things differently in New York City," Dr. Thurson said to Daniel "They are more susceptible to political pressure and hysteria. But, you see, we have our methods here. We follow an established routine whenever we're called in by local officials. If, for example, we had an outbreak of Legionnaire's Disease, we'd go to the site and run tests. We'd build a network for collecting data and set up treatment centers . . . but, you see, we'd have clear-cut symptoms, a known treatment. We're not miracle workers."

"I guess I don't have to remind you that Legionnaire's Disease had no name and no treatment not very long ago, Dr. Thurson . . . Do you all realize how many generations of bacteria have grown since we called this conference? Do you expect me to lose another twenty-four hours trying to convince you people that this is really happening?"

"Sit down, please, Lieberman," Hayes said. "I received a call from McGinnis early this morning. He's on our board of directors . . ."

Daniel sat down. He looked anxiously at his watch.

"He called me to reassure me that he'd been thoroughly questioned about the P3 and that he'd thought you were satisfied with the answers. But now he hears murmurs, as he calls them, from the public."

"He didn't say the *peasants?*" Daniel asked.

Larry Roberts smiled. "He also called *me*, as I told Mr. Hayes. He said he was planning on having his son Billy's records transferred to my office, because he feels you're conducting a personal vendetta against him, and as a parent, he's worried that your antagonism may be displaced onto Billy."

Daniel nodded. "Dr. Thurson, Dr. Sealy, I'd strongly suggest to your agency that they begin an investigation at the McGinnis Laboratories on Broadview Road as soon as possible. Something came out of there last Thursday night, and whatever it is, it's infecting the town."

Dr. Thurson gave him a neutral glance and looked at Hayes.

"There is," Hayes said, reflectively pulling on his earlobe, "a certain arrogance in maintaining theories, embellishing them with charts, and accusing a respected citizen of irresponsible behavior, and in fact, of downright lying, without one shred of proof."

Daniel pushed his glasses up and cocked his head slightly. "There is a certain arrogance in venturing outside of my own branch of medicine to offer you my observations in the hope that you can use the information. But there's a greater arrogance in sitting on one's ass while Sheffield burns." He gathered his notes and stood.

"Where are you going, Lieberman?" asked Hayes.

"To get some fucking help!" He ripped his chart off the blackboard and stormed out of the room.

McLoughlin had not intended to cause panic when he'd summoned his men to headquarters for standby duty. He had assured each of them that it was not an official civil emergency but that, nonetheless, he wanted them all at headquarters on standby. He told them he would be conducting an immediate and thorough investigation concerning a subject he would explain.

As they stood there in the very early morning, he explained the problem in a carefully neutral voice. Their job would be to explore the possibility that an epidemic of an unusual illness might be in progress in Sheffield.

Ned McLoughlin looked around at the faces of his men. Lieutenant Johnson and Officer Buford were next in command after him, and they in turn had charge of the seven patrolmen who made up the entire force of the town. The men stood in a disciplined fashion as McLoughlin gave his orders, listening to him quietly. He spoke very concisely and calmly, as if about an unusual spell of weather, but each man felt the repressed emotion and the impact of the words:

"We're a small department," McLoughlin concluded. "And *if* this theory of an unusual virus or bacterial illness turns out to be correct, it will be too much for us to handle. In that case, we'll call upon our neighboring PDs for help right away. And if their resources aren't sufficient, we'll go to the State Police. At this time, I hope that additional manpower will prove unnecessary."

The nine men nodded agreement and waited.

"All right, Officer Buford, you'll be responsible for the team tracing the Horgan girl's contacts. Here's the file. Lieutenant Johnson, you'll be taking the Dougherty case. You have the entire force at your disposal for the next twenty-four hours. I want to be kept informed right along. I don't want any of you going home until we get a handle on this. . . ."

A young patrolman spoke up: "Chief McLoughlin, if this thing is contagious, what protection do we have against it?"

"I was getting to that. None of us have protection," McLoughlin answered. "We're going to have to leave that to the medical people and get on with our work. I'm distributing medication to each of you before you leave. It's only a tranquilizer, and it doesn't cure or prevent this illness. But if you feel any of the symptoms I've described, take it as directed. Stay put. And let me know. There are directions on each bottle . . . And if I start acting strangely, the senior healthy man should take over immediately. Get me properly restrained, and call Dr. Lieberman and Chief Denton at the numbers up here on the board."

No one spoke.

"Men, if you weren't conducting these interviews and you

didn't happen to be on this force, you'd still be susceptible to this illness. If it exists, it's everybody's problem."

The men began their work methodically and with great discipline in the early morning. By ten thirty they had questioned and interviewed over fifty potential contacts. In each case, it was their duty to describe the mystery illness to which these contacts might possibly have been exposed. They worked in a friendly, calm way, not running into any actual cases at first. They began to suspect that the mystery illness was a myth, and as the morning progressed, the reality of a "crazy sickness" grew remote. Their optimism increased until they suddenly encountered some acute cases: the nearly starved Hill sisters; the now incoherent boy, Gary West, and his younger sister; a few elderly residents of the Wests' neighborhood . . . Then they began to reconsider the behavior of some of the contacts they had already interviewed—and they became aware of the slight but telltale irregularities. They began bringing cases to the General—seventeen by noon. The "crazy sickness" was real after all, and it scared the hell out of them.

From pay phones they quickly told their families, their girlfriends . . . the families and girlfriends told their relatives and acquaintances. The exposed contacts themselves made telephone calls. Soon the telephone lines were tied up all through town. By two o'clock almost everyone in Sheffield had heard about the mystery disease. Rumor traveled faster than infection, and it was more thorough: the telephone operators, the supermarket checkout girls, the counter waitresses and dishwasher at the Olde Freeze Shoppe, the gas station operator and his partner, housewives, the butcher, the movie box-office lady . . . they all knew.

"Ladies who lunch," Greta said from a chaise near Pam Vail's pool, "are missing good sun."

Pam sighed with boredom, looking at Greta and Angelique from her seat under the umbrella, surveying the free-form swimming pool which, no matter how pleasant, was simply never going to be as dramatic as the McGinnises'. "Greta, we really should go. It's past eleven thirty. We have to talk about the Heart Disease Dinner."

Greta opened one eye, noting how young Pam Vail sounded—and was. "Why don't we postpone it till the dead of winter?"

Angelique smiled politely. Her hotel restaurant, Chez Claude, was the chosen site for the big dinner, and it was important to her when the event was to be scheduled. "How is it possible to lie in the hot sun the way that you do?" she asked Greta with a mixture of admiration and scorn.

These women do nothing, she thought with annoyance. She was the only one of the three who worked: who kept books, arranged the flowers at Chez Claude, ordered supplies for the hotel, helped manage the staff . . . they did nothing, yet she was grateful to be with them, and when Pam had invited her to lunch, she was happy to be accepted by her and Greta McGinnis. Perhaps they only wanted her to donate the hotel facilities . . . if so, she could not afford the gesture. This past week, many people had canceled after that horrid drowning. Without the usual summer reservations, winter would be difficult.

Angelique sitrred restlessly. Even now she was missing work that she'd have to make up. What was Jean-Claude doing, anyway? How could he have gotten involved with this Pam Vail? It was hardly the first time he had played around. But this time she knew he was serious. He could not afford to get involved this way, and he did not realize that this young American woman was only playing. How would Angelique approach the subject tactfully and make herself understood without seeming a fool? This Pam Vail was so cool, impervious to feelings. Angelique watched her smooth heavy brown hair swinging just past her shoulders as she stood, and her walk, so elegant as she went to Greta.

Angelique tugged at her skirt, feeling old. Greta, she knew, was older, but she felt stodgy with these two. She had put on weight. These two, they were never serious. Why did Pam bother Jean-Claude when she had her own husband and child—everything, in fact. What did she want? It's a game to her, thought Angelique sadly, and I'm losing. She had a feeling of intense self-pity; the very air around her seemed to have turned gray again. This clouding had been happening all morning ever since she woke with a headache. She felt powerless with these two women, and now she even felt a physical weakness being near them. She felt as if she could not stand up. They played. They only played. The people in this town had no feelings.

"Angelique! You're *not* wearing stockings in this heat," Pam exclaimed suddenly. "I don't know how you can stand it!"

Angelique thought, if only Greta would leave us alone, I would tell Pam what I think about her seeing Jean-Claude, and that I will not stand it any longer. She smiled. "Inside it is air-conditioned, no?" she said brightly.

Greta rose, stretching like a cat. " 'Scuse me a minute. I'll be back, and then we'll go for lunch." She headed for the house to dress.

Quietly Angelique turned to Pam, who was applying lip gloss. "Pam, I do not wish to discuss this with you. This is what I wish to say, and I do not want that you answer me, please. I simply wish to tell you that you must not go on seeing . . . the man you are seeing."

Pam shut her lip-gloss case and sighed. "Would you like some iced tea, Angelique?" she asked.

"That would be nice," Angelique replied.

Suddenly she felt very dizzy—perhaps it was the unexpressed words, the rage and screaming she held within her. If she had had a different temperament, she would have thrown things and shouted. "I hope that you do understand me . . ." she said slowly and emphatically. She passed her hand over her eyes as she spoke, because it had turned cloudy again.

Pam looked at her a moment. "I understood you perfectly. I'll get you some iced tea . . . are you all right? You look strange."

Angelique nodded yes.

"Would you like to come in the house?" Pam asked.

Angelique shook her head no. For some reason she could not talk or stand. It was the anger, she thought, and the heat. Yes, that was undoubtedly why she felt so very strange. She looked up at the hazy, painful sun; its light diffused all around her, surrounding her, choking her. She was barely able to breathe now and could not wait for the promised drink. This intense thirst was so sudden. Who had gone to get her a drink? Had someone said they would bring her something cold to drink? When? Yellow sky and burning rays assaulted her, piercing the haze. She was . . . where? Where was this cocoon of heat? It was getting rapidly worse, so strange; the feeling of being nowhere, enveloped in heat. And the intensity! . . . But then she saw it. Of course. She should have realized . . . She lifted her arm, her pale, plump arm, and she examined the blue flames that rose from it like little hairs. They were small, like the centers of candle flames, the hottest part, and they radiated all up and down her arm. And then she saw that they were on her skirt as well; on her legs She must put them out. The water. If she could only raise her heavy body and get to the water. The pool glittered like ice only a short distance away. . . .

Greta was standing just inside the kitchen door as Pam entered the house.

"I thought you came in to change your clothes . . ." Pam said.

"I changed," Greta replied, putting her hands in the pockets of a wraparound skirt.

"Then what are you doing?" Pam asked.

"Waiting . . . I thought she might want a few private words with you."

"About what?" Pam asked, blank-faced.

"Jean-Claude."

Pam nervously stirred some iced-tea mix into a glass of water. "I think she's very upset. Please come out with me."

Greta looked amused and sat at the kitchen table. "Count me out."

"Please. I told her I understood. That means it's over. I really mean that. She looked a little weird."

It was just then that Greta noticed the bottle on the center of the kitchen table. It was shaped like the plastic container for her new vitamins at home. She picked it up and examined it. "Where'd you get these?" she asked Pam.

Pam put ice cubes in the tea. "Oh . . . those are some new vitamins that Charles is pushing. You know how he worries about his health and aging and all that crap. But now he insists that I take them along with him, three times a day no less."

Greta took the cap off the bottle thoughtfully, sniffing the contents, then taking out a few pills to examine them. They were white oval tablets, exactly like hers. "When did you start taking them?"

"Um . . . Sunday, I think. They're megavitamins, whatever that means. Come on, Greta, don't just *sit* there. I really need you!" Pam said, losing her studied cool for the first time.

Greta thought enviously how young Pam was; not even worried yet about aging. Vitamins . . . Greta had thought that Paul insisted on her taking them as a subtle hint that she was getting on . . . but Pam!

"I have the exact same ones," she mused aloud. "Paul's

esting them." She rolled two of them about in the palm of her hand reflectively.

"Please do me this one favor; don't leave me alone with her!" Pam pleaded.

Greta rose from the chair, absently putting the two pills in the pocket of her skirt. She took off her bikini top and put on a white silk shirt, not bothering to button it. "Okay, okay. You sure know how to ruin a lunch, Pam. I'm sorry you talked me into coming . . ."

"Sorry," Pam said, like a humbled child.

Greta opened the door to the patio for Pam, who was carrying a small tray with a glass of iced tea. They both stood a minute, dazed by the bright sun, and then both saw that Angelique was no longer by the pool at the table where she'd been sitting.

"I bet she left," Greta said. "That make you happy?"

"She's too polite . . ." Pam began.

Then they saw Angelique.

Characteristically, Greta was the first to take action. She unwrapped her skirt as she ran toward the pool and made a running dive to the center. Angelique was floating face down, her shoes weighting the lower half of her body. Angelique's body was heavy and limp, but Greta was strong and an excellent swimmer. Pam stood at the shallow end of the pool and helped Greta pull Angelique out and lay her on the flagstone. But then Pam stood there transfixed and had to be shouted at before she finally ran to call an ambulance. Greta applied expert artificial respiration, vigorously working on the flaccid body while the sirens sounded in the distance. Not until the rescue squad came and actually pulled her off, did she stop her furious efforts. Then she stood silently and watched while the ambulance team worked on Angelique.

The police followed shortly. They asked questions mostly of Pam. Officer Buford wanted to know whether Pam had any explanation, whether it was an accident or attempted suicide, whether Mrs. Santé could swim, and had there been any mood change or depression that preceded the incident. Pam slumped into a chair and answered tearfully, afraid of scandal, terrified that Angelique might not pull out of it. The police exchanged glances, and Officer Buford made a note in his report about another possible case of the new illness . . . Pam, for her part, wondered how this man, Jean-Claude, could be so important to Angelique. No man was worth that.

Greta stood stock still until finally the choking noises began and Angelique began breathing on her own. She thought how strange it all was; how very strange. Was it really for Jean-Claude that Angelique had attempted suicide? How extraordinary it must be to love someone that much. She thought of Daniel Lieberman, of the feelings that he'd stirred in her, feelings she would never express, of her envy of Laura—and suddenly she remembered his question: had Paul done or said anything unusual that past week? She forgot Angelique and reached slowly into her skirt pocket, where the two vitamin tablets still lay intact.

By the time Daniel left the conference and finished his hospital rounds, Emergency was beginning to fill up. The usually frosty Barbie Doll receptionist in the lobby was looking terrified. People were milling around like ants. A siren cut through the air announcing the arrival of Angelique Santé. Daniel stood at the glass doors a moment, looking back at a group of incoming patients, at the patrolmen accompanying them. He decided to leave immediately. Hayes, Nelson, and the rest would soon know what was happening down here. These first few cases now would convince them that they'd have to deal with reality. He and Bill Edwards would have to get some answers while they started to cope with the influx of patients. He began walking to the parking lot.

"Daniel!" Greta called after him.

He stopped. She was running toward him, mascara-streaked black smudges under her eyes, shouting, out of breath.

"Listen! Wait a minute," she called, approaching. "Where are you *going?* Angelique was just brought in."

"What happened?" he asked.

Greta hugged herself with her arms, trembling slightly and breathing hard. "She . . . jumped into the pool at Pam Vail's house. And she can't swim, I guess. She nearly drowned."

He stared at her, surprised that she was shaking. "I'm sure she'll be all right now, she's in good hands."

"But she tried to commit *suicide!* You know her, Daniel. She's so godawfully organized and controlled. My God, she's such a *lady*, you know what I mean? It wasn't like her at all to do something like that. I panicked. Then I remembered you asked me about Paul, about whether he had done anything unusual . . ."

"You remembered something?"

"Here," she said, putting two white oval tablets in his hand. " See, I just saw these at Pam's house. Let me explain," she said, biting her lip in an effort to regain control. "Last Sunday morning Paul was home for breakfast. *That's* really unusual in itself, you know I can't remember when I've had breakfast with him . . . but there he was! And I was kind of hung over from the Doughertys' party and I was having black coffee. Well you know he's a health nut, into physical fitness, jogging, and wheat germ. Always has been. But he never included *me* before. And he never waits to have breakfast with me. So last Sunday he put this bottle of *vitamins* on the table and said I should take them." Greta slowed down, and as she recovered her self-possession, her voice took on the familiar self-mocking sarcasm. "I thought right away they had to be slow-acting poison, because God knows he'd like me to die young. So why would he give me ordinary vitamins, right?"

Daniel shrugged impatiently. He was in a hurry. "Maybe you misunderstood him . . ."

"Hah! I thought immediately: he's trying to kill me. And then he took one himself. And he was kind of *solicitous*, if you can believe it, and he said we were going to take these things three times a day. I thought, Christ, I must look repulsive. Why this sudden concern for my health? Maybe he's only hated me all these years because I had a vitamin B12 deficiency, right? Well anyway, then he said he was *testing* this vitamin for some other company. A new product, but perfectly safe. I asked him if it had been through the ape contingent yet. He laughed. He never laughs at anything I say. He asked me to keep a record of how I felt and see if I didn't have more energy. He's been taking these things along with me."

Daniel looked thoughtfully at the pills in his hand. "And these vitamins Pam has are identical to yours?"

"Absolutely!" she said. "And she also started last Sunday."

Daniel looked at her closely. Greta seemed genuinely shaken, but he couldn't help wondering whether her story was a ploy to gain his attention—to be with him. He didn't want to hurt her feelings again. "I'm heading into the city now—to try and put some things together and get some answers fast. I promise I'll keep you posted, all right? Meanwhile, sit tight . . . Oh, and listen, thanks."

He got into his car and started the engine. Greta leaned over to the open window. "Would you take me with you?"

"I think you're better off here, Greta. Stick around home, though," he said gently. "It may get pretty rough in town."

Greta stood motionless. Her figure grew smaller and smaller in the rear-view mirror as he sped down the long hospital drive.

She watched with surprise as a maroon Dodge suddenly started up and left the parking lot in a cloud of dust. It had been so still, and she had been so involved in her recollection, that she had thought she and Lieberman were alone.

Paul McGinnis shook hands with Charles Vail. He picked up the bundles of cash and put them neatly into his attaché case. He kept his slight, superior smile. "I hope this doesn't inconvenience you, Charles. I appreciate it." He arranged the packets in the case. "I would have called ahead, but this trip came up so suddenly . . ." his voice faded out as if with boredom.

Vail sputtered a laugh. "No problem, no problem. I would have had it ready for you faster if you'd called. That's all. It's no problem. I hope you have a good trip!"

"I should be back Monday. Just a gambling junket you know, a once a year binge . . ."

"Really?" Vail said, his voice politely intrigued. A junket! "Well, I won't tell a soul. Las Vegas?"

Paul McGinnis closed his eyes briefly. "No . . . no. The Caribbean. I don't know it if's a good idea. It will probably be hot and boring. I'd probably be better off on the courts . . . well, why don't we make a game for next weekend anyway?"

Charles Vail smiled. A gambling junket was a preposterous explanation for the amount McGinnis had withdrawn. Besides he was too old-family rich and conservative to pull off such an excuse with any credibility. But two could play at that game. "You have a good time and come back with a bundle!" he said cheerfully. "Watch out for the young chicks."

Paul McGinnis snapped the locks, swung the case off Vail's desk. "Love to Pam," he said as he left the office.

The Jaguar XJS door was unlocked. He threw the case on the bucket seat beside him. He had parked in front of the bank on Main Street in a no-parking zone. Just as he put one leg in the silver car, he saw Lieberman coming around the corner in his Volks. He quickly got in and locked the doors with a push of a button.

Daniel Lieberman pulled up alongside and shouted at him. "I want to talk to you!"

With no perceptible change in his expression, McGinnis started his car.

"Stop!" Lieberman yelled.

This time, Paul McGinnis turned as if surprised, pushed a button on the center panel, and silently rolled his window down three inches. "Would you like my space?" he asked with a polite look on his face.

"I have to talk with you!"

"I'm really sorry, old man, but I have a plane to catch. Can it wait till Monday?" He looked at the street ahead of him.

Daniel Lieberman got out of his car and walked to the partially open window. "It can't wait," he said.

McGinnis allowed the window to slide down a bit farther. "I don't know what I've done to you, Dr. Lieberman, but you do seem to have it in for me, don't you?"

"I think you have the answers to a few questions. It's urgent. It's not a personal matter."

"Look, Lieberman, I'm on my way to a conference. I'll be back on Monday, and we'll get together then. I swear I haven't the vaguest idea of what you're talking about."

"Like hell you don't," Daniel exploded. "We've got a lot of sick people in town right now. It all traces back to your lab. You've got a responsibility!"

"You are making a scene on the main street of Sheffield. You're harassing and embarrassing me, Lieberman, and I won't stand for it."

The Jaguar's windows slid up, and the car simultaneously began to glide away from the curb.

"The Perrinis are dead!" Daniel Lieberman shouted. "They were in a car accident, you hear me? Your colleagues are *dead* . . . and they were never coming back here anyway, were they, McGinnis?"

McGinnis's chin was slightly raised and his eyes were on the road. The silver Jaguar XJS pulled away smoothly.

"I'm sorry to have forgotten this," McGinnis said casually, standing in Charles Vail's office a few minutes later.

He had reparked his car at the back entrance to the bank, left his hazard lights flashing, and now stood shaking his head, as if scolding himself, as he smiled at Vail. He took a white envelope from his breast pocket. "I forget things occasionally. Early senility I suppose."

Charles Vail stood looking at the bulky envelope with the

lumpy square shape in the center. "We're all forgetful when we're in a hurry," he said graciously as he rang for the vault clerk.

"I'll just stick this in my regular safe-deposit box."

Vail helped McGinnis through the tedious procedure quickly. Box 74. McGinnis opened it, dropped in the envelope, and pocketed the key.

"See you Monday!" McGinnis said.

"Place a bet for me," Vail replied, smiling. "Number eleven. That's how long Pam and I have been married . . ."

McGinnis nimbly descended the back steps of the bank. He took the other envelope out of his attaché case and placed it next to him on the front seat. He felt the duplicate tape inside it. This envelope was stamped. He'd mail it soon.

Charles Vail watched as the Jaguar sped away. Paul McGinnis had grace and charm. Extraordinarily bright, too. But he was no professional. Charles Vail had never fully approved of him. But now at least he had secured the tape. Now it was safe to move. There were advantages of using amateurs, especially those with conservative prep-school backgrounds and a certain American naïveté about banks. Vail sat at his desk and unlocked and pulled out the bottom drawer. He dialed the private telephone he kept there . . .

"NPI. Chameleon control."

Buzz, click. "Yes."

"I have the tape. There may be a duplicate. He's withdrawn a lot of money and seems about to cut out. I'd detain him if I were you."

Paul McGinnis turned onto his usual highway exit on the Merritt Parkway, where a public telephone stood at the back of the normally slow filling station. He immediately placed his call.

"NPI."

"Chameleon . . . I'm leaving town now, in case you missed my exit," he said quietly.

The voice on the other end sounded surprised. "What's the problem?"

It was that same strange voice, belonging to someone he had never met.

"The Perrinis were in a car accident. They're dead."

"Yes . . . I'm afraid that's true."

"If anything happens to me, I don't think you'll like the tapes and detailed protocols that will be found."

"McGinnis, we depend on you. Now I don't understand what you're talking about." The voice was patient.

"It's in epidemic spread now—and you're cutting loose."

"Use your common sense and don't panic. We have the situation well under control. We have people at the hospital now. We need your cooperation."

There was a silence.

"McGinnis, I'm telling you we're in absolute control of this whole problem. Now do us all a favor, yourself too, and go home. Wait out the weekend."

"Dr. Lieberman is on your tail . . . as for me, I'll make my own plans."

"Think about your family while you're at it—Billy, for example."

There was a click.

McGinnis smiled bitterly. They had left him little choice but to return to Sheffield.

Daniel Lieberman pulled off the West Side Highway on Ninety-sixth Street. He had sped to New York at fifteen miles over the speed limit. Because it was Friday, Bill was most probably at the midtown lab; but knowing his friend, he could just as easily be at home in the Village, writing and catching up on his reading. Not wanting to lose any time in backtracking, he decided to call from uptown. He drove down Broadway until he found a parking space near a pay phone. The Volks huffed an unhealthy sound as he cut the engine. He called Bill first at the lab. No, he hadn't come in, they said. He redialed Bill's home and waited fifteen rings.

"Bill? It's me. I'm in New York."

"Am I glad to hear your voice!" Bill answered warmly. "I was worried. You're all right?"

"Yes, I'm all right, don't I sound okay?"

"For you, maybe," Bill said jokingly, with obvious relief. "But I don't know how long you're going to feel that way when I show you the material I dug up on the Perrinis . . ."

"How about NPI?" Daniel asked hurriedly.

"Yes. Well how about NPI? It exists. It has an address in Chicago, a telephone number, but no one I've talked to seems to know what the company produces. In fact, no one's ever heard of it. Daniel—be careful."

"I'll be at your place in half an hour."

Daniel stopped at the bagel place a little farther down Broadway. It was going to be a long afternoon and he hadn't had breakfast or lunch. He left his Volks illegally close to a hydrant, lights flashing, calculating he'd only be in the shop a couple of minutes and he did have M.D. plates. The line moved quickly. He bought an assortment of pumpernickel, poppy seed, and onion bagels, salivating at the warm smell rising from the plain white bag. He paid and walked out.

The car wouldn't start. Daniel knew from the engine noises that the inevitable moment had arrived. He'd pushed the ancient vehicle too far on the open highway. He slammed the steering wheel with his fist. To fizzle out at a hydrant, what else? He'd get a ticket any minute. Then he saw a maroon Dodge, empty, parked adjacent to a hydrant on the opposite curb. That was some comfort, he wasn't the only one. But if they towed him, he'd have to pay to get the wreck back. Not much cash in his pockets. Most of it was in a cookie jar for Maia and household emergencies. Suddenly he realized he had taken off so fast he hadn't made any arrangements for Maia.

He got out of the car hurriedly, black bag in hand, and went to the corner telephone booth to dial. There were very few pedestrians out in the heat. Very few taxis. How the hell was he going to get to the Village fast?

He called collect to Mrs. Benedict and told her in capsule form where he was and what was happening. The "crazy sickness" rumors hadn't yet reached her, but he realized that the Benedicts were not really close to anyone—they were regarded as the town "radicals." He asked Mrs. Benedict to take Maia in if he didn't return as expected, by early evening, and he gave her Bill's telephone number . . .

Deciding the subway was fastest, he walked quickly to the station. He'd change for the express at Seventy-second and jog from Fourteenth to Perry. Save time. He sprinted down the stairs, white paper bag in one arm, black satchel in the other. A man rushed past him and Daniel's elbow caught the man in the stomach very hard. The guy was built like a quarterback. He turned angrily toward Daniel on the landing.

"I'm really sorry," Daniel apologized to the stranger facing him. He was in his twenties, well dressed, his seersucker jacket unwrinkled, his shoes shiny. "But you should watch where you're going."

Then the first blow came from behind. Daniel started to turn in pain and shock to see who had hit him, his reflexes ready for a fight. But as he moved, the man who had been facing him took his turn. This time the punch was to Daniel's diaphragm, and the air was knocked out of him. He doubled over, gagging; and the next blow came. It was to the back of his neck. It was all happening so fast he couldn't get a return punch in. Daniel fell to his knees and then both the men began kicking, slowly and deliberately. It registered, in his confusion, that they seemed too well dressed, their shoes too well shined. He managed to lunge forward and topple the man in front of him, then he kicked out furiously and flailed a few wild punches at the other. He tried to rise, but then came a brutal kick to his head. They weren't going to let him escape. This overwhelming realization drove out all other thoughts. Another hit. He felt his lip split, and as he fell backward onto the concrete, he tasted blood before everything went dark . . .

That evening as the brilliant red sun set, the empty streets of Sheffield and the deserted beach seemed peaceful except for the occasional sound of sirens screaming. Lights clicked on one by one as dinnertime ended, giving the external appearance of normality; of the special secure warmth of a small suburban town.

Many people, feeling dizzy, disoriented, and panicky, had called the police. The small force coped with false alarms as best they could, already beset with the actual cases that had swelled in number all afternoon. In fact, many of the cases were not new—they had simply been waiting for discovery. Families, now assured that their relatives had not suffered embarrassing breakdowns but had a "real' sickness, were finally willing to call for help.

Even with a full staff at the General, the treatment rooms would have been filled and the telephone lines jammed. But there was a ten percent absentee rate on the evening shift, due to fear and, in some cases, illness. Patients brought to the General were treated with Valium and sent home if there was someone to care for them there; others were given beds at the hospital, on a floor hastily set aside for the outbreak. The police used their vans and borrowed others from the Fire Department. They were rapidly becoming exhausted. At twilight, in many homes, people packed hurriedly to leave the infected area. On Main Street, in the darkening shadows, the usual crowd of teen-agers grew and grew. It had a menacing quality that disturbed the policemen riding by on their way to the hospital.

In the early evening, a meeting took place in Town Hall, which had been kept lit and open for the occasion. It had been scheduled that afternoon as evidence of a real crisis accumulated. Uninvited, worried citizens came in to listen. The auditorium was half full. A small committee sat around a conference table on the wooden platform at one end of the room.

"I'd like to remind our visitors, this is not an official meeting and our agenda is quite informal. I'll call first on our Health officer for a detailed report—Mr. Majeski," said Mr. Danielli, the president of the Sheffield Board of Health.

Mr. Majeski gathered his notes, looking more in command than at the General. "Ladies and gentlemen," he said formally to the small group with a passing nod to the public, "some very unusual and tragic events have taken place here in Sheffield this past week, and this morning we discussed at the hospital the possibility that they all have a common cause . . ."

He carefully outlined the situation to the hushed audience. "The big question," he concluded, "is how can the local board of health help out at this point. I want to turn to our vice-president, Mr. Hayes, for a medical update."

Hayes looked calmly around at the expectant faces. The secretary was ready with her steno pad. The town sanitarian, Mr. Hanks, who would soon be responsible for conducting whatever tests they could think up, was looking at him with a quizzical smile, as if he'd been told a bad joke. Next to him was the young, successful veterinarian, Dr. Hinsdale, repeatedly tapping his nails with his pencil. And there were Mrs. Williams, the dietician of the high school; Mrs. Feniman, of the Visiting Nurses Association; and the widow Mrs. Johnston, outspoken and brusque. Finally, Hayes noted unhappily, there was the crown of uninvited, scared-looking people who had somehow found out about the session. He cleared his throat to gain time. He could handle the crowd, he thought. His main job was to avoid inciting panic.

The police began moving the teen-ager's off Main Street at 9:00 P.M. No moon shone, and it was unusually dark. Every time a patrol car cruised down Main, the kids were shifted. But then they reassembled and continued to grow in numbers. The situation was increasingly explosive.

". . . so, finally, the question is," Hayes concluded quietly, "is this epidemiological survey going to be covered by our municipal budget?"

"Why don't you call the CDC in?" Mrs. Johnston interrupted very loudly. "I don't understand your position on that at all. First you tell us it's nothing, then it's a mystery virus that we can't control, and finally it's some unknown toxin!"

Mr. Danielli was pink with irritation. "Mrs. Johnston! All of you! We must allow the meeting to continue in an orderly way. We can always call in a federal agency. But Mr. Hayes explained to you that there is no reason to do so at this time. We don't even know that it is a communicable disease . . . all we have here are a few cases of behavioral changes, not even the same kind. We'll look like a bunch of dumb hicks calling in the CDC."

"I don't care what we look like!" a man shouted. "My cousin was killed in a car accident on Newtown this morning . . . car went into hers, out of control!"

"The CDC could come in here and cover all bases. Test what those college students have been dousing our trees with . . ." Mrs. Williams began.

An old man stood up in the audience. He looked frail, but interrupted in a harsh, gratingly loud voice. "You people shouldn't dismiss the possibility that Sheffield is being used as a model testing ground for a germ warfare experiment!"

His comment was met with general groans from all around him.

"Oh, for God's sake," his neighbor said.

"Wait a minute!" Hayes said, standing to gain attention. "So far, out of a hundred or so reported cases of this thing, I can't confirm a single one of them. A lot of people showed up today with symptoms that all turned out to be false alarms. Maybe we have a bunch of mass-hysteria cases, aggravated by heat . . ."

On the hospital floor set aside for isolation, the scene was eerie as the masked doctors, nurses, and attendants walked around the many extra beds, spaced at the minimum four-foot distance apart, and did their routine tasks in the subdued light. In the lobby, families and friends of the sick milled around asking questions of anyone who passed, spreading contradictory information among themselves. The receptionist was absent. No one was available to replace her. The now-littered corridors were in a state of chaos. Unsupervised children screamed and fought. A number of women sobbed noisily.

Meanwhile, two nurses decided that it was wise to stock up on Valium for their own families, and for profit. After their clandestine raid, the supply was found to be dangerously low. Larry Roberts was furious at his own inability to deal with the situation and at having been made a fool of by events. He kicked his locker door in anger and wondered where the hell Lieberman was holed up.

It took only five minutes for things to fall apart completely. The teen-agers stood very still on the corner. Then suddenly their hostile mood ignited, their tension erupted in whoops and roars as they raced up the street ramming in doors and windows. Alarms shrilled unheeded. Shattered glass covered the sidewalks. Some of the teenagers stripped the store mannequins of clothing and pulled the arms and legs off them, using them as clubs to smash display cases. Others took hi-fi equipment and sped off; the jewelry store was looted bare; so was Krantzer's Sporting Goods. They smashed their way into the ice-cream store, helped themselves, and smeared the rest on the walls. The box-office lady in the movie theater turned out her light and ran. The crowd took less than half an hour to go through Main Street like a swarm of locusts.

Daniel woke once in the night in the darkened ward of Roosevelt Hospital. His eyes ached painfully in the bluish light. He tested the ragged inside of his cheek with his tongue, wondering, semiconsciously, where he was. Even the effort of lifting his head caused him intense pain. He closed his eyes and slept again. Several yards from his bed, overhead, behind a partition, the television news flickered on, bringing information to the night staff:

"Sheffield, the model Connecticut town recently plagued by tragedy, has taken a surprise turn for the worse tonight. Rioting and looting have broken out on the normally tranquil Main Street. Before the small police department could summon aid, teen-agers had done an estimated three hundred thousand dollars worth of damage. Main Street is reported to be nearly impassable at this time, with shattered store windows and merchandise blocking the pavement. An angry mob has gathered on the village green in front of Town Hall. Our mobile team has been dispatched to the scene and we expect a report momentarily. Police Chief McLoughlin is not available for comment, but . . ."

Maia began crying softly when the rock came through the bookstore window, nearly hitting Sam Benedict. They had just locked the front door—Thursday was their regular late night—and had been preparing to leave.

"Let's all stay away from the windows," Sam said, guiding Laura and Maia to the back of the store.

There was a shout, and another rock came in.

"Sam, I really think we should all leave. You know the police are probably too busy to respond," Mrs. Benedict said.

"I'm not leaving my store. The rest of you go."

Maia shivered at the sound of Sam's voice. She watched the glow of his pipe in the darkness.

"Mother, you know Dad won't leave," Laura said gently. "If it would make you feel better, I'll take you over to Daniel's with us. He should be back soon."

"No, dear. I'll stay with Dad. But I'd feel a lot better if you took Maia over to her father's house immediately."

Maia watched the three grownups in the semidarkness, thinking that Mrs. Benedict sounded just as firm as Sam, although her voice was soft and gentle.

There were some shouts from the street and then the sound of glass breaking nearby.

"Laura, go along now," Sam said. "Just a couple of stones. Don't worry, Maia." Sam kissed her good night.

Maia took Laura's hand and they left silently through the back door, making for the van. Laura started the camp van without lights and didn't put them on till they were several blocks from Main Street. Then, when they got near Maia's, Laura doused the lights again. "Just to be on the safe side," she said. "With all these characters out breaking glass, I think we'd better pull the van into the garage."

"Daddy always leaves the remote-control switch under a rock for me when he's out, so it's easy to get to my bicycle. I'll get it."

They pulled in quietly and closed the garage doors behind them. Maia had the housekey on a chain around her neck and let them in through the door that opened into the kitchen from the garage. They sat in the kitchen awhile and had milk and cookies. Then they went upstairs. Laura told bedtime stories, and they sang softly. But to Maia, it felt like war.

McLoughlin's head ached as he dialed. He looked at the emptied gun on his desk; it was twice as large as he remembered and had an odd, vivid sheen. He had locked the bullets in a drawer and put the key in another room. Plowing through the night without the gun, battling the sick and the well, the insanity all around him, had certainly been enough to give him this confounded headache. He hadn't eaten or slept, either; hadn't even been home. But though he could go on telling himself that his bouts of dizziness and weakness were from exhaustion and that the headache was produced by tension, he was afraid that he might get worse before he acted. He took a Valium and dialed Jim Denton—the chief of police in Norfolk.

"It's me, Jim. My second call . . ."

"You all right? . . . I just saw the TV news. What the hell is going on there?"

"I think I'm getting sick, Jim. I need your help right now. I want you to take over for me . . . We have a real state of emergency here. It's not just the crazy sickness . . . It's panic, plain rotten out-of-the-woodwork behavior, and just everything falling apart. They're not all sick. We've got some squad cars from Summit and Harleyville, and the County boys, but it's not enough. I think we'd better have the town cordoned off, and the State Police in to take over."

"I'll get them . . . when do you want it cordoned off?"

"Immediately. Before too many more cars get in or out of here. We sure don't need everyone else's teen-agers coming in here and finishing off our stores for us, and besides, they'll risk getting infected. And we can't allow citizens out of here on the major highways, because some of them are incubating this thing and won't be able to control their cars . . . you wouldn't believe the number of auto accidents in town. We just have to keep our problems contained till we find a solution."

"I think I can convince the governor to act immediately."

"And, Jim, we need a whole lot of manpower, because my command isn't going to hold up much longer . . ."

"Look, you just stay put and don't worry. I'll get the National Guard if necessary. Promise me you'll take medication and you won't drive . . . just wait. I want to hear you say it."

"You got it. Thanks, Jim . . ."

Ned McLoughlin rested his head on the desk and let the next wave of dizziness take him.

# Friday, August tenth,

Daniel Lieberman's eyes flickered open and uncomprehendingly took in the blurred details of the strange objects around him . . . wrinkled white cotton under his right hand; the bandaged hand itself; across, in his line of vision, somebody's plaster foot cast raised up; overhead, the fluorescent squares flickering constantly. He could hear footsteps, the sound of a buzzer, heels sharp and moving fast on the linoleum flooring, a distant page. Slowly he turned his head, smelled disinfectant, urine . . . He was in a New York City hospital ward. But which one, and why?

The mugging. He winced as the memory hit him and his body ached all over. What the hell time was it? What day? He felt a rising panic in his gut and grew more alert, attempting to sit up. What was happening in Sheffield? Where was Maia? He had to get to a phone. He raised his shoulders up off the bed, leaning heavily on his left forearm, noting a constant dull ache in the back of his neck and an acute light sensitivity as he peered around. He needed information desperately, yet he could barely make out surrounding patients . . . his glasses. Obviously broken. He couldn't see the wall clock in the now visible nurses' station. He felt a huge wave of frustration, tried to breathe in the airless room, lay back down, and drifted into a dreamless sleep . . .

"Daniel, wake up! Daniel . . . wake up. Daniel." An insistent voice in his ear. "Daniel wake up."

He opened his eyes again, this time to see Bill Edwards's dark face near his own.

"Bill!" he rasped. "Get me out of here!"

"Take it easy."

"What time is it?"

"Just past seven in the morning, Friday. Not too bad, because you were due at my place yesterday afternoon," Bill said comfortingly.

"Where the hell am I?"

"Roosevelt Hospital. I finally figured out if you ran into trouble it was somewhere between Zabar's and Perry Street. Lucky for you, your bagel-maven habits narrowed the hunt."

Daniel turned his head sidewards and whispered. "Two thugs mugged me and left me for dead . . ."

"They must have thought you were a tourist," Bill replied jokingly, but his eyes were very troubled. "They really did a job . . . you're listed as John Doe around here. They took every piece of I.D. off you. Can you sit up?"

"I don't know."

"Who's the President of the United States?"

"Grover Cleveland. Cut the crap, Bill. You don't have to do a mental status test on me. I'm okay."

"You have a mild concussion and some superficial bruising, but you don't seem to be any dumber than before, so let's go."

Daniel squinted at Bill to focus his expression clearly. "But first I have to get to a telephone . . . I have to call home right away!"

Bill gripped Daniel's arm firmly and began to pull him up as he spoke in a level, quiet voice. "I called. Maia's fine. Normally, in your condition I wouldn't let you move one inch out of bed, my friend, no matter what you said. We'd just sit right here while you filled me in. But I just went through seven miles of red tape downstairs for you. Now that they know we're both doctors and that I'm taking you home with me, I'm getting you sprung *immediately*, and we're going straight to my place and you can call home from there."

Bill had managed to get him to a sitting position, but Daniel felt too weak to talk. When he breathed deeply, his ribs hurt.

"There you go. Now, when you stand up, you just be slow and steady and don't mess up, we've got to get you out of here. Let's not have you fall over and give the floor nurse second thoughts, because she's watching. Are you going to make it?" Bill asked, standing him up.

". . . I feel like a large bruise. A little dizzy, too . . . If Maia's okay, why do you want me out of here so fast?" He looked down and noticed an elasticized bandage on his ankle. His own bandage was still on his infected big toe.

Bill was getting his clothes together. "Let me put it this way, Daniel. You were fine when you were John Doe. But, baby, if I can find you, so can they."

"Yeah?" Daniel answered, groggy with the effort of dressing. "Who's they?"

"I'll tell you about 'they' later. Just hold on to me now."

The minute Daniel walked into Bill's apartment on Perry Street, he felt better. Bill gave him a careful bear hug and asked him if he'd like coffee.

"God, yes. And a phone. And an explanation!"

He looked around the apartment, still in a state of comfortable disrepair, cluttered with pillows, plants, papers, and masses of medical and scientific books and journals. Bill eased Daniel down on the couch and pointed to the phone on the low table. "There you go. How about some food, too? They didn't even let you eat your bagels."

Daniel smiled as Bill disappeared into the small kitchen and his jaw gave a painful twinge, reminding him of why he was there. What the hell had Bill meant by all that stuff about 'they can find you'? It was Maia who answered the phone when he called his house.

"Hi, honey, it's Daddy."

"Daddy! What happened?"

"I'm in New York at Bill Edwards's apartment. Everything okay?"

"I guess . . . Bill called before . . . lots of bad things are happening in town."

"But are you all right? And Laura?"

"Oh, we're fine."

"Could I speak to her a second, honey?"

"She's still sleeping. We got to bed *very* late. You want me to wake her up?"

"No, no . . . it's not that important. Just write down this telephone number for her. You have a pencil?"

"Yes, Daddy, but I know Bill's number by heart. It's WA 4-2049."

"Good. But write it out for Laura, all right? And if you need to dial, remember to dial 212 first."

"Oh, Daddy," she reprimanded him, "I know that. Are you coming home soon?"

"Yes, soon as I can. Now don't you go out meanwhile, all right? Lock the doors, and stay right where you are. That goes for Laura, too, when she gets up. I'm sure you'll find something for lunch in the house . . ."

"There's peanut butter and jelly and V-cillin."

"Delicious. This is your last day, isn't it?"

"Yep . . . see you later. Daddy? Someone threw a rock at Sam Benedict."

Daniel's breath caught, but he tried to keep his voice normal. "Is he all right?"

"Yes, he's fine. They didn't hit him. They were breaking glass on Main Street."

"Well, just at the moment some people aren't acting the way they normally do, honey, that's why I want you indoors."

"I promise."

"Anything else?"

"Nooo . . . but I miss you. I don't want anyone to throw a rock at you. I told Bill that when he called before."

Daniel laughed and felt a sharp pain in his ribs. "Don't worry about me, honey. I'll see you soon."

Billy McGinnis stood with balanced grace on the very top of the side turret of the Lanes' beach house. It looked like rain. Billy did not notice the wet, gray air or the sea gulls swooping fast over the silver water. He just saw with intense pleasure the brilliant chalk-white cupola on which he stood gripping the smooth round sides with his wonderful taloned feet. He had begun his journey upward by crawling a tall, forbidden rock, and then had scaled a trellis, helped by his new agility and keen vision. He had looked three stories up from down on the scrub grass and seen the scalloped etching in the weathered turret and the painted white cupola, textures clear and sharp, as if viewed through binoculars. He had decided then to stand at the top: to see everything! And now, after his climb, he had finally reached the summit.

A small group of people watched helplessly from the beach. Greta had been hurriedly called, and stood there in her kerchief and sunglasses looking up at the small figure. Attempts to reach the Fire Department had been to no avail; they did not answer their telephone. One man had attempted the long climb up the outside of the beach house but had given up. Greta was calling Billy's name, but the child did not respond with even a glance.

Billy looked down again with a thrill of delight as he inspected his exquisite talons, roughened golden wonders with flecks of ruby-red on the cruel, curving claws. He took a deep breath, stirring his new, brilliant green and azure-blue iridescent feathers. His gawky little body, that had been the object of so much scorn and teasing, had miraculously changed. How long ago had his transformation begun? It didn't matter.

His mind was clear on the now marvelous being he had become; the powerful bird creature that could fly anywhere! He shrugged his back muscles where his new wide wings began and he breathed deeply again, getting bigger and bigger as the earth grew small and distant. He laughed loudly, but the sound was a fearful screech. He threw back his head and laughed again. Then he took off over the water.

There were shrieks from the onlookers, but Greta was silent. She briefly raised one arm in front of her face, and then ran forward toward the small still figure in the sand.

Bill Edwards came back into the living room at the apartment on Perry Street balancing two mugs of coffee and a sandwich. "Everything still all right at home?"

"Yes, but apparently not in town . . ." Daniel said, looking at him questioningly.

"I know," Bill said gently. "Your hometown had some bad press last night . . ." He filled him in on the details. "You must feel like Rip Van Winkle; a lot of things happened while you were out."

Daniel looked thoughtfully at Bill. "What did you mean before about my not being safe and all that? Is that related to what happened?"

Bill smiled ironically, his head tilted to one side. "Later, later. Now we're just going to talk. You're safe here; nobody knows my name . . . First off, I checked out the Perrinis for you. I had met them personally a while back. They looked like two eggs, right?" Bill's smile broadened and, over his coffee cup, his eyes twinkled with amusement. "That was not a racist comment. I really meant they looked like eggs with glasses, right?"

"Right."

"Eat, please. I know it hurts when you chew . . . but eat. Anyway, would that the Perrinis had been as harmless as they appeared. Some of their work is fairly well known, but some is a little harder to find. To make a long story short," Bill said, finishing his coffee with a gulp and leaning forward intently, "I found a citation for a paper of theirs in an obscure journal—the subject being the genetics of certain biochemical pathways of tissue-cultured cells of an Amazonian plant called *Tetrapteris*. Oddly, that issue of the journal was 'missing' when I tried to see it, so I don't know *which* pathways. Anyway, Daniel, that was their last research project before Sheffield."

Daniel looked puzzled, waiting for Bill's explanation. "Can you make anything of that?" he asked finally.

"No, not by itself. But the *Tetrapteris* species are vines and trees that contain powerful macroptic hallucinogens. They distort reality and produce incredible visions."

Daniel munched on the cream cheese-and-jelly sandwich thoughtfully. "That's suggestive. But chemical hallucinogens aren't contagious, and we've already decided that this is an infectious disease. I had an idea," Daniel went on, feeling groggy, "that perhaps they were culturing an oddball viral material . . . some laboratory mutant strain."

Bill was listening, but had a faraway look in his eyes.

"Bill, you think the Perrinis' being in South America before coming to Sheffield has something to do with the situation? I don't understand the connection with the *Tetrapteris* . . ."

Bill focused sharply and suddenly on Daniel. "You're still the one who interests me, Daniel," he said, pointing his finger. "Let's start with you. You telephone me and tell me you're treating a sick girl. Then her nurse gets sick and the librarian gets sick and you're in contact with *all* of them, but you stay on your feet. Why?"

Daniel shrugged. "Being a pediatrician, I'm exposed to just about everything . . ."

"I know you guys never get sick, but forgetting that terrific immune state, I wonder if anything else accounts for your walking blithely through the center and staying healthy. What makes you different?"

Daniel shook his head. "Search me. I've thought about that since Dr. Singh got sick, and another nurse named Miss Manderson, who had relatively minor contact with Wendy . . ."

"Maybe you *caused* this mysterious virus. You said it didn't start till after you arrived in town. Maybe it wasn't the lab . . . maybe you're typhoid Mary," Bill said in baiting tones, crossing his arms, waiting for a reaction.

Daniel recognized Bill's technique for unjamming his thought processes with an unexpected remark, for jarring him into rethinking, rerouting information. They had done it often enough, and it still worked. He felt himself stimulated to alertness and concentration on the problem, and he fought the grogginess and the pain. Suddenly, he sat up straight. "Hey! Where's my jacket?"

"Here," Bill said, holding up the folded torn jacket.

"Look in the inside pocket . . . they were so small, I put

them in tissue inside . . ." Daniel said, watching Bill anxiously as he fumbled through the torn pocket. "I hope they're still there."

"These?" Bill asked, putting the two white oval tablets on the coffee table.

"Yes!"

Bill examined them without expression. "Speak to me."

"Greta McGinnis, the wife of the lab owner, gave those to me yesterday, right before I left town. She said she'd been told they were experimental wonder vitamins. That McGinnis gave them to her last Sunday. But she'd just discovered that her friend Pam Vail was also taking them, and *also* started last Sunday. I don't know what they are, Bill, but last Sunday was the first day McGinnis could have known for sure that Wendy or anyone was sick because of the lab break-in. There has to be a link. Maybe this pill is an antitoxin, something he made to protect himself and his family—although I don't see the Vail connection."

"These tablets have a manufacturer's name on them, and a number . . ."

"Yeah. She said he told her he was testing them for another outfit."

"It's a standard product," Bill said. "That doesn't make any sense."

Daniel peered at the pills. "I don't recognize them. I don't use them in my practice."

"Let me find my PDR . . . it's here somewhere," Bill said, tossing pillows and papers from the bottom shelf of a bookcase, foraging through tumbling volumes. He picked up a thick blue book and dusted it off. "This is it, but just hope it isn't anything new, because this *Physicians' Desk Reference* is from my practicing days . . . Look, here's the product identification section. Look at all these pills, will you?" he said as he held a tablet up against the colored illustrations. "Let me get the right manufacturer . . . let's see . . . Lakeside, Lederle, Len-Tag . . . here we go! . . . Ready for this one, Daniel? It is not a vitamin. It is five hundred milligrams, that's eight hundred thousand units, of good old potassium penicillin-V!"

They were silent.

"One hell of a big dose three times a day, isn't it, Bill?"

"Yeah, from what you told me, this lady could be taking treatment for venereal disease."

"And her friend, too?"

Bill raised his eyebrows. "Isn't it a swinging crowd up there?"

"Shit!" Daniel said, sitting bolt upright. "Wait a minute, wait a minute, shit! Of course. I've been on penicillin for my toe. I'm still wearing the bandage, for Christ's sake. I haven't been able to shake it . . . and the children!" He slapped his forehead with his bandaged hand, not even noticing the pain. "The children . . . nearly all of them. No wonder Roy Dougherty didn't get it. Damn. Thank the Lord for small blessings, you know? If we hadn't had a strep epidemic, why even Laura . . ." He stopped, looking suddenly anxious. "I'm not sure they're all still on medication . . ."

"Penicillin!" Bill said, and began to pace. He strode vigorously around the room as Daniel craned his aching neck to follow him. Bill's pacing charted the progress of his thoughts like an oscilloscope tracing. He began taking short, rapid strides. "So that means we're probably dealing with a bacterial infection, not a viral one. No virus is sensitive to penicillin. All right. All *right!* Now we have this high-powered dude McGinnis spooning himself and his wife some penicillin after a break-in in his lab. And we have the Perrini team in a P3, a recombinant lab . . . to say I don't like this would be a gross understatement . . . the whole thing gives me chills in my coccyx . . ." Bill finally stopped in front of Daniel, looking grim. "You're lucky you stuck with babies, man. They give you hope. This adult stuff gives you terror in your bones, you know?"

Daniel had never seen Bill so agitated. He waited patiently for Bill to continue.

"All right!" Bill finally said, holding one hand up. He sat down and spoke quietly at first. "What we have to date, in its right chronological order, is that first, the Perrinis are in a P3, and then, the P3 gets ripped off and the kids who did it get sick. The symptoms of this sickness are disorientation and violent or bizarre or withdrawn behavior. Each different. Then, one by one, with thirty-two to forty-eight-hour incubation periods, contacts come down with the sickness, and finally, we now have good reason to believe the thing can be prevented or cured with ordinary penicillin! That's all we need to know but for one fact," Bill said, pulling his chair in closer. "One ineluctable, alarming fact: every test came back normal, no white-cell rise, no nothing, and yet we're talking bacterial infection . . . Daniel, how much do you know about recombinant DNA?"

"Basics . . . I haven't kept up. Tell me simply, please. Pretend I'm a first-year medical student."

"You see, we're not talking your ordinary everyday bacterium. We're talking about a synthesized man-made monster that your friendly neighborhood lab cooked up to drive people out of their skulls!" Bill stood and paced, gesticulating to drive home his points. "First of all, we have a bacterial host, right? In recombinant work, a lot of stuff has been done to date with a nice innocent intestinal bacterium named *E.coli*, because it's well understood and easy to grow. My guess here is, if you're right about respiratory-route spread, and I believe you are, that they went for another quiet, laid-back bacterium that the body recognizes and accepts as normal. I think that they found their baby in the lining of the throat and nasal passages . . . *Strep viridans*. Been with all of us from birth, not the kind that causes strep throat, mind you, just a real quiet one that gives no hassle to the system—no white-count changes. In short, a bacterial host that any asshole would know is too dangerous to use even in a P3 or P4, if they cared!"

Daniel braced himself. "So they use the *Strep* as a host. For what? What did they do to the *Strep viridans?*"

Bill's voice was clean and cold as a scalpel, and his words were precise. "They snipped a small piece of DNA material and inserted it into the genetic DNA material of *Strep viridans*. And what was that little added piece of DNA? It was a string of genes from *Tetrapteris*—genes that give instructions for making natural hallucinogenic substances in the plant."

"Wait a minute, Bill. You mean they can insert plant genes into bacteria and still have them work as if they were back in the plant?"

"Where have you been, Daniel? Any species DNA can be added to any other, it doesn't matter a darn; they all use the same chemical code. Oh, there are technical problems, but not insurmountable ones. Once the DNA is isolated from cells in tissue culture, which I remind you the Perrinis *had* done before, they simply trim it with restriction enzymes, figure out the part they want, and shove it into the nucleus, tacked on to the bacterium's own genes. Then happy birthday! We have something new in the world! We have a rapidly multiplying man-made bacterium that lives among all the other cells in the back of the throat, absolutely unnoticed! The cell *looks* exactly like its neighbors. Just another *Strep viridans*. But it's a wolf in sheep's clothing. It's got those plant genes in it. And the cell goes unrecognized for what it is; the body accepts it as a normal inhabitant, and that's why no temperature, no elevated white count with this little baby. Uninterrupted, it goes on doing its thing, producing hallucinogens, because that's what it's programmed to do, see? They get absorbed into the bloodstream. And within forty-eight hours anyone who's victim to this recombinant cell is going to be crawling the walls!"

Daniel closed his eyes and sighed deeply. He could empathize now with Hayes's disbelief; the thing was so incredible he had trouble believing it himself. "So it's the victim who's manufacturing his own hallucinogen. No wonder each case is so different . . . different underlying personality, different time course, different quantity. Why the violence, do you think?"

"You have to picture this stuff pouring into your bloodstream in greater and greater quantities . . . something like an increasing dose of LSD. Only the thing is, in this situation, the victim didn't do anything to initiate it and isn't emotionally prepared for it. And then it hits, slowly at first, but soon in massive quantities—crazy visions, loss of time sense, strange sensations, maybe voices. If there were violence already *in* a personality, this could bring it out. Anyway, even with an ordinary acid trip, you can't predict any individual reaction; you are dealing with the unconscious mind. You know something? That must be what they wanted. Highly individualistic reactions. Much harder to trace. That must have been a priority for them."

"Who's them?"

Bill shrugged.

Daniel spoke flatly. "McGinnis must have given Louise Garner penicillin when she got sick. He's known right along. . . . What's the hallucinogen? Not LSD. We tested for that."

"No. I looked up *Tetrapteris* yesterday. It's full of active compounds. Alkaloids: harmine, DMT, *B*-carbolines—we'll probably never know—not easy to analyze for them."

Bill had walked restlessly to the window and now peered out for a moment, thinking. He turned. "In my field, I live very close to recombinant DNA research these days . . . some of it's constructive, I suppose, although I'm not sure. But the technology is available to anyone. This puts poor old Frankenstein and his monster in the pre-nursery class. But it fits everything you told me. I wish it weren't so, but clinical evidence plus the Perrini papers and the antidote . . . it all adds up to one recombinant monstrosity."

Daniel put his bandaged hand over his eyes, still trying to take it in, to understand. "But . . . Jesus, *why?* Why the hell is anyone doing this kind of project anyway . . .?"

Bill's face tensed, and he looked strained and older. He sat down on the edge of the couch. "It could of course, be some multinational pharmaceutical outfit working through your local lab. They do most of the recombinant research. And nobody knows their motives; they've always operated clandestinely and outside the law—look at the death camp I. G. Farben ran in Nazi Germany. But my guess is that this is a government baby . . . some of our own intelligence people playing spy games—dirty tricks . . . I don't know, Daniel, this recombinant material is basically untraceable. Makes it very attractive."

"But, Bill, as a germ-warfare tool, it's pretty unimpressive. I know Sheffield is in bad shape, but still, only one tenth or less of the population's been affected. This wouldn't knock a city out of commission."

"Suppose only one person was the target?" Bill said, pacing back and forth. "What would be your chance of figuring out what was going on? Suppose they wanted to discredit one important person, maybe at a large public gathering or on TV, without being traced. Everyone would think the guy had flipped out; his own cronies would immediately dump him."

"Yeah . . . but how would they keep it from spreading?"

"They couldn't, the way it is now. But that's just it. They didn't plan the P3 break-in. This isn't a test, it's an accident. Maybe their plan was to reduce infectivity and administer it to the target in one massive dose . . . there's no way of telling."

Daniel let his breath out slowly and picked up the telephone receiver. "I'd better get hold of Hayes. But I don't know, Bill . . . if they didn't believe me before, I think my credibility gap has just broadened."

All circuits were busy, the operator said. Finally he put the call through as an emergency, but the hospital switchboard disconnected him twice. He began perspiring heavily under his bandages.

"I can't get through to Hayes. It must be chaos at the General . . . my best bet is Dr. Cameron . . ."

The elderly retired pediatrician answered after many rings, apologizing for being out in the garden. But Daniel was relieved that the reclusive life and habits of his predecessor had prevented him from becoming infected.

". . . I see on television they have us cordoned off," Cameron said calmly. "I was thinking of heading over to the General in a bit to see if I could lend a hand."

"I'm in New York, Dr. Cameron," Daniel said, trying to keep the alarm out of his voice. "I'm on my way home, but I have some extremely urgent requests, and I'm going to ask you to help me out. I can't reach Hayes at all."

"I'm glad to be of help, Daniel."

"I'm going to ask you to do these favors without going into detailed explanations now . . . this illness that's going around Sheffield is bacterial, it's responsive to pencillin. I want you to go to my home and administer penicillin to Laura Benedict, a large dose. Go also to Graham Hodson and see if he's all right. If not, give him the same dosage. And bring Valium with you. Be prepared for strange behavior. Then go directly to the General and give Wendy Dougherty penicillin; she's a primary case, and if we can pull her out of it, and *if* she remembers anything, she may tell us something of its origin tomorrow . . ."

"I'll do all you said, but I'd like to know more about this. If you can divulge a bit more, I'd be interested . . ."

The line went dead.

Daniel pushed the buttons on the top of the phone several times. "Sheffield phone lines are all messed up," he said.

"Yeah?"

"I'll give it a minute and then try Hayes again."

Bill sat down opposite him, looking grim. He picked up the receiver and held it to his ear. "This line's stone cold, my friend."

Daniel stared at him, disbelieving.

"They must've had me bugged since I did the first toxin tests . . . now it all makes sense. Why it was so fucking hard to get info on the Perrinis . . ."

"Bill, these people you call 'they'—you think they tried stopping me yesterday?"

Bill smiled crookedly. "At the obvious risk of being told I read *The Village Voice* too much, I think they're out there right now. It's easy knocking out an apartment phone if you already have the basement lines marked . . . shit! You told Maia you were here, right?"

"Only about half an hour ago."

"Fast. They must want to stop you pretty badly, Daniel."

"Why?"

"Now they know you know."

"Why wouldn't they want me to stop the spread?"

Bill paced. "It occurs to me that they're still covering their tracks, man. They are playing for time."

"The lab!"

"Yeah . . . look, Daniel, maybe I should go to that lab alone. You're in no shape."

"Damn it all, Bill, I'm going too. I've got to get home right away . . . Maia's still on medication, but I'm not sure about Laura or some of the kids—they may have finished."

"How about we try a neighbor's telephone to the General first?"

"No, let's go! Hayes can wait another hour."

"Okay, okay, say no more." Bill went into his bathroom and came back with a bottle of pills. "Before you go, physician heal thyself. Two penicillin tablets for each of us, and the bottle for the road. We're not walking around Sheffield without protection."

Daniel swallowed the pills, put what was left of his jacket over one arm, and started for the door, limping. "Later, we'll hit the lab and confront McGinnis. If he isn't there, we'll crack his fucking safe."

"Sure, Superman. Fine. Will do. But first, you think you can get down the stairs? We may have a time getting to my car. Let's just hope they're afraid of disturbing the Village peace!"

*Another phone receiver was lifted in answer to a ring. The man listened for a few moments in silence, then:*

*"He said* if *she remembers anything."*

*He listened again for a moment.*

*"All right then."*

*He hung up.*

Laura was lying on her back on Daniel's bed, undisturbed by the morning light. It was drizzling lightly outside now. She lay stretched out on the blue cotton spread, one arm flung back behind her head, her hair floating out over the pillows, her lips parted. She had been asleep for ten hours and showed no signs of waking. From time to time, her eyelids fluttered, her breath quickened, and her head tossed from side to side, but the two times Maia had looked in on her, she had not stirred.

* * *

As Laura slept on, a constant and deadly microscopic ctivity was ocurring. There, in the membrane-lined crevices f the nose and throat, in the profound darkness, lived ountless millions of firm-walled spheres: bacteria. A light iicroscope could have revealed them. They were scattered ke subterranean dust along the surfaces of the living caves. ome were separate, others were grouped together in chains, ke strings of beads: *Streptococcus viridans*.

Every few hours, each sphere would develop a constriction hrough its center, pinch itself in half, and there would be wo spheres. And every now and then, for no obvious reason, sphere would die and disintegrate and its fragments would e scavenged by the wandering white blood cells, much arger than the spheres and capable of movement.

Squeezing through the pores of the capillary blood vessels hat ran like a network of trails through the microscopic andscape, the white cells would pick up debris and engulf lien bacteria, but they left the living spheres alone. These pheres were permanent residents, normal, harmless; cells ike these had been present in the body since shortly after irth. They were not to be attacked.

However, although the white cells could not distinguish mong them, all the little spheres were not alike. In isolated atches, clumps of the *Streptococcus viridans* were subtly lifferent. Even the most sophisticated electron microscope ould not have detected the difference; but they had been ltered by man. The double-stranded spiral of their very enes had been altered, snipped in two—and a string of genes from an unnamed Peruvian species of vine of the genus *Tetrapteris* had been inserted.

Steadily, with remarkable speed, the altered bacteria copied and translated the double spiral of instructions, making from it the vital components of their walls, membranes, and protoplasms. And they copied and translated the *Tetrapteris* genes also, for they were written in the same universal code. They automatically produced the unfamiliar kind of molecule that the alien genes told them how to make, even though it was of no use to them. And when large numbers of these molecules had accumulated in the altered spheres, they began passing through outer bacterial membranes and walls, escaping to the surrounding human tissues. Some of the unfamiliar molecules found their way through the pores of the capillary vessels and were swept, along with the blood, to all parts of the body, including the brain.

Laura moaned in her sleep, her hands clenched, drops of sweat on her smooth forehead. She tossed her head back and forth, stifling a groan.

Maia opened the door again and, pushing her glasses back on the bridge of her nose, stared curiously at Laura. She stood awhile, solemnly wondering if Laura was having a bad dream. Then she tiptoed to her father's bed and sat next to Laura for a little while. She touched her friend's hand lightly. Laura's eyes fluttered open and she fixed her gaze on Maia. Maia stared back at her, puzzled, for Laura's eyes were wide with terror.

In her first waking moment, Laura was aware that the room was unfamiliar. The proportions and size of everything had radically altered and continued to change before her eyes with a kinetic energy that thrust new shapes and colors at her with breathtaking speed, as if the room itself were alive. And in front of her was a nightmarish creature. Its face was huge, menacing, and lustrous; its mouth horribly distorted. Behind it was a spinning and dissolving background of melting, lurid hues. Laura edged away, propped on her elbows, and the grotesque face bobbed at her like a carnival freak. Tears came to her eyes. She was rigid with fear and began to feel as if she were suffocating. An ominous red glare, shot through with flashes of gold, filled the room. She extended her arms toward the monster, palms outward, as if banishing it from her view, and as she did, there was a sudden shrill noise that shattered the colors. A scream. It jarred her senses. For a split second, as if some other reality had clicked into place with the speed of a camera shutter, the room stopped spinning and she saw a little girl cowering at the foot of the bed. Maia was screaming! Laura swallowed hard with terror. The creature was only a child, a friend. Oh my God, she thought in that instant, I am sick. I am sick . . . Then she lost consciousness.

At the corner of Main Street, Dr. Cameron was waved back impatiently by a patrolman. He rolled down his car window. "I have to pick up some medicine at the drugstore," he said.

"I'm sorry. No cars allowed in there . . ."

"I'm a doctor. I have M.D. plates."

"Sorry, Doctor. This street is too dangerous for cars."

"May I leave my car with you and walk there?" Cameron asked.

"Suit yourself," the patrolman said reluctantly. "But hurry, please. I can only watch it a little while."

Dr. Cameron took his black bag with his own small supply of penicillin and syringes and started briskly down Main Street. It was drizzling on the ruins of the street, and the scene shocked him profoundly. A dump truck fitted out with loudspeakers moved slowly up the center of the street like a tank, its heavy tires bumping over pipes, fragmented merchandise, and broken glass. Its speakers blared monotonously: "All citizens stay indoors today. All citizens stay indoors today. No unauthorized persons on the street. No private vehicles are permitted for the next twenty-four hours. Repeat, only vehicles with special permits allowed. Stay in your own homes until you have received further instructions. All citizens . . ."

The truck lumbered on like a prehistoric beast, and the sound gradually faded. No one on Main Street was listening, and the three or four policemen guarding the undamaged stores were not enforcing the curfew. The store owners walked gingerly around, picking up pieces of merchandise, writing on pads of paper, talking softly to each other. Some wept. Other people sat in the rubble, unresponsive to the truck or the store owners. A few of their faces were familiar to Dr. Cameron. They were neighbors. Most were oddly dressed, some in wrinkled and dirty clothing, and some in nightclothes. Their expressions varied, but none of them looked sane.

He reached the drugstore and saw that it was a total shambles. All the shelves had been swept clear of prescription medicines—the floor was awash with glass, trampled tablets and capsules, and puddles of sticky, colored liquids. The pharmacist was not there. He would have to pick up his supplies at the General.

"NPI."

"Chameleon."

Buzz. Click.

"McGinnis, where are you?"

"Your surveillance lax this morning?"

"We're doing all we can to minimize the damage without revealing ourselves. We can't post our men and advertise. Anyway, we've been advised that serial passage *in vivo* will eventually attenuate the material, and it will peter out without intervention."

Silence.

"My son died this morning," McGinnis said.

There was an almost imperceptible metallic click on the line.

"Oh . . . I'm . . . very sorry. Very sorry." The voice was shaded with an uncertain edge now.

"My son jumped from a roof. He was ten years old. I believe he was under the impression he could fly," McGinnis continued in a cool voice.

"As I said, I certainly am very sorry . . . it's a terrible thing. What are you planning to do now, McGinnis?"

"I'm leaving."

"Where are you now?"

"I'm certain you've traced this call already."

"You've just suffered a severe personal trauma, I know. But you must try to listen and understand. We can't have anything endanger a matter of national security."

"How long do you think I'll stand here on the side of the highway in open range?" McGinnis interrupted in an oddly lethargic voice.

"Listen to me. You'd better pull yourself together now. That reaction was paranoid. You telephoned yesterday, McGinnis, and were instructed to stay home. If we had wished you any harm whatsoever, you wouldn't be standing there now . . ."

"How far are you going to let the epidemic spread before you find a way to let the public know what's going on?" McGinnis asked in a neutral voice, as if checking the correct time.

"We don't anticipate further spread. Sheffield's cordoned off. Frankly, I don't know how you got out."

"What are you waiting for?"

"The material's contained and we're going to introduce antibiotic dosage on a mass scale through the central water supply system."

"There isn't enough antibiotic in the country to dose the water supply system, and even if there were, half Sheffield is on private wells. Who are you trying to kid?"

"Look, McGinnis . . ."

"Never mind. I called to say that I have a bag full of money, a supply of antibiotics, no car, and all the Chameleon material."

"We collected the material on Wednesday."

"What you collected was a half-dozen vials of ordinary

bacterial cultures and some sealed vials of a lyophilized powder which is Fleischmann's yeast. You can bake a cake with it."

The uncertain voice on the other end was guarded and less steady now, and if McGinnis had intended to taunt the listener or derive any pleasure from his fear, he would have enjoyed this small victory. "McGinnis . . . let's try to meet and discuss this one-on-one. We can work together. We can cover our traces and go on from here. That's the bottom line. We have huge respect for your ingenuity, McGinnis . . . Don't be a fool."

A shadow of a smile played on McGinnis's lips. "You respected the Perrinis too? Poor bastards . . . you'll have to find me first."

McGinnis hung up and carried his traveling bag out onto the wide border of grass at the edge of the highway. He struck a casual pose at the low fence, as if he were leaning on the net post of his own tennis court. A man who looked like Paul McGinnis was a no-risk pickup. It would be assumed that a well-dressed businessman hitching near a gas station had had some difficulty with his own car. He surveyed the cars speeding past and stuck out his hand, thumb pointed in the direction of traffic. His eyes were searching and intense, totally incongruous with the casual posture. The telephone call had taken just under three minutes, and the odds were great against deploying an agent here too quickly . . . unless he had been followed. He would be careful.

Hitchhiking was new to McGinnis. Cars passed his raised hand, and he considered alternatives. He could call a taxi, go to the next town, call another, then hitch from a safer location. But a taxi would take time in coming.

He hadn't had to make that NPI call. Whether it had been a sporting gesture or a form of suicide was something he did not ponder. He had wanted to make it. And now, as cars hurtled by, an unfamiliar panic began to glimmer in his eyes, and he found himself gritting his teeth. One car slowed down, or seemed to, but then, as McGinnis turned, it picked up speed and went on without him. He considered and rejected the idea of recovering his own car from the place he had abandoned it—too dangerous. Two, three, four minutes passed. Finally, there was a car—an old Plymouth station wagon slowly cruising down the right-hand lane, near him. His ride. The car wobbled to a halt.

He peered at the driver and felt his tensed muscles relax.

He was a short, squarish old man, barely able to see over the wheel. Next to him sat his wrinkled little wife, smiling out the open window at McGinnis. No air conditioning. McGinnis felt an odd mixture of irritation and relief. It would be a hot, boring trip.

In the back seat was the rest of the extended family, down to a baby on the lap of a young, slightly retarded-looking mother, who did not smile. A small quiet dog, some sort of a mutt, lay wilted in the middle of the back seat. The young mother had dark, semicircular sweat stains on her pale shirtdress. The baby whimpered, and a smell of vomit wafted through the open window. The young father didn't look up. McGinnis opened the front door, and the old woman moved to the center.

"New York?" the driver asked with a sharp appraising look at McGinnis's clothing.

"Yes," McGinnis said. "My car broke down . . ."

The old man shook his head with a smug smile. He was a good judge of character, the nod said, and had just won an argument with the old lady. "Thought so! Isn't that what I said, Em . . . come on then, we'll drop you off downtown near where we're heading."

McGinnis slipped in beside the old woman and closed the door. She smiled at him in a polite, disinterested way, but seemed too engrossed in the crossword puzzle on her lap to talk to him.

"We're heading downtown somewhere round the World Trade Center . . . but I don't know if the highway's open or closed. Have to see. They're always digging," the driver said.

Paul McGinnis closed his eyes briefly. He didn't want to continue the conversation. He looked out the window, trying not to smell the vomit. The car was traveling at about thirty-five miles an hour, and the scenery barely moved. In the back seat, the baby began to cry loudly. It was going to be interminable.

The hospital was operating as well as possible under the circumstances. But Dr. Cameron gasped when he entered the lobby. There were over one hundred people there, in a state of total anarchy. It was impossible to sort out on sight which of them were sick and which well. An elderly woman, noticing his bag, fell upon Cameron as he entered, screaming, "Help me, help me . . . my daughter!" He replied softly that he would see what he could do and gently disengaged her hand from his arm. Then he went back out to the parking lot and put away his bag, locked the car, and walked in again, an ordinary man. People milled about and asked each other for help, pleading and threatening, but he was no longer special and identifiable and was able to get through. He saw many people walking quietly about the corridors, disoriented. On a wooden bench Larry Roberts was sitting in his white coat. He did not respond to Cameron's hurried greeting. At the pharmacy, two unfamiliar nurses and an attendant were hastily stuffing bottles of Valium into a paper bag. Dr. Cameron's quiet entrance didn't stop them. Perhaps they assumed he was just another "crazy" who had wandered into the supply room. He felt a wave of physical revulsion and anger at their activity, but he did not speak to them or attempt to stop them. He simply recorded their faces. The injectable penicillin was untouched and, strangely enough, so were the disposable syringes. The Valium was gone, and he substituted an equivalent tranquilizer. Finding an unmarked cardboard carton, he silently packed what he needed.

Charles Vail acted immediately after receiving the telephone call. They had never before called his home, and he knew upon hearing the voice that it was an emergency. When the phone call transmitted from New York had been intercepted, there had been no time to contact him in the usual way. Vail took the Mercedes.

He walked through the hospital lobby with a sure step, unflustered by the chaos. He went directly to the empty reception desk and looked over the counter. The patient directory was within his reach. Wendy Dougherty had been moved to an isolation unit on the fifth floor, Room 516 . . .

He stood confidently, waiting for the self-service elevators—a well-dressed, self-assured visitor, somebody's uncle, notable only in that he was still functioning. He looked up impatiently. The indicator had stopped on two. The lobby was bedlam. Children cried. Parents, near the breaking point, yelled and raged. Many people crouched unselfconsciously along the walls, obviouly ill, and others wandered aimlessly as if in shock. Vail considered taking the fire stairs. Just then, the indicator light changed.

The door opened, and a few patients in hospital gowns giggled at him from within the elevator. One turned away and faced the corner. So they had been holding the elevator, probably playing with buttons. Ordinary psychiatric cases—

not the new sickness. But he didn't care. He had time. Even i
Cameron had already administered the antidote, he ha
time. He smiled at the patients in his avuncular way, elicit
ing absolutely no response. He pressed five and ignore
them. They would not recognize him again. The door to th
unit was marked ISOLATION. Wendy Dougherty's name wa
one of those on the handwritten card. He entered. Charle
Vail stepped over an attendant who lay, apparently asleep
on the vinyl floor of the corridor. A few patients wandered th
halls, and farther down the corridor he could hear screamin
from within a room. In the ward at the far end, he could see a
doctor and two nurses coping with a struggling patient. The
didn't see him

Wendy was asleep, alone in her semiprivate room. He
hair was tied in bunches, and her face was paler and thinne
than he recalled. She breathed heavily as he approached, bu
did not open her eyes. Her IV was still going, the containe
half-full of glucose solution containing a dosage of Valium. I
dripped slowly into her arm. She slept as Vail walked to the
head of her bed in a businesslike manner, took a syringe
assembly and vial from his jacket pocket, and injected the
vial's contents into the clear plastic IV tube.

Dr. Cameron could have sworn he saw Charles Vail walking out of the lobby as he came up from the supply room. But when he called, the man did not turn. Well, maybe it wasn't Vail, or maybe, because of the noise, the man didn't hear him. After checking the directory, he went up to Room 516, examined Wendy briefly, and administered the penicillin. She was sleeping soundly. Cameron left the floor by the fire stairs, because the elevators were stalled. He got back down to the lobby and stopped to move Larry Roberts into an unoccupied room and give him an injection.

It had all taken much longer than he anticipated; still, before leaving the General, he made an attempt to phone Hayes. He wanted to talk to him about the dangerously chaotic conditions at the hospital and, most importantly, about his aborted conversation with Daniel Lieberman. Soon it became clear that his efforts were futile. After the disorganized switchboard disconnected him several times, he gave up. He had made a promise to Daniel Lieberman that he intended to keep. He walked toward the parking lot.

There were teen-agers there. They looked tanned and healthy in blue jeans and T-shirts, moving with sure strides around the cars, including his. Cameron knew they were not victims of the illness from the way they moved and spoke. What were they looking for, he wondered. Syringes? Drugs? Keys left in the ignitions? They were obviously not professional thieves, but it would be dangerous to show himself with his box of medicine and syringes, and his keys, with their Cadillac emblem. There was no one to stop the scavengers. The police would not come, and he, by himself, was not about to do anything stupid. His priority was to Hodson and to Laura, not to indulge in futile heroics.

He stepped out of sight behind a tall hedge. He felt ancient and vulnerable as he waited—a relic from another era, filled with helpless fury. The kids didn't leave for a very long time.

Bill drove at a steady sixty-five, windshield wipers rhythmically clearing the glass; he was silent and tense, thinking.

"Nobody's stopped us so far, Bill. You think maybe I should call Maia again before we get to Sheffield?"

Bill glanced over at Daniel. He saw a deeply furrowed brow beneath the bandaged forehead; worried, near-sighted eyes, one of them swollen, half closed, and discolored. "Maia was fine just a little while ago," he said gently. "And Cameron told you he'd look in. Frankly, my friend, I'm much more worried about you and me."

Daniel sniffed back the slight trickle of blood that started down his right nostril, and rested his throbbing head on the back rest. A mild concussion, Bill had said, how the hell was he going to break into a lab? And what was he looking for? "How can this be happening?" he said aloud. "It's like a fucking nightmare."

"*Chacun à son goût*," Bill replied sarcastically. "You realize the time and money that went into this little plague? Must have cost them a goddamn fortune . . . Fucking asshole!" he shouted suddenly. They had nearly been sideswiped by a maroon Dodge. Bill swerved, then jerked the Volvo back into line on the highway. The Dodge had cut directly in front of them and was speeding ahead.

Bill recovered quickly, keeping a steady sixty-five. "I'll tell you something, Daniel," he said totally ignoring the incident that had left Daniel staring nervously out the rain-drenched window. "If there's anybody doing this kind of project, I'd bet it's our own boys. Remember that little number they pulled with the *E. coli* aerosol spray in San Francisco? Remember how harmless they claimed it was when it hit the news?

They don't give a damn what happens, even in their own country, as long as they can cut loose and run. We all knew from the start that this recombinant stuff is tailor-made for their kind of games. That's why the NIH guidelines are such a joke—these guys don't follow guidelines. So you can call it a nightmare, but I'd bet there are some people jumping for joy in some Washington office right now."

Daniel turned from the window, marveling at Bill's ability to concentrate on any subject that fascinated him regardless of the situation at hand. He just was getting over being side-swiped himself. "It would seem to me, Bill, that if they spent a fortune on the development of this monstrosity, they'd be pretty unhappy right now. The fact is, we *can* stop the sickness, and they won't be able to use the product again."

"Never say never . . . they may use Sheffield as a model and see how they can improve on the idea—this is just one variation on the theme. Next time it'll be different organisms and different genes, and we may not be so lucky then. They're like kids with a new toy. Wait till you try explaining this illness; you better believe, without hard evidence, everyone's going to look at you funny. Real funny," Bill said, raising his eyebrows. "Especially when the panic's off and nobody needs you anymore. Watch them stick their heads back in the sand!"

"Wait'll we see what's at the lab. And remember, there are witnesses. Wendy may remember after the illness that she was actually there. And that boy, Chet. After we cure him, maybe he'll remember the break-in. All we need is one good witness—even some good circumstantial evidence."

Bill swung on to the Hutchinson River Parkway. "Look at that, Daniel!"

Daniel sat bolt upright and peered short-sightedly ahead. The maroon Dodge that had sideswiped them was now just in front of them in the right lane, hanging back, going slowly, too slowly.

Bill passed it quickly on the left, but the car pulled out from behind and cut him off. As he attempted to pass the Dodge for the second time, it swerved left and rammed them on Daniel's side. They skidded diagonally across the road, careening toward the metal traffic divider. Bill accelerated expertly out of the skid, regaining control and gun-barreling down the dead center of the left-hand lane. They were now driving parallel to the maroon car, and Daniel caught a glimpse of the impassive face of the driver.

"That's 'they,' baby," Bill said, his mouth tight with fury. He slammed his foot on the gas and took off.

Bill's head was bent slightly forward with concentration, his gaze intent on piercing the solid sheets of rain on the windshield. They were doing eighty-five, weaving through the sparse traffic, with the Dodge not far behind.

"What the hell good would it do them to stop us now?" Daniel asked.

"Stop us! They just want to *detain* us. For stopping, they have other techniques," Bill said grimly. "Jesus! They are really into road stunts . . . I just realized. Of course! The Perrinis couldn't have been sick. That was no accident."

"Why not?"

"You don't work with this stuff without being on an antidote; look at McGinnis. He never got sick. He was taking penicillin. The whole team must have been on penicillin. And the Perrinis . . . they didn't have any sudden onset of symptoms on the road. They had some other kind of 'accident.' "

The Dodge appeared behind them again, the driver's face a blur behind the rain. The car stayed on their tail, buzzing them, but Bill was undaunted. "It's like the *autostrada*." He laughed tensely and pulled ahead with a renewed burst of power. "Always wanted to race. I'm a frustrated closet racing-car driver. The Black Baron!"

The Dodge faded back into the rain once more.

Bill kept up the speed, mile after mile, a determined look on his face. Finally, they pulled to a halt with a squeal of brakes on the slick road surface at the roadblock outside of Sheffield. Bill rolled down his window. A middle-aged state trooper in a slicker stood beside the car, looking surprised and suspicious, his square jaw set and his eye noncommittally surveying the passengers.

Maia sat wide-eyed and trembling as Laura went limp and fell backward onto the bed. She was paralyzed with fear. Her child's mind churned with earlier terrors, brought back by Laura's sudden strange transformation. She experienced again the desolation of wandering through empty rooms after her mother's sudden departure—her breathing quickened as she remembered the shadows, the horrible imaginary things under the bed, in the closet. And she remembered Miss Hill's masklike face in the deserted library stacks . . . But she's only sick, she struggled to reassure herself, like Janie's

Mom, and *she* got better . . . Her glance shifted desperately to the telephone.

Just then Laura sat up, staring at her in that awful, frightened way. Maia tried to speak to her, but Laura only put her hands over her ears and ducked away. She watched Laura stagger across the room, pressing her body against the walls, until she came to the door. No time to telephone. She pulled and tugged urgently at Laura but could not stop her. Laura flung open the door, fell, and crawled rapidly toward the stairs. Helplessly, Maia stood at the top of the staircase, looking over as Laura stumbled down the carpeted steps and headed for the kitchen, darting terrified glances over her shoulder. Maia ran after her, tears streaming hot down her cheeks.

Laura was just standing in the kitchen resting her cheek against the refrigerator door, her eyes closed. Maia hesitated, then approached cautiously as she might approach a poised butterfly. Finally she touched Laura's arm gently and spoke.

Immediately Laura opened her eyes, looked at her, and began to scream. Rushing to the door that led from the kitchen to the garage, she opened it and staggered into the camp van, closing the door. Maia raced after her and grasped the handle of the van, but paused and turned as the steel-sheeted door to the kitchen slammed closed; then she turned back, horrified by the unmistakable sound of the van locks clicking shut.

"No! Laura!" Maia shouted. "No!"

But Laura, inside the van, pushed her hair back with shaking hands and turned the key that was still in the ignition.

The sound of the racing motor filled the dark garage. Maia pounded her small fists against the van window. Then she stopped abruptly, a helpless look on her face, as Laura fell against the steering wheel, unconscious once more.

Maia coughed in the rush of exhaust fumes, tears streaming down her face, and tried to think. Her housekey, the one she usually wore around her neck, was inside on the living room couch. The dark garage held a control box for the outside door, but she knew it was well above her reach. The remote-control switch was in the van with Laura . . . and Laura was sick. There was a small, sealed window near the ceiling of the garage; it was shedding some pale light, and Maia's eyes were growing accustomed to the darkness. She knew that she must think; not panic. The exhaust smell was nauseating; the motor was still on, but at least Laura's foot was off the pedal. Maybe, Maia thought, there's some way out.

The state trooper looked them over. "I can't let you through here," he said evenly. "This is a roadblock."

Bill sighed. He had been scratched lightly during the collision with the maroon Dodge, and a thin line of blood ran across his cheekbone. Daniel's nose was bleeding profusely, his torn jacket was disreputable-looking, and his split lip was caked with a brown crust. He raised his bandaged hand in a polite greeting. "I'm a resident of Sheffield—Dr. Daniel Lieberman. This is my colleague, Dr. Edwards. We have to get through to the General right away!"

The trooper remained silent, unimpressed, his gaze shifting from Daniel's clothing, to Bill's face. "May I see some I.D.?" he finally asked.

"I don't have any," Daniel said impatiently. "Check it out with Mr. Hayes at the General, if you want, or try Chief McLoughlin. He's a friend of mine. He knows all about this."

"Chief McLoughlin is hospitalized," said the trooper in a level voice.

Daniel sat there in the drizzle trying to convince the trooper to let them through, knowing that his words sounded preposterous. The names he mentioned were public knowledge by now. Each time he spoke, he discredited himself further. Bill kept a profound silence while the trooper worked with his apparently defective walkie-talkie and checked Bill's license. Daniel patiently explained why he had none himself; he'd been beaten and robbed . . . New York, he summarized, with a woeful look. That was the breakthrough. The trooper nodded sympathetically.

They waited nervously while the man tried to get through to someone in authority. Why hadn't that car caught up to them? Maybe their assailants figured that the roadblock itself would detain them, they didn't have to worry. About what? Daniel wondered again. Why would they stop them from stemming the illness? It was grotesque. Like the behavior of the town. Maybe that was worse. The well against the sick. Looting. Rock throwing. He ached to see Laura. And to hold Maia safely in his arms.

His fist clenched with impatience at the trooper's slowness. It was infuriating. Bill looked calm enough, staring quietly ahead, but his stillness was unnatural, and Daniel saw a small muscle rippling in his cheek. He was about to explode. Daniel wondered if he was going to drive through the roadblock, when some squawking noises from the radio finally satisfied the trooper.

"Stay under twenty and lock your doors," he said in a monotone, and waved them on.

Daniel tried to focus with his one good eye through a blurred windshield on the streets he'd only recently learned. "You make a right up ahead . . ."

Something was wrong. He sensed it immediately. The house seemed too still. There was no movement, no lights, but that was true of every house. He got out and searched under the familiar border rock for the garage door remote-control box. But nothing was there.

They must be at the Benedicts, he thought. Sure, why hadn't it occurred to him immediately? They were at Sam's. But nobody was allowed on the road without a permit . . . Then he became aware of a soft droning sound. Bill's motor? Knowing the answer in advance, he stuck his head hastily in the open window. "Motor's off, isn't it?"

"Yes."

"Oh my God!" Daniel yelled and stumbled across the driveway to the garage door. He pounded on it with his good hand. There was that sound, clear now; a motor idling, almost as quiet as the rain. But no voices, and no response. Bill grabbed him by the shoulder; he was carrying his medical bag with the penicillin and Valium.

"Come on, let's go!"

"No housekeys . . ." Daniel said, as they ran to the front door.

Bill swung his bag and knocked out the glass panes. Daniel entered first and ran through to the kitchen; as he opened the connecting door to the garage, he gulped a huge breath of air and held it. They dashed in. He flicked on the lights and Bill went right to the van, smashed the glass with a wrench he found hanging on the garage wall, and opened the door. Laura fell out onto his shoulder. Holding her, he turned the ignition key to "off."

Daniel, meanwhile, scooped up Maia, limp and small, where she had fallen in a corner. So damned small, he thought, as his tears fell on her upturned face. Closing the door behind him, he carried Maia into the kitchen and opened a window.

"Laura's pulse is strong," Bill said, propping her up in a chair near the door.

"They're both breathing." Daniel's voice shook uncontrollably. "Maia's got a little reddening of the lips, but her skin coloration is okay, and Laura looks good. They couldn't have been in there very long. I don't suppose you keep any oxygen in your car?"

" 'Fraid not," answered Bill. "But I don't think they need it. I've seen plenty of monoxide poisonings. They'll be okay."

They carried Laura and Maia into the living room and put them both on the couch. Bill opened a window while Daniel ran upstairs for blankets. When he returned, Maia was regaining consciousness. Bill was holding her in his lap—she made little hiccupping sobs and her eyes were moist, but she managed a weak smile for her father.

Then she saw Laura. A look of desperate urgency came into her face, and after a fit of coughing, she managed to whisper to Daniel: "Sick. Help her. She didn't hurt me . . . She wouldn't . . ."

Daniel placed a finger gently against Maia's lips and said, "I know, honey. Don't talk; you were wonderfully brave. Don't worry, Laura will be fine in a day or two."

Daniel injected Laura with Valium and penicillin before she awakened. He looked at the gentle, beautiful face as the thick, honey-colored lashes fluttered open, and he grimaced at the thought of the nightmares she must be having.

Bill sat pensively holding Maia, cuddling her. One by one he picked up her slender, small fingers. "Just think," he said very quietly, "if we'd gone to the lab first."

A car screeched to a stop outside. Daniel moved cautiously to the window, peered out and then smiled. "Dr. Cameron," he said with relief.

A few minutes later, Daniel sat in the vestibule trying again to reach Hayes. After being disconnected three times, he finally was put through to Hayes's extension. The man's voice was barely recognizable.

"It's Daniel Lieberman, Mr. Hayes . . . are you all right?"

"Yes. I'm just exhausted . . . I don't know what to say to you, I feel terrible about . . ."

"Don't worry. I know it sounded fantastic. But . . . are you sure you feel all right? Please tell me if anything is bothering you."

"I swear I'm fine. No crazy thoughts, nothing odd. Just exhaustion. But I'm afraid the news about the rest of the regular staff isn't too good. Nelson and Roberts are ill, and I tried reaching Hodson again at home, and have reason to believe he's sick there. We have a lot of professionals here, but many of them are from the outside."

"Well I think I have some good news for you. Bill Edwards—he's the biochemist who was working on Wendy's toxic screen—was able to put some material together for me, and now we're pretty sure we know what's going on. But, Mr. Hayes, you are definitely going to need CDC help to handle this."

"They're on their way," Hayes said in a tired voice. "I contacted them late last night, woke someone up in fact . . . They're sending a large team. Didn't you see the news on television?"

"No, I missed it."

"It's pretty bad here. We've got all the help anyone could ask for, we just don't know what the hell to tell them to *do*. We have people running tests, the CDC group arriving shortly, teams distributing Valium, but that's only a stopgap—we can't keep everybody on Valium forever. And obviously, with so many unanswerable questions, we have a major panic."

"All right, Mr. Hayes. This is what you do. You have the CDC people assist you to give depot penicillin injections to the whole town and any outside contacts . . ."

"What?" Hayes asked, confused. "There's a lot of noise out here, I don't think I heard you right."

"It *is* bacterial. It *does* respond to penicillin. You heard me."

"Lieberman, you're sure?"

"You're not going to give me a hard time, are you? They're going to need quite a supply. Everyone who isn't penicillin-sensitive should be treated as a preventive measure, symptoms or not. For those who can't tolerate penicillin, any antibiotic that works against gram-positive bacteria like strep is okay. Handle it pharmacologically as if it were a strep-throat epidemic. Same doses. And Mr. Hayes, you start on penicillin immediately yourself, before you begin administering this program . . . any questions?"

"Obviously lots . . . You're sure about this, Lieberman? It sounds incredible."

"So did my prediction of what's going on now."

"Is there . . . a name for this illness? Something I can tell them? How did you and Dr. Edwards find it?"

"Let's worry first about prevention and cure. We'll talk about the medical details later, all right? Remember, deep

IM injections of depot penicillin-G. That's Benzathine penicillin. B-e-n-z-a-t-h-i-n-e. The dose for adults is 1.2 million units. A single shot. Scale it down accordingly for kids. We'll have a very small number of allergic reactions, but that's better than what you've got now. Just be prepared for them. You have any problems with what I've told you?"

"No. I've written it down. I wouldn't question you again. Frankly, if you told me the cure was chicken soup, I'd start the vats boiling . . . I'll get on it right away!"

Leaving Dr. Cameron in charge of Laura and Maia, Bill and Daniel set out in the rain for the laboratory. Daniel wondered vaguely how realistic it was to expect that they could actually get tangible evidence. He felt pessimistic as he gazed out the window at the town.

They passed by parched, yellowed lawns, all baked dry by the heat wave; the rain was too late. Rivulets of muddy water trickled down the grassy slopes. For the first time in weeks, the air was chill. "Left, over here, I think," Daniel said. The residential part of Sheffield looked unchanged, but was eerily quiet. There was no movement on the sidewalks or streets. Cars were locked behind garage doors. Shades were drawn. It had the feeling of a ghost town. They passed the school. It was the right direction. "It's just up ahead a bit, we have to turn onto Broadview." And there was the garbage dump . . . they crawled along at twenty-five till they turned onto the wide, uphill road called Broadview.

The lab was at the crest, but they could see the flames and black smoke a half mile away. Bill speeded up to forty. Silently, they pulled across the road from the massive chrome gate and got out of the car. All the buildings, set way back on cleared acres, were on fire: billowing torrents of flame and acrid dark smoke obscured the wide landscape. Their faces were lit by flames as they stood silently, witnessing the destruction. Lone spectators in the drizzle, they were the only audience for the awesome spectacle. No one else would arrive. No rubberneckers would pass on the road. No one was at the firehouse to respond to the alarm . . . but then, Daniel thought bitterly, they must have considered all that.

"Pretty fucking unsubtle," Bill said at last. His words came up from an anger so deep he'd been nearly unable to speak. "Now we know why they let you through to Hayes this time. They were done."

Daniel watched the marble facing licked by rising flame; the carved letters of the laboratory's name were etched even more deeply in the flickering glare. "I guess we didn't leave them enough time to think of anything else . . . you really led them a chase," he said morosely.

A window exploded, sending them back several feet for safety.

Bill put his arm around Daniel's shoulder. "So . . . there goes hard evidence. If there ever was any."

"They must have thought there was *something* in there," Daniel said. "Or they wouldn't have gone to so much trouble trying to slow us down."

The drizzle steadily hit the flames and turned to steam, and now the dark smoke began to roll toward them like fog in a sudden wind shift. They got into the car, turning to take a last look at the wreckage.

"Well, they're finished here," Bill said, starting the car. "I don't think they'll bother you anymore."

A feeling of despondency swept Daniel, and he thought of Maia and Laura. They were all that was important to him; and it was their faces he imagined, not a place, when he said, "Let's go home."

"Sure," Bill said gently. "It's all over . . ."

Charles Vail stood near the drawn brocade curtains in his bank office on Main Street. Ordinarily he kept his curtains open, but today the broken glass of his windows was covered with plywood. The interior of the bank building hadn't been touched. Unlike the merchants of the street, his merchandise was kept safely locked away behind vault doors.

He handed the white, lumpy envelope from Box 74, containing McGinnis's tape, to the man sitting across from him. "Well, it looks like we lost this one. The material is of absolutely no use to us now," Vail said.

The man shrugged slightly but did not speak. He fingered the envelope with his baby-sized hands and stared at Vail.

Charles Vail shifted his weight nervously. "But at least we cut our ties," he said. "Except for Lieberman."

"What can he do? The lab's gone. He has no witnesses."

Vail hesitated. "Did you try to stop him?"

"Yes, but our people were interrupted. He had a lucky break. That's all."

Vail regarded the small hands with an unfamiliar nervousness. When things went wrong, there had to be scapegoats. He was on guard. But then he was always on guard, and because of that, he did not make errors. Except, he thought bitterly, marrying Pam. "You see any future in Chameleon?" he asked. "Can it still help us before November?"

The man smiled slightly. "We'll see."

Vail looked carefully at the man whose face he continually forgot—as he expected, the man wouldn't tell him anything about the future of Chameleon. Vail was a servant, a prosperous, effective launderer of money; experienced, convenient, but replaceable. He had no illusions. The man was staring at him, his expression indecipherable.

"What about that boy, Chet Gabrini?" Vail asked. "Won't he remember everything after he's treated?"

The man shrugged slightly. "We took care of him this morning. You're about the only local left . . ."

Vail stiffened and looked at the man.

"Except for McGinnis," the man continued evenly. "He may be out of the country—you haven't, by chance, heard from him?"

Vail tried to keep the fear out of his voice. "No. Certainly not."

"That's too bad."

"What about the lab?" Charles Vail ventured. "Are you considering rebuilding it and maintaining the relationship?"

The man stood to go. "The lab is a respected institution in this town. That makes it valuable to us. It's a useful facility. We may use it again."

Vail smiled. "Yes. Things are a little chaotic right now, but nobody believes there's any connection between the lab and the sickness. There won't be any trouble here." Vail began to relax. He was still useful to them. As long as he was useful, he was safe. "Who will we get to run the lab?"

"Garner and McGinnis both were too independent. And McGinnis . . . I don't trust people with charisma. Now, this fellow Lawson may have possibilities . . ."

# Friday, August twenty-fourth,

*the limousine pulled up in front of a starkly modern office building whose glass entranceway was shaded by an arbor of purple bougainvillaea. Flanking the building were symmetrical groves of carefully tended orange trees, their dark green foliage contrasting with the bare plains and parched, sand-colored hills beyond.*

*Paul McGinnis stepped out into the searing breeze and intense light. An attendant in a kaffiyeh and robe closed the door after him, led him under the bougainvillaea into the air-conditioned building, and conducted him to a low table in the lobby, where a guard inspected the contents of McGinnis's attaché case. Another guard, in dark glasses, carrying a snub-nosed black machine gun, leaned against a marble and chromium pillar and watched disinterestedly while McGinnis was given an apologetic but efficient frisking. The attendant led the way to a bank of elevators with McGinnis not far behind, striding his tennis player's comfortable walk and looking very much at home. At the basement level, McGinnis and the attendant stepped out of the elevator and walked over to an electronically controlled sliding metal door. The attendant inserted a thin magnetic key card in a wall slot; the door slid silently back, and he and McGinnis stepped into the laboratory.*

"Today in Sheffield, Connecticut, the local outbreak of the so-called crazy sickness that scared the nation is finally under control. But victims of this past week will leave the small town in mourning long after the debris has been cleared away . . ."

At the moderator's last words, many heads in the Town Hall's auditorium bowed as they might have in church, and most eyes looked down briefly from the television monitors that hung above the stage. The crowd was well dressed, quiet, and self-conscious; they seemed much aware that the eyes of the nation were on Sheffield. Laura sat next to Daniel

Lieberman, her hand grazing his from time to time, her other hand in a clenched fist. Bill sat on the other side of Daniel, shifting impatiently in his folding chair. Two policemen stood quietly on either side of the stage, watching the audience. Daniel thought of McLoughlin, who was still hospitalized for an ulcer, and wondered if he was watching the broadcast from the General.

As the studio anchorman in New York reeled off Sheffield statistics, there was footage of the town. Then suddenly the local cameras took over and people saw themselves live again on the monitors. Daniel recognized on screen the Taylors, Louise Garner, Pam Vail, the Lawsons, and even some of his own young patients . . . He closed his eyes, trying again not to think of Wendy.

"The summer heat and the Sheffield scare have stimulated a great many reports of hallucinations—phone calls have been pouring into this station and the rest of the network all week from Manhattan, Connecticut, New Jersey, and even a couple from as far away as California," the New York announcer said. "In answer to our viewers' understandable concerns, we've set up a special panel in Sheffield that will attempt to discuss the questions: where does the 'crazy sickness' come from, and where is it going?—George?"

There was sudden activity on stage as the cameras rolled in close, and the monitors showed five people sitting at a conference table set up on the wooden stage. The panel moderator opened the discussion by turning to an attractive woman on his right who wore a white physician's jacket.

"Dr. Rachel Case is from the federal Center for Disease Control in Atlanta, and is here heading the CDC team in Sheffield. Dr. Case, the question on everyone's mind: has your team located the organism responsible for the 'crazy sickness'?"

Dr. Case ducked her head toward the microphone and spoke. "Well, at this time we haven't yet isolated any organism, but we're getting a good response to penicillin. I think that should be stressed. We can use penicillin effectively against this. It's not a runaway sickness raging in the East or anything like that."

"And it doen't present any danger to other communities?" the moderator asked.

"It appears to be pretty much confined to Sheffield. Reports of other incidents haven't yet been verified, and the situation here is completely under control."

"And what prospects have you for finding the organism?" the newscaster repeated.

"The CDC is investigating many potential sources of the illness. We're conducting exhaustive tests on the local water supply, checking foods and, as we did in the Legionnaire episode, we're looking into air-conditioning units and other unusual potential harboring sites. Meanwhile, we've set up treatment centers in town and have so far injected over three-quarters of the population with antibiotic. Unfortunately, we can't reliably separate real cases from panic reaction. As you know, there are no physical signs or medical tests for this illness. In fact, it's possible that the antibiotic is having a purely psychological placebo effect . . ."

There was an immediate rustling in the auditorium, wooden chairs creaked, and people began whispering. Near Daniel, a few people spoke aloud. Bill shook his head.

"Wait just a minute," the newscaster interupted hastily. "Are you now suggesting that there may actually be no 'crazy sickness'—that this is just mass hysteria?"

Dr. Case nodded. "Well that's certainly one possibility we have in mind. We haven't come to any firm conclusions . . ."

"Mr. Hayes"—the newscaster addressed the man next to Dr. Case—"as administrator of the Sheffield General Hospital, would you agree with the CDC evaluation?"

"They're doing a terrific job in Sheffield!" he said, smiling, and looked around the audience for agreement. "We all sure were alarmed at first, but now, whatever this thing is, we seem to have it licked. And that's all that counts, isn't it?"

The newscaster thanked Hayes and turned to his left. "Other public-health experts, such as Dr. Albert Sealy from the Harvard School of Public Health, have a different perspective. They suspect the disease is not so new after all! Dr. Sealy?"

"Back in the Middle Ages, there were episodes like this, George, when whole towns went crazy." He puffed his pipe and smiled. "We've always blamed those incidents on ergot poisoning, but my guess is that it's a previously unknown bacterium we're dealing with. Outbreaks of this illness have undoubtedly been occurring sporadically for centuries and always been misdiagnosed. I'm confident that we'll find antibodies establishing the prior existence of the so-called crazy sickness in many parts of the country. That ought to squelch any thoughts that this whole thing originated in Sheffield."

The newscaster turned to Charles Vail at the end of the

table. A close-up of Vail's solemn face and wide shoulders flashed on the hanging monitors. He gazed earnestly out at the live audience. "I don't know why God singled out this town for tragedy. But I can assure you that the authorities are continuing their intensive investigation of this incident and . . ."

"He's in on it!" Daniel whispered to Bill. "The bastard's been on the antidote from the start, and he put his wife on it too! And how about Hayes—why didn't he get sick?"

"Don't get paranoid," Bill whispered.

Laura took Daniel's hand and squeezed it tightly.

Daniel ignored the attempts to calm him. "There are deaths involved here! And Wendy's death is still unexplained—I never ordered that goddamn much Valium . . ."

"Daniel . . ." Laura said.

"But it's a cover-up . . ."

"Forget it. Tell it to *The National Enquirer*," Bill said harshly.

"Shhh!" a woman in front of them hissed with an angry glance.

Suddenly Daniel stopped, staring ahead at the stage.

Greta McGinnis was walking up the platform steps, ignoring the newscaster's frantic gestures to her to go back. She turned at the conference table. Her face looked like a tragic mask, her eyes were black shadows. Without makeup, her skin appeared coarse and blotchy under the harsh television lights as the camera caught her on the monitors. No one in the house moved or spoke.

"My husband . . . was responsible," she said in her normal husky voice, loud enough for everyone to hear. She grabbed a microphone from the table. "My husband caused this sickness . . . he was responsible, he . . ."

A burst of whispers came out of the stunned silence, and there were sounds of movement throughout the auditorium. Daniel stood and tried to leave his seat but Bill pulled him down. The two policemen walked over to Greta rapidly and took her arms. She offered no resistance as they led her off the stage, while on screen the monitors recorded only the faces of the panel moderator and Hayes in hurried conversation.

"I've just learned that Mrs. Paul McGinnis, the woman who interrupted our panel just now, has suffered a double tragedy recently. Her son Billy, age ten, fell to his death from a beach-house roof. Her husband, one of Sheffield's leading citizens, is still missing tonight. Local conjecture is that Dr McGinnis himself may have set fire to the laboratory while victim of the illness. However, there are no eyewitnesses, and the only body recovered so far from the ruins has been identified as Jim Walters, a security guard. Mrs. McGinnis is understandably in a state of emotional shock. They are taking her home now . . ."

The New York anchorman resumed from his studio. "Before we get back to the Sheffield story, we'll take a small break for a word from our sponsor . . ."

In the Town Hall auditorium, people argued heatedly.

Bill sat back in his seat and looked up at the monitors. There was a Ford commercial on the screens. The panel moderator stepped forward on the stage to quiet the house.

Daniel and Laura ran out after Greta. They arrived at the door in time to see Greta put gently in the back seat of her limousine, which promptly slid away from the curb. Daniel was shaking with anger. He stormed across the village green with Laura at his side. Without speaking, they walked to the bottom of Main Street and looked around. The debris had been cleaned up and restoration was in progress. Silently, they walked past the old-fashioned store fronts of weathered shingle. Inside, many shopkeepers were watching the broadcast on portable television sets. Daniel and Laura stopped in front of Gregory's Appliance Store. The door was open and the owner waved to them. They looked at the large color TV set flickering behind the new plate-glass window and heard the broadcast from a speaker mounted over the door.

Vail's image gazed out at them with an avuncular smile. "I have every faith in this community," he said, "and I know in my heart we'll be able to rebuild, although we'll always mourn our neighbors and our loved ones. Tomorrow the laboratory's board will meet to elect a new director. Our aim is to pick up right where we left off and to recreate an institution that meant so much to our town. The ordeal is finally over, and we can give thanks that it has left Sheffield whole in spirit, healthy . . ."

Laura turned her back to the window. "Daniel, this new bacterial variant they made, will it weaken and peter out eventually?"

"Maybe. Bill says it's a misfit because it has to keep producing all those useless plant chemicals. Natural selection should weed it out in time, but who knows—" Daniel broke off abruptly and turned away from Laura, then he spoke intensely. "You think they didn't believe anything we told them? When they called us in for questioning, Bill and I must have talked to those doctors from the CDC for a full hour! They *seemed* to believe what we were saying—they know the cure works!"

"Maybe that's it: the cure works. Daniel, when you think about it, what else do they have? The lab's gone, and it's too late to culture the organism even if they could . . ." Laura looked back at the set.

"Remember, viewers," the studio moderator was saying, "this illness is no more severe than a common cold, but unlike a cold, it's treatable. If you or any of your friends or family do have any of the symptoms we described earlier, and if you've had any contact with anyone from Sheffield, Connecticut, get in touch with your doctor, or call this number . . ."

Daniel took Laura's hand firmly and crossed the empty street to the old elm. They sat in silence on the bench for a moment. Daniel stared straight ahead. Laura could see the taut muscles of his shoulders trembling with anger beneath his shirt.

"Hey . . ." she said, putting her hand up to his chin and gently turning his head toward her.

He looked at her for a moment and his expression softened. He put his arms around her.

"Darling," Laura said, "it's time for us to go."

KUWAIT, May 5—*The sudden departure for home yester*
*day of Sheik Fouad, the Saudi Arabian oil minister and hea*
*of its OPEC delegation here, has been viewed with concern i*
*Western diplomatic and economic circles. Leadership of th*
*Saudi delegation has been assumed by Prince Hassan, a*
*outspoken opponent of Fouad within the royal family. Hassa*
*has long been known for his militant pricing stance, similar t*
*that taken by Libya and Iran. At this morning's meeting*
*Hassan made it clear that Sheik Fouad's pro-Western polic*
*was no longer in effect.*

*The reason for Sheik Fouad's abrupt departure has not bee*
*officially released, but it is widely rumored that he has suf*
*fered a nervous breakdown. According to a spokesman for* Th
Petroleum Observer, *an authoritative newsletter that cover*
*the international oil scene, Fouad was present at the OPEC*
*session on May 3, but his behavior was described as "strang*
*and inappropriate." At the close of the session, he was assiste*
*from the room by aides and did not return for the afternoo*
*meeting. The Sheik last spoke to reporters on May 1, at*
*reception hosted by the Libyan delegation. He appeared to b*
*in good spirits at the time.*

*Industry sources predict that another severe escalation of oi*
*prices is in the offing. Some believe that the Saudi shift wil*
*push the price of a barrel of light-crude past the sixty-dolla*
*mark . . .*